GOODY ONE SHOE

JULIE FRAYN!

DEDICATION

This is for the odd ones. The nerds, the geeks, and the weirdos. You know, for everyone.

BILLIE FULLALOVE SAT ON AN UPTURNED CRATE and shifted her attention to the man at her feet. She slid the knife into his abdomen, between his ribs and into his cold, dead heart.

Adam Ant ear-wormed his way into Billie's subconscious. All it took was a few notes to cross her mind, that unmistakable guitar riff and those screeching horns. What were those, trumpets? Taunts and jibes reached out from her childhood. More than two decades later, she couldn't escape feeling like a bullied third-grader.

"Goody two shoes! Goody two shoes!"

If only they could see her now. Sure, she still had one shoe firmly planted in good-girl ground, fertile with etiquette and kindness and prayer. But the other foot dangled over the pier and dipped into the evil pool. Evil with a purpose. Evil with a heart. Or at least, half a heart.

And one goody shoe.

The city skyline shone in the distance. The lights of downtown reflected in the wide expanse of the Grantham River, sparkling against the muck, each twinkle of wattage oblivious to the stench of dead fish, spilled fuel, and rotted flesh.

The justice system couldn't deliver the punishment the corpse on the dock deserved. They would never be able to prove he was guilty of the crime he'd committed. How he'd ruined Billie's life before she was old enough to live at all. She'd righted an atrocious miscarriage and delivered justice on the eve of a super moon. Carried out his death sentence under its eerie glow.

He would never kill another innocent victim.

Billie ran her fingers along the bars of the gold crucifix that hung from her neck. She closed her eyes and found her father's face. A breeze picked up, tossed strands of her long, chocolate hair about her face, and cooled her cheeks where tears wet them.

FIVE MONTHS EARLIER

BILLIE GRABBED A PENCIL FROM HER DESK AND rammed it between layers of stockings and the foam cover of her prosthesis. It was always at the height of frustration when her stump itched. Perhaps the stub on the end of where her calf used to be was the outlet for words she couldn't scream into the open office space. Words like *"they're*, not *there*, you stupid fucking asshole writers!"

Not that she'd ever say the F-word. Not out loud anyway. Her private cussing was between her and God. He understood that even good girls needed to be profane on occasion.

She glanced around at the green-tinged fluorescent lighting bouncing off shiny foreheads, at the shoulders scrunched up near everyone's ears, scowls on their faces. Did they all hate their jobs as much as she did?

It hadn't always been this way. Her heart used to quicken when she was assigned a new author, a new manuscript. Maybe this one would be *that* one — the one that put her on the publishing map. The one that elevated her out of the proofing primordial soup and onto the evolved editorial beach. But it never was. How could she take a pile of crap and elevate it to anything more than less-than-crap without just writing it herself?

"Ah, to heck with it." She tugged her plaid skirt above her knee, pushed down the foam cover — the thing that was supposed to make the average passerby think she had two functioning legs — slid the black compression sock off, and popped her leg free of the socket. She stripped the rubber sheath and two layers of soft stocking from her stump, scratched and rubbed the end until it stopped screaming. She leaned back in her chair and closed her eyes. "Oh yeah. Much better."

"Gross! Billie, cover that thing up."

She slit her eyes open to find the office whiner staring at her vacant calf. "If you're so disgusted by it, why do you always look?"

He pushed his thick-framed hipster glasses up higher on his pointed nose and blinked. "It's like a train wreck, complete with dismembered body parts. Awful. Disgusting. But you can't look away."

Her mental red pen appeared and drew little mouse ears on either side of his head. "You're an idiot, Jeffrey." She added whiskers and tiny buckteeth, then scratched out a thought bubble with "squeak, squeak" in the centre.

"Wilhelmina Fullalove. We've talked about this." Katherine Busby stood behind Jeffrey. She put one hand on his shoulder and jerked her head at his desk. He obeyed in that silent way he had of ingratiating himself at every opportunity. Like an annoying little brother who always got the last word, always got the biggest slice of pie, always got mother's full love and attention. Katherine crossed her arms and glared at Billie's stump. "Cover it up. Keep it covered. Respect your fellow workers or you'll find yourself freelancing. And let me tell you, that's no walk in the park. Even if you were walking on two legs."

Billie winced. Her mouth said "Yes, Katherine," but she screamed all manner of profanities on the inside. Even a few threats against the safety of Taffy, Katherine's prized Chiweenie and provider of incessant yapping. Billie couldn't air out her own skin, but the boss brought her little urine-spewing, ankle-nipping, piss-poor excuse for a dog to the office every day and expected her minions to take it out to the two-by-three foot piece of grass that supported the only city-planted tree on the entire block to do its business. And clean up after it too. Handle its little steaming shit piles with plastic gloves so thin the heat from the dog's excrement warmed her fingers. And then there were days when the gloves split open.

Katherine turned her back so fast, Billie imagined the sound of a whip snapping in her ear. She massaged and scratched her scars and mangled flesh one last time. Her body had grown in the twenty-two years since she lost her leg, but the skin on her stump hadn't kept up. It simply stretched. She sighed, reassembled the layers of her fake leg, and slid her sensible skirt back over her knees.

She turned to the manuscript on her monitor. The one she'd opened on Monday morning, full of promise and potential. Now, three days later, laden with spelling corrections and grammar edits, it sat there staring back at her with the vacant eyes of a corpse.

Her body swayed and jerked against the plastic seat. The subway rocketed underneath the streets of Grantham. Each time her shoulder crashed against the four-hundred-pound man beside her, she cringed and clenched her fingers around the handle of her briefcase. Garlic and cheese and sweat and feet crawled into her nostrils and poked at her sanity.

Freelancing. Not a one-legged walk in the park. But not a gut-turning, nose-plugging ride in a hurtling metal tube either.

Maybe it was time. Not to quit her job or anything, that was professional suicide. Or maybe just regular suicide, since she'd have no regular income, no regular way of feeding herself. Or supporting Peg Leg. She kept her smile inside but allowed a flash of her three-legged cat to brighten her commute.

They'd found each other eight years before. Billie was two years out of university and had been living on her own a mere six months, in a tiny, walk-up apartment. Peg Leg was hobbling through the alley behind her building, scrounging around the Dumpsters for any scraps that hadn't landed in the bin. She'd just gotten her latest prosthesis, one that looked more like a real leg, with a foot that would fit into kitten heels. It was one of her desperate periods where she yearned to meet a man, to find love, to be transformed into someone feminine and pretty. That was tough to accomplish with a foot that only fit into runners or ballet flats. No flip-flops, no stiletto heels. Not even open-toed sandals. She forked over a ton of cash for that leg, added it to her growing collection, like normal women would add to their shoe closets.

But that damn thing hurt. Her real toes ached inside the snug little pumps. The fake toes didn't quite fit the pointed shoe so she had trimmed them. Not the nails. Not corns or callouses. The toes. She hacked off the pinky and filed down the big toe until the pointed patent pump slid on. Too bad she couldn't do the same to her real toes. Maybe then, those heels would have been comfortable.

So there he was, a three-legged cat, struggling and failing to bound up the crates and into the garbage bins. And Billie, her fake leg strong, her real leg crippled by the kitten heel and her need to be normal, to be pretty, to be a real woman. She approached the cat, his inky fur matted and bald in patches. He hissed at her, bared a declawed paw and swatted at the air. She cooed and poured milk from a grocery bag into her palm. The cat lapped it up, his eyes on her face, assessing her trustworthiness with each tickle of his raspy tongue against the soft skin of her hand. In the end, he followed her. And she took him into her home. Into her life. Into her heart.

There was a lot of available space.

The subway car lurched and convulsed, then shuddered to a stop. The fat man laboured to his feet and left two empty seats behind. A new crowd of commuters poured in through the doors.

Billie said a silent prayer that they would choose to sit somewhere else. She tugged the shank of her prosthesis up to expose a foam foot and titanium tibia. Each rider that eyed the empty spot to her right glanced at her leg and moved along. The car thrust forward. She kept her eyes trained on the pole resting against her thigh and kept her satisfied grin internal.

That moment she made her choice. Time to dip a toe in the freelance water, find a few clients outside of the publishing house. Perhaps she could muster enough work to never have to step foot on the subway again, never sit on a seat thousands of passengers before her had farted on.

Was she allowed to take on private clients? She made a mental note to check her contract when she finally, blessedly, got back home.

Four stops later, Billie walked two blocks and stood at the threshold of her building, her little apartment three flights up, overlooking the roofs of a two-story business block. The deli smells, though garlicky and cheesy, were enticing, now that feet and sweat weren't mixed into the aromatic soup. She climbed the stairs, nodded at Mrs. Rogerson, always sitting outside her apartment door, spying on the comings and goings of the inhabitants. Billie felt like an ant in a farm, stared at through the glass as she went about her day, scrabbling through the tunnels of her life.

She tossed her keys into the pottery bowl next to the phone. "Peg Leg. Where are you, sweetheart?"

The cat mewed from his favourite perch on the window ledge. Did he stay there all day, his tail swishing in the sunlight, his amber eyes trained on the bustling crowd below, like so many mice just waiting for him to snatch them up and stuff them into his watering mouth? She imagined him lounging on the couch, the television clicker in one paw, the other paw wrapped around a cold beer, one eye on the clock. *Five twenty-seven. TV off, assume the cat position at the window. Don't tip human off to the reality of cat life. Must maintain the façade.*

Billie joined him at the window, cooed at him, and scratched between his ears. His eyes became slits and a rumble of satisfaction shook his body. She gave his stump a rub and a scratch before tossing her briefcase onto the sofa. A plate of last night's remains from Thai-Bow, her favourite take out place just up the block, heated in the microwave while Billie poured a rare glass of chardonnay. She deserved it. It had been a long week.

She sipped the wine and flipped through the mail until three beeps announced that Tom Yum soup and satay chicken skewers over coconut rice were ready. She salivated like Pavlov's bloody dog. Maybe it was time for a change, to shake up the routine. Learn to cook her own meals. It would save some money.

Cutting expenses — a good first step on the path to freelance heaven.

1993

BILLIE'S MOTHER HELD HER HANDS OVER BILLIE'S eyes. "Don't peek." It was four in the afternoon and already nips of whisky slurred her words.

Billie said a brief prayer and asked God to make her mother stop drinking. Just for today. It was all she wanted for her eleventh birthday. No ponies, no new clothes. Not even the new Teen Talk Barbie that all the girls at school already had. Billie's big birthday wish was for her mother to find a better way to cope. Not buying cigarettes and alcohol with what little money her father made.

She inhaled the comfort of her father's cologne.

"Okay, Billie Angel," he said. "Open them."

Her mother released Billie's eyes and she stared at the cake, ablaze on the kitchen counter. Not even a homemade cake, but a fancy store-bought one with big roses and "Happy Birthday Billie 11 years-old" written in cursive blue-icing letters atop the white slab. The flames from eleven candles danced and swayed and threw their glorious light on Billie's face.

Her parents broke out into the birthday song. When they finished, they urged her to blow out the candles.

Billie shut her eyes tight and wished for a sober mother. Then she made another wish. The same one she made last year. She wished to have friends. Real friends, not just her daddy or mother, or the five-year-old next door who wouldn't leave her alone. Not just her grandmother, who doted on Billie since grandpa passed away the year before.

Real. Friends. Please. God.

She opened her eyes and stared at the flickering candlelight. Were two wishes even allowed? She took a deep breath and blew out every candle. Their extinguished bodies sent wisps of smoke into the air. Then every single one of them relit. Billie blinked.

It was a miracle. A sign.

"Woohoo!" Her mother's volume was whisky-fueled. "Billie's got eleven secret boyfriends." She threw her arms in the air, clapped, and laughed.

Billie fought back tears. "I do not." She blew out the candles, and once again they relit by themselves.

Her mother doubled over, one arm across her belly, laughter shaking her oversized bosom. "Ah, shit, Billie. Do it again."

"Florrie," Billie's father touched his wife's arm. "That's enough. It's not funny anymore."

Billie crossed her arms. Her mother was never funny.

Her mother yanked her arm out of his grip. "It was fucking hilarious." She turned a finger on Billie. "You need to get a sense of humour."

"Florrie! For God's sake, make some coffee." Her father squatted in front of Billie. "We're going out to dinner. All fancy for your birthday."

Billie glanced at her mother. She put her forehead against father's. "But we can't afford it," she whispered.

He put his hand on the back of her head and patted her hair. "Don't you worry about that. We can afford one night out." He cut his eyes to his wife and set his lips in a thin line.

Billie's father pulled her chair out for her, like she was a real lady. He told her to get anything she wanted. Her mouth watered at the choices on the menu. Some she didn't recognize. Escargot. Lobster bisque. She settled on something familiar, yet exotic. Roast chicken with demi-glace, garlic mashed potatoes, and asparagus with hollandaise sauce. She hoped that meant cheese.

It didn't. And it smelled like farts. But the chicken and potatoes were delicious.

"I have one more surprise for you." Her father beamed across the table at her. He reached into the pocket of his pants and pulled out a small box. He slid it across the table.

Billie picked it up. It was made of soft velvet. Short sprigs of royal blue material stood on end, and shifted under her fingertips when she rubbed the surface. She swallowed and eased the lid open. Inside, nestled against ivory satin, was a gold cross. Billie gasped. She ogled the shiny pendant and looked up at her father. "Gold? For me?"

"Just for you. Because we couldn't ask for a better daughter."

Her mother rolled her eyes and pulled a cigarette from her purse.

"Jesus, Florrie. Can't you skip it for one night? I hate it when you smoke in front of Billie."

Her mother pinched her lips together and pitched the cigarette into the gullet of her cheap purse.

Her father stood and came around behind Billie's chair. He plucked the necklace from inside the box, undid the clasp, and placed it around her neck.

She touched the cross, ran her fingertips over the pattern carved into its surface. She closed her eyes, held it in her hand, and imagined Jesus on the crucifix. A tear sprang to her eye. She turned in her chair and threw her arms around her father's waist. "Thank you, Daddy. I'll take good care of it."

He kissed the top of her head. "I know you will."

Her mother shook Billie's shoulder. "Hey, it's from me too you know. Don't I get any hugs?"

Billie released her father, stood, and put her hands on her mother's shoulders. She placed a kiss on her mother's cheek. "Thank you, Mother."

"You are welcome, darling. Now how about dessert?"

"We had cake at home, Florrie."

"So? Special night, right? Buy the kid a piece of pie, cheapskate."

Her father squinted.

"It's okay, Daddy. I don't need pie."

His face softened and he turned to Billie. "Of course you do. Apple, right? Ice cream and cheese and anything else they'll put on it."

After she finished her slice of pie, her father counted out the last of his cash. A flash of panic crossed his eyes and he whispered to his wife that the tip would be a little light. Billie's mother shrugged and examined her fingernails. When they stood to leave, Billie rested her small purse, a hand-me-down from her grandmother that carried nothing but cherry Chapstick and a small mirror — and the twenty-dollar bill her grandmother had slipped her for her birthday — onto her chair.

Outside of the restaurant, Billie tugged on her father's sleeve. "Daddy, I left my bag. I'll go get it."

"We'll wait. I'm sure your mother would like a cigarette."

"Hell, yes." Her mother dug in her purse.

Billie ran back inside. She picked her purse up from the chair, unzipped it, and pulled the money out. The waiter was taking the tab and the funds her father had left behind. "Excuse me, my father asked me to give you this for a tip."

The man's face lit up. "Why thank you, young lady. And happy birthday to you."

12

"Thank you."

She pushed open the door to the restaurant. Her parents stood on the street corner, arguing. Her father had one finger wagging in her mother's face, and her mother was tapping her foot against the pavement. She slapped his hand away, turned, and stormed down the sidewalk.

Billie slid her hand inside her father's and smiled up at him.

He returned the smile. "Shall we take a walk? Your mother wants to window shop."

Billie nodded. She knew her mother wanted more than window-shopping. But there wasn't enough money. It was the biggest issue between them. She wanted more. He couldn't give it. But he'd do anything he could, spend more than he had, to make his daughter happy.

Were all mothers jealous of their daughters?

They strolled along the street and spied the shiny goods inside the lit-up windows.

Her mother oohed and aahed at the jewelry shining behind the glass, at the shoes and boots and furs. She put both palms flat against one window. "Look, Danny." She wagged a finger. "Red patent leather stilettos. Oh, and a matching purse." She sidled up to him and slipped her arm through his, rested her head on his shoulder and ran her fingers around the buttons of his shirt. "Will you buy them for me? Pretend it's my birthday?"

Her mother's batting eyelashes and sly smile were all too familiar.

Billie's father's cheeks turned as red as her mother's lipstick and his jaw clenched.

Billie took his hand. "It's all right, Daddy." Similar scenes played out a few times a week, like a television rerun of an old, worn-out sitcom. Minus the com. "Let's just go home."

Her father squeezed Billie's hand. "We'll cut through the alley.

Maybe we can be home in time to watch *Full House* before bed."

Billie nodded with vigour.

They stepped into the darkness of the alley, musty and reeking like an unclean bathroom. Dim bulbs over the back entries to stores and bars and office buildings cast deep shadows across their path. Halfway through, the thumping rhythms of hip-hop music vibrated from the bricks. Yards ahead, a door opened and the music spilled out, its heavy beat tickling Billie's feet and bouncing in her ears.

Three men burst from the building. One of them wore a bright red bandana on his head. The closer Billie and her family got, the louder the men became.

"Da fuck, man? I said twenty per. You shortin' me?" He grabbed another man by the collar.

Billie couldn't take her eyes off bandana man's funny teeth. She tugged on her father's hand.

He stopped and turned to his wife. "Take Billie."

"Danny, don't." Her mother yanked Billie backward a couple of feet.

"I have to. It's my job."

"You are off the clock, God damn you. Can't you just walk on by for once?"

Her father reached into his jacket pocket where he kept his badge. "You know I can't."

He approached the men. "Good evening, gentlemen." He flashed his badge." Can I see your hands please?"

The man with the teeth dropped the other guy's collar and spun around. The light glinted off one tooth. A gold tooth. His eyes were wild behind bushy brows.

The guy who was being roughed up backed away, turned, and sprinted down the alley.

Gold Tooth jerked his head at Billie's father. "Mind your business, cop. We ain't doin' nothin'. Just out having a little smoke, that's all."

"Sure, that's all. Empty your pockets."

Gold Tooth smirked and craned his neck. He took a step forward in front of the third man who just stood in the dark and didn't say a word. "That's a pretty lady you got there." Gold Tooth put his hand inside the pocket of his hoodie. "Maybe you oughtta just take her and the little one home."

Billie's father rested his hand where his gun holster would be if he were in uniform. "Let me see your hands."

Gold Tooth yanked his hand from his hoodie and flicked open a knife. He lunged and slashed at her father.

Her father pulled away, grabbed his forearm and swore. His sleeve was cut and blood seeped through. He turned to his wife. "Run for help."

Billie froze in place. The whole world slowed on its axis and every second took ten to tick by. The barrel of a gun flashed in the dim light. It was all she could see, the end of that gun, pointed at her father. It got bigger and bigger until it took up her entire field of vision.

The muzzle flashed and a boom echoed off the walls around her. Her father fell to his knees and landed on his face on the alley floor.

A high-pitched whine rang in Billie's ears.

Billie's mother ran to her husband. She kneeled in the filth and the spilled blood, shook his shoulders. Her mouth was open and screaming but all Billie heard was that whine.

She stood there, transfixed and paralyzed. Her feet had grown roots and her body was numb.

The gun went off again and her mother collapsed on top of her father. Gold Tooth held the knife at his side and yelled something at the man with the gun.

Billie looked into the eye of the gun. She prayed for him to shoot her too. Kill her too. Send her to heaven with her father.

Gold Tooth waved his arms and yelled. Billie could hear nothing but blood coursing through her veins and the squeal and echo of gunfire. Could feel nothing but hot urine running down her legs.

The muzzle flashed at the same time that Gold Tooth pushed the gunman.

Billie went down. She didn't feel any pain. Didn't even feel her body hit the ground. A cat screeched and music pulsed through the pavement. She fell asleep to a good vibration and a sweet sensation whispering in her ear.

First Friday in May

MORNING COMMUTES WERE MUCH LIKE EVENINGS — except most passengers were fresh and sparkling clean and didn't stink of lost hope and dried perspiration.

Armed with the knowledge that her contract allowed freelancing, so long as she wasn't stealing the company's clients, Billie felt more alive than she had in months. A few internet searches to pillage billing rates and buzzwords from other editors, a down-and-dirty website announcing her services to the waiting world, and several unsolicited emails to independent writers she found on LinkedIn and Twitter and all manner of other time-suck social media sites, and she was on her way. Or at least, she'd made the first step. One tiny step.

At the third stop of fourteen, a horde of teens hopped onto the train. She was familiar with this group. They were not a friendly bunch. They pushed their way into the metal cylinder every morning, rode the rails four whole stops before disembarking a block from school. She knew this because they were so bloody loud that everyone heard where they were going, whom they'd slept with, how horrible their parents were. Half a dozen privileged white boys trying their hardest to be street. They made snide comments to commuters who were minding their own business. Rude remarks about fashion choice and haircuts, weight, height, four eyes. Juvenile bullshit with a hard edge. An edge that would turn vicious and leave a deep wound if they were in just the right mood.

She hated them all. Why didn't they get off their lazy asses and walk twenty-seven blocks? Leave the subway for those who needed it. Folks who had a long commute. Struggled with mobility. Couldn't afford to drive. Didn't want to be annoyed, interrupted, accosted by their presence.

One of the boys sat opposite her and gave her the same look he did every day. Not even a look at all. His gaze passed through her as if she weren't even there, as if she were made of glass that didn't shine, didn't reflect. She was lucky. If he did focus on her, who knows what unmannerly verbal detritus would spew from his bully mouth.

He was their leader. Each of his crew did his bidding, sometimes without the benefit of words being spoken. That morning he wore a new accessory. A red bandana, do-rag style.

She closed her eyes to avoid looking at him. The spectre of a gold-toothed man in a bright red headscarf loomed behind her lids. Her hand trembled and she blinked the memory away.

Senseless tribal tattoos snaked up from under the hood of the subway bully's jacket and crawled around his neck. He probably thought they meant warrior or strength or leader. She'd bet they meant puppy. His hoodie fell open and underneath, a T-shirt emblazoned with the symbol of Batman.

She hated Batman.

The people who killed Bruce Wayne's parents didn't shoot him full of lead. Didn't cost him a leg. They just shot him full of angst and cost him a normal life.

Billie had fought for normal. Fought to keep friends, freaked out by the eleven-year-old's missing limb, by the metal and rubber that replaced flesh and bone. No fancy skin-like cover, no-siree. Grandmother couldn't afford that. When Billie hit puberty, the boys avoided her. Budding breasts be damned, they couldn't get past the missing part, the gnarled, scarred, misshapen knob at the end of what was left of her calf. But still, she fought for normal. It just never found her. No date for the prom, no sleepovers with her girlfriends. There were no girlfriends. Just books. Books and her father's mother, who tried her best to be a replacement for Billie's own mom. Except Grandmother didn't drink. So that was an improvement.

Billie vowed to be as normal as possible, just to spite the bastards who took her family. To spite the kids who couldn't see past her handicap, past her deformity. Who couldn't see her at all.

The subway shook and Billie focused her eyes. Bat Head was gone. She found him standing in front of the door, waiting for it to open. When it did, he led his crew out into the big wide world to annoy the crap out of decent people everywhere. She blinked, glanced around, and rested her head against the window behind her. Her fingers found the carved surface of her gold cross.

Seven more stops.

A manuscript landed on her desk with a slap. Billie jumped and jostled her teacup, sloshing oolong onto her mouse.

"An old-fashioned one. Paper and all." Katherine crossed her arms. "Due by the fifteenth. You can handle it, right? It's only six-hundred pages." She smirked.

"In two weeks? Without a computer?" A knot grew in Billie's stomach. So much for spare-time to freelance.

"Two weeks. Assuming you still want to work here." Katherine loomed over her and leaned in. "You think I wouldn't see that piss-poor excuse for a website you threw together? Think I'm not checking up on all you proofing-pool rats and what you say about me?"

Billie swallowed. "I checked my contract. I'm allowed. I'm not taking any clients away from the company." Her head lightened and her cheeks warmed. "I promise."

"You know where you can shove your promises. By the fifteenth. Or consider yourself released to work freelance. Permanently."

Katherine stormed back to her office. Jeffrey poked his weasel head out of his hole, one side of his mouth upturned.

Billie put one palm atop the almost three-inch-thick manuscript. She flipped through a few pages. Typewritten, single-spaced for crying out loud. Who uses a typewriter? Single-spaced? She rubbed the bridge of her nose and shook her head. Good thing she had no social life. It would have been sacrificed to the editing gods anyway.

She ogled her computer, ran one finger across the keyboard. She reached for the monitor and depressed the power button, a long sigh feathered across her lips. A second before the screen's light died, she noticed the date. May first. May Day.

How bloody appropriate.

MONDAY, MAY 4TH

B Y SUNDAY, BILLIE'D HAD ENOUGH AND ESCAPED her apartment, unchained herself from the insufferable prose of Edward Morse, soon-to-be not-so-bestselling author of fantasy drivel, and fled to find sanctuary in church. She hadn't attended services for months, and even then, only to absorb the beauty that was the Reverend Gabriel Keene, the message he conveyed less spoken than effervesced from his full lips. His take on the word of God.

But that wasn't her God. Not anymore. She wasn't afraid of her God. He was her friend, her confidante. Her God understood that all good people aren't perfect. That those who are the most broken need the most leeway.

She'd sat in one of the front pews, distracted by the pretty priest. Visions of dangling modifiers and mangled expressions impeded her prayers. No, that Sunday hadn't been about God. Billie had just needed a better view for a couple hours.

Her cubicle walls quaked when she slammed her briefcase, heavy with the six-hundred-page manuscript, onto her desk. It had become her cross to bear. The anchor that kept her from drifting off into calmer waters. The old ball and chain, without the side benefit of rote sex and fake orgasms. It became a metaphor for her life, heavy with sorrow and unrequited grief for lost parents, lost childhood, lost limb. It was the weight of her loneliness, the burden of her mutilation, the utter heft of her failure at normal. It was her new handicap.

She picked up her mental red pen and edited the clichés out of her own thoughts. If she were one of her clients, she'd have dumped herself a hundred pages ago.

The latches opened with a hollow click. She peered inside. The fat ream of paper stared back at her, her own red deles and carets and strikethroughs taunted her with just how little she'd accomplished, just how much more literary offal she had to slash and correct and, worst of all … read.

She hauled out the manuscript and slumped into her ergonomic chair. Only seventy-eight pages in three days. At that rate, she'd be freelancing before the week was up. All weekend she'd tried to focus, to find the mental energy to face the slop on the pages. She'd sit on the sofa with thirty sheets, nod off, awake to paper all over the floor. Have to sort it, stack it, put it back in order. Not an easy task since the fatuous author didn't number the pages.

She tapped the manuscript with her red pen and sighed. Reading aloud, perhaps that would work. Billie cleared her throat. "The earth shook when he took me in his arms. Or maybe it was just me, trembling at the cold, clammy touch of his undead fingers. His teeth penetrated the silky white flesh of my virgin neck. An explosion of light emanated from him like a glitter bomb. A glitter bomb of love."

Billie threw up in her mouth a little.

"How goes it?" Jeffrey stood at her elbow, failing at his barely veiled attempt to size up her progress. He was on standby, waiting for her to blow it. He'd probably measured her desk, one of the few near a window, before she got to work. Presumptuous, brown-nosing little wiener. She suppressed a grin at the thought of him in a rhinestone-studded dog collar, trailing behind Katherine, a leopard-skin leash in her hand.

Billie lowered the lid of the briefcase. "It's going, Jeffrey. Just like you are. Back to your hole." She flicked her fingers at him.

"Shoo."

He huffed at her and stuck his lower lip out, turned and retreated to his hovel in the corner.

She clicked her computer on and stared at the screen while it went through its daily start-up process. When the cursor turned from spinning blue circle to hollow arrow, she clicked on the Outlook icon and watched her inbox fill up.

She'd missed the due date on a ninety-thousand-word nonfiction self-help book. Not that it would make any difference to sales. Publish now, publish five years from now, same old love-yourself, art-of-attraction, smile-and-the-world-smiles-with-you flapdoodle that filled literal and digital bookshelves. And flew off them too. Why did people fall for such falderal? If anyone needed some feel-good self-help, it was Billie. But even she couldn't buy into the shallow end of that psychobabble pool. Thrice-weekly workouts at the gym, that was her salvation. A beating heart and the promise of heaven was all she needed. Or so she kept telling herself.

An hour later, her emails answered, other authors put off with the excuse of competing deadlines, which was no lie, she buried herself in the huge typewritten pile, the third vampire novel she'd edited that year. Come on, people, vampires are so twenty-ten. What would be the claim to fame for this group of neck biters — glowing? Sparkling? Or maybe some good old-fashioned blood sucking murder for a change.

Seven hours, six cups of coffee, three stale doughnuts, and one new red pen later, she'd fought her way through forty-seven more pages. She rubbed her neck and eyed the pages, like the aftermath of a bad slasher flick. Serves the author right, all that passive-voiced, head hopping, cliché-riddled claptrap. Thank God for small mercies, after the glitter bomb of love, the story was rife with actual sucking of blood, death, and gore. No angst-ridden, teenaged, ashen-yet-shiny vamps. But the prose was painful. It wasn't bad enough he was ripping off Bram Stoker's original character, this author was channeling the adverb-heavy, run-on sentenced, writing style of the late nineteenth century. The kind of stories only palatable in the modern day when computer-generated on the big screen at the multiplex. Not wrought on paper — actual bloody paper — and fraught with twisted metaphors and obvious similes and repeated misuse of common idioms. Intents and purposes, damn it, not intensive purposes. Penal system, not penile system.

She pitched her pen on her desk. It skittered across the surface like the perfect skipping stone across a mirror-flat lake and landed at Katherine's feet.

Katherine stooped to retrieve it, placed it on top of the manuscript, tossed her Coach bag over her shoulder, and left the building without a word. She didn't need to speak. Her one arched brow, lips clamped into a thin line, and loathsome glare spoke volumes.

It was all Billie could do not to yell "bitch" at her back. But Billie would never say that aloud. She was already swirling the profane drain with all of the damns and bloodies, and even the occasional F-bomb she'd been screaming in her head. Plus all the fantasies about Katherine's demise and Jeffrey's undoing. She hadn't had those thoughts about anyone before, except the men who'd murdered her parents and took her leg. But God would forgive her those transgressions. It was only imaginary. She'd never hurt a soul in real life.

She snatched the pen from her desk and wiggled it across Katherine's retreating back. She drew a red gun in the air, shot a couple of rounds into the kidney region. Red ink blood spewed and spattered and oozed from the wounds, drenched Katherine's Holt Renfrew skirt and dripped from the hem.

And yet, she kept walking.

Billie clutched the pen in her fist. She plucked three more of them from the old NaNoWriMo mug on her desk — the one she bought to commemorate her excitement four years ago, the only year she tried to write fifty thousand words of a shitty first draft of a novel in one short month. Epic fail. But it did make a lovely pencil cup.

She tossed the pens into her purse, dog-eared the page she was working on, stacked the bloody sheets and fastened them together with one giant binder clip. It was only Monday, but she felt the need for a good sweat. She needed to clear the cobwebs and let the proofreading juices flow.

THURSDAY THE FOURTEENTH

*P*EG LEG CURLED UP AGAINST BILLIE'S THIGH. HIS bodily warmth and moral support gave her the strength to push through the final chapter of Morse's future flop, a work she had unofficially subtitled "Dreckula." She turned the final page, laid her head against the soft cushions of her grandmother's old sofa, and heaved a massive sigh. One day to spare. Job saved.

Sanity?

The jury was still out.

She ran her fingers between Peg Leg's pointed ears and slid away from his heat. She refreshed her email, surprised to find three new messages. Her eyes widened as she scanned the subject lines. Potential clients. Her very own clients. She glanced at the clock. Too late for her usual Thursday treadmill time. She sat at the breakfast nook and clicked on the first email.

I'm a indie author, so I'm not making much money and can't afford you're full fee. What services you could give me for under a hundred? Or I could pay you out of future royalties. The book is awesome. Its sure to sell a million copies in no time.

Billie ground her teeth at each error and composed a reply in her head. *Dear Indie Author. Screw off, you moron. I'm not running a charity, for Christ's sake. I have to eat, too. For under a hundred I can offer you some advice. Don't quit your day job.*

Her actual reply was polite, concise, and grammatically perfect. One potential client down, two more to go. The second was no better, offering to trade his "excellant" writing abilities for her "excellant" editing. Pass.

She stared at email door number three and sighed. She was going to need Earl Grey reinforcement before reading it.

Minutes later, a steaming, sweet, milky brew in her hand, she clicked the message open.

Dear Ms. Fullalove,

I am seeking a professional editor for my first novel. It is a psychological thriller, in the range of 325 pages. The fourth draft is almost complete and I feel it will be ready for a professional's eyes within the month.

The indicative rates on your website are competitive. If you are interested, please provide a firm quotation for a full edit (proofreading and content) of an 82,000-word document. I would also appreciate two references. I am attaching a brief sample of the book.

Sincerely,

Annabelle Wright

Well, hells bells. An actual prospective client.

Billie sent emails to four authors in her roster that she knew and trusted. Authors to whom she had secretly offered editing advice outside her lowly proofreading role. Authors who had rewarded her with their silence and more than one gift card to her favourite coffee shop as secret compensation.

She acknowledged Annabelle's message and promised pricing and references to follow. She grinned and picked up the warm teacup, held it in both hands and leaned back in the chair. Step one in extricating herself from proofing-pool obscurity underway. No more Edward Morses. No more typewritten manuscripts. Unless Katherine was already planning the next roadblock in Billie's quest for freedom. To heck with Katherine. She wasn't going to dampen the mood tonight.

Billie gathered Peg Leg into her arms and headed to her room. She set the cat on the bed, sat beside him and dismantled her at-home prosthesis, a simpler form of the one she wore to work, with a smaller foot and fewer layers of socks. Usually she didn't even bother with that. Just hopped around the apartment on one leg, or used her grandfather's cane for support, the one with the brass horse's head for a handle.

She pumped baby lotion into her palm from the bottle that was a fixture on her nightstand and massaged the emollient into her stump. There were other choices, unscented, with aloe vera, with vitamin E. Too many choices. The hospital used baby lotion during her recovery. The baby powder scent was soft and soothing to her eleven-year-old self, and calmed her now. Now that she knew recovery wasn't a thing. It wasn't a point in time. It was an evolution. A journey without end. Her own never-ending story.

Each night, when that lotion hit her nostrils, she regressed to a time when she felt reborn. A new baby learning to walk. Learning to live. Learning to forgive.

She had learned to forgive her parents for dying on her. For leaving her to grow up without their guidance. For abandoning her when she needed them most. The hardest was forgiving God. She'd had many discussions with Him. Had sworn at Him, sworn off Him. If He was everything, was everywhere, why, why, why did He kill her family? Why did He leave her on her own with only an old grandmother, far past her prime and exhausted by daily life, let alone life with a mutilated young child, a recovering lost soul? Heck, grandmother was messed up too. She'd lost her son, after all.

But Billie could never forgive those murderous men. Some things were unforgivable.

No matter how often she strayed from His side, Billie always found her way back to God. They had a complicated relationship. And a silent understanding — as all understandings with God are. She agreed to be a good girl on the outside. But on the inside, if she kept it to herself, she could think bad thoughts. Swear and curse and imagine a tortuous revenge inflicted on the evil beings of the world.

The evil that God couldn't control.

God agreed to let her have those silent indiscretions. So that she could survive her wretched life.

FRIDAY

THE COOL, PRE-DAWN AIR BRUSHED BILLIE'S cheeks. She blinked hard, failing in her attempts to focus on the twinkle of light to her left. She stared at the soft beam, followed the illuminating ray it offered until her eyes finally connected with her brain and she recognized the graffiti-tainted trash bin under the light standard half a block up from her apartment building. She wavered, her balance off. She grasped the wrought iron post of the fire escape and looked at her foot. One foot balancing on the railing, her stump dangling mid-air.

Billie drew in a sharp breath. What the hell had her deranged nighttime brain planned to do? Plunge her three stories to her death? Well, guess what, night brain — that would have only crippled her. Again.

Next time, get up to the roof.

She took hold of the pole with both hands, eased her quaking body down, shifted her butt onto the railing, and hopped to the grated floor. Her window was wide open, the gauzy curtain blowing into the apartment. Peg Leg sat on the window ledge, his head cocked to one side. He meowed at her, gave her a withering glare, and disappeared into the living room.

Sleepwalking. She hadn't done that in three years. A full year after her last episode, she'd stopped seeing Dr. Kroft. Billie shut her eyes and conjured the doc's voice. Dissociative fog. Or something or other. Coping mechanism. Resulting from trauma. Triggered by anything that triggered the memories attached to her trauma.

Years ago, Billie would awaken, or have her conscious brain take over, and find herself in the park a couple of blocks from her grandmother's house. Sometimes she'd have only ventured out into the yard. But often she'd be gone for hours, come to on the subway, or in a part of town she was unfamiliar with. It was when she was fourteen, after her night brain took her on a field trip to a dark alley, the heavy beat of loud music vibrating the asphalt, that her grandmother made the first appointment with the doc.

Billie rubbed her hands against her arms to ward off the morning chill. To heat the ice that always replaced her blood when the adrenaline of waking from a walking dream raced through her body. She crawled through the window, righted the potted petunia, and brushed dirt from the ledge into her open palm. She stared at the dirt, balled her fist and squeezed. She looked out the window at the horizon. A purple dawn overtook the darkness. Peg Leg poked at her clenched hand with his head and rubbed her knuckles between his ears.

Billie swallowed. Maybe she needed to get back on the psychology train. Before her night brain did something crazy. Something permanent.

"Wilhelmina!"

Katherine screaming names from inside her office was never a good way to start the day. Especially when it was Billie's name.

She gathered her skirt and her courage and stood. She took a deep breath, eyed the beautiful day outside the window where everyone was free. She chided herself for her envy of the birds, envy of the wind, envy of the clouds. That was her reincarnation wish —

to return untethered and in full control of her every choice. To take flight. Not be anchored by one lost leg. Or anchored by legs at all.

She touched her fingertips to her hair to ensure everything was in place, straightened her shoulders, and marched to her doom in the chamber of horrors.

At the threshold, she tapped her knuckles on the doorframe. "Yes, Katherine?"

You bellowed?

Katherine stood at her own window, the six-hundred-page albatross in her hand. She turned and lifted it in the air.

Billie held her breath. If Katherine dropped that bomb, binder clip be damned, red-stained pages would explode all over the office. And Billie would be the one putting the unnumbered pieces back together.

"What the hell is this?" Katherine's eyes burned, her laser stare piercing Billie's bravery.

"It looks like Mr. Morse's manuscript." Billie glanced at her feet. She'd chosen the black pointed-toe flats with the faux snakeskin texture this morning. But there was only one. In her haste to make the train, she had failed to change the shoe on her prosthesis. It remained the dull brown ballet flat with the rounded toe and the teardrop-shaped holes cut into the leather. She couldn't help but grin at the dichotomy worn on her feet. A perfect match to her internal courage — pointed, black, reptilian, overwhelmed by, and contrary to, the dull brown reality of the terror manifesting in trembling hands and the threat of tears.

Goddamn tears.

Katherine slammed the document onto her desk.

Billie jumped, her heart hammered. This was it. She was done for.

"Just what is your role here, Ms. Fullalove?"

"Proofreader?"

Katherine nodded. "Yes. *Just* a proofreader. *Only* a proofreader." She tapped one finger on the pile of pages. "And in what universe did you think that proofreader extended to editor, huh? Did I miss the memo that you got a promotion?" She cocked her head and tapped that same finger against her cheek. "Oh, wait." She turned the finger on Billie. "I'd be the one writing the damn thing." Katherine took a step forward.

Billie braced for impact. But Katherine wouldn't hit her. Couldn't hit her. That was crazy. It was just intimidation. A tactic she excelled at. Stand your ground, Billie. Stand your damn ground. "I just thought, since I'm already editing —"

"Proofreading."

Billie bit her lip. "Proofreading. And I can see issues with the plot, with consistency. And the characterization?" Billie furrowed her brow.

"That is for the editor, not for you. If I wanted to know if you could edit, I'd ask you to damn well edit. You're just another minnow in the proofreading pool. Now I have six hundred pages with your shitty red chicken scratch marring the manuscript. How is the editor going to sift through entire paragraphs slashed out, through your puny thoughts scribbled in the margins?"

"I added some pages of notes, cross-referenced with —"

"Not. Your. Job." Katherine punctuated each word with a poke to Billie's shoulder with that offending, pointing, crimson-lacquered finger.

Billie swallowed. "Katherine, please don't touch me."

Katherine's right eyebrow arched so high even her Botoxed forehead crinkled. That brow was the harbinger of doom. The forecast of the storm to come. Shit was going to hit the publishing fan.

"Get out."

It was a whisper, but one so menacing, Billie thought her heart had stopped beating. "Yes, ma'am." Billie turned to the door, hesitated, turned back to face the tempest, her gaze on her mismatched feet. "Do you mean out of your office. Or out of the building?"

Katherine's heavy sigh blew her caramel macchiato breath across Billie's face. "Get your gimpy ass to your desk and do your job. *Only* your job. Understood?"

Billie swallowed the urge to scream, "Fuck you, bitch, I'm no goddamn gimp," and simply nodded. She turned, strode to her workstation, sat with purpose and a straight spine. She double-clicked on a file icon, opened a manuscript, the priority work of the day, and began to proofread. And edit. Couldn't help herself. But she kept those edits off the digital page, hidden away in her mind. Right next to Katherine's dead body.

MAY 21ˢᵗ - THURSDAY

BILLIE PICKED A LILLIPUTIAN PIECE OF FLUFF FROM her skirt and flicked it into the air. It floated and swayed on the stillness before the evil forces of static electricity dragged it back down to the floral polyester. She sighed and looked up into the sagging face of Dr. Kroft. The past twentyish years hadn't been kind to the old broad. What was she, pushing sixty? The crevasses around her eyes and canyon-deep laugh lines parenthesizing her dry lips made her look closer to seventy-five.

The doc pushed her Sally-Jesse-Raphael-red glasses up higher on her nose and glanced at her lilac notepad. Not a book, never white paper. Lilac. Only lilac. Billie had always wondered why. Had never asked. But at that moment, the question burned a hole in her thoughts. "Why lilac?"

The doc sent one eyebrow into space. "What's that, now?"

Billie gestured to the notepad. "Lilac paper. Always lilac. Twenty plus years of lilac. Did you buy them in bulk back in 1994 or something?"

Doc's eyebrow landed back on earth and the corners of her upturned lips disappeared into folds of old skin. She shook her head. "I like purple. When you were gone, I tried yellow. Even plain old white. But lilac is calming." She tapped the rim of her glasses with her pen. "It's kind on the old eyes. Now enough about my quirks. Let's discuss your messed-up psyche."

One thing Billie could always count on was Doc Kroft not pussyfooting around her crazy.

"So you awoke on the fire escape. You think you were going to jump?"

"Either that or fly. Maybe my night brain thinks that's possible. I can run with one leg, so why not fly without wings?"

"Have you had any new trauma?"

"Nope." Katherine's pokey finger and crimson face came to mind. Is being mistreated at work, being intentionally held back from any opportunity to move up, to be promoted, to find any nuance of job satisfaction, trauma?

"No public teasing, no verbal abuse."

Billie squished the piece of skirt fluff under her thumb and pushed it around. "That's not trauma. That's life."

Doc tossed her lilac notepad on the coffee table between them and lobbed her blue pen at it. "Billie, we've talked about this. It's not the same as witnessing your parents' murder, or having your leg shot off. But for someone who has been traumatized in that way, it can be a trigger."

Billie sighed. "Yeah, I know. You being pissed at me doesn't help."

"Darling, Billie. I am anything but pissed. I'm worried. You've not been to see me in more than two years. Are you taking your meds?"

Doc had her scrunched-up concerned face on. Did she practice that in the mirror? Billie liked that face. It was endearing. It reminded her of her grandmother.

Billie fidgeted with her skirt, made eye contact with the curtains, cleared her throat.

"Billie. You stopped again."

"Yes, I stopped. I think it's the meds that make me crazy."

"No, it's not. There are side effects, but without them, things end up worse." She tented her fingers.

Billie often wondered if there was a special class for that at psychologist school. Finger tenting one-oh-one.

"How about the social life?"

Billie winced. "Does the cat count?"

Doc shook her head. "So no new friends, no boyfriends. Not even one date?"

"No ma'am. Unless you count the sweet sticky things in the grocery store."

"Have you tried the tips I suggested? Volunteering, singles groups, support groups?"

Billie stared at her.

"Ok, then. You're still active at church, I imagine, so that is something."

Billie bit her lip and looked at her lap. "Actually, I don't go there much anymore."

"What's not much?"

Billie shrugged. "Never? Well, once. A couple of weeks ago. Before that it was a few months."

"But not since." It wasn't a question. The doc was ruminating on her disappointment. She picked up her lilac pad. "Well, if you're not going to get out there and look for support and you insist on staying off the meds," the doc eyed her over the rim of her glasses that hung on for dear life at the tip of her nose, "you'll need therapy. Consistent, ongoing therapy." She turned to a fresh sheet and scratched out a few words, ripped the page off and handed it to Billie. "Three other therapists to consider."

Billie stared at the names, looked up at the doc, a tear burning the corner of one eye. "You're dumping me?"

"Dumping you? Of course not. But maybe you need someone new. I figured since you'd avoided me for so long, you could stand some fresh ideas."

"I wasn't avoiding you. I was avoiding everything." Billie wadded up the paper and tossed it on the coffee table. "I don't want anyone new or fresh. I want you. But I don't want drugs. They make my skin crawl and itch. My stump is itchy enough already."

Doc smiled. "All right, then. Let's ease back into it. How about every third Thursday? We can take it from there."

Billie tapped her real foot against the area rug. "How about I come back in two weeks?"

Doc nodded. "Two weeks it is. See you on the fourth."

THE FOLLOWING MONDAY

BILLIE SPREAD THE NEWSPAPER ACROSS HER LAP. The subway rocked and jerked as it always did, an annoying reality that brought a sense of uncomfortable comfort. Some sameness and predictability to her increasingly unpredictable days.

She scanned the headlines, rolled her eyes at misspelled words and inconsistent capitalization. She froze when she read "Couple Gunned Down In Alley." It was a small article, near the bottom of page seven, tucked away like it didn't even matter. She ran her fingers down the column and devoured the text. Young family out for a matinee on a Saturday, they left the theatre by the back exit and were robbed of wallet and purse. The muggers shot the parents and took off. No leads. Children traumatized. Father dead. Mother clinging to life in the hospital.

Billie closed her eyes. They were going to get away with it. Like the monsters that killed her family. Those poor children. Maybe she should visit them. Talk to them.

Goddamn bullies in the world can't leave good people alone. Have to harm them, steal from them, push them around. Snuff out their lives. And where's the justice system? Sitting back and watching, scratching its balls and flexing its scrawny biceps. Stupid cops and stupider courts with all the rights afforded the accused and none left for the victims.

She blinked her eyes open and unclenched her fists. She smoothed the crunched up corners of the newspaper against her lap. Her inner fury prevented her from noticing the band of teenage hoodlums who were too lazy to walk home from school milling around her. Bat Head, his shirt gray and batless, smirked in her direction.

"Hey, cripple. Nice shoes." His posse laughed and one of them slapped his back, congratulated him on his prowess at insensitivity. His awe-inspiring superpower to be mean for no reason.

"I am not a cripple," Billie said through grit teeth.

Bat Head tapped her prosthesis with the toe of his lime-green kicks and leaned in. "Cripple," he sneered.

The car descended into silence except for the rustling of newsprint somewhere at the back and the clomp of heavy footsteps up the aisle. "Leave her be, boy. She's not bothering you."

Billie blinked at the sound of a man's voice that rumbled like a bass tuba with a handful of gravel caught in the bell.

Humanity on the subway. Go figure.

The boy turned on the man, but when he had to look up a good five inches to meet his gaze, his bravado faltered. He held up his palms. "It's cool, dude. Just playin' with the gimpy chick. No harm, no foul, right?"

The man took a step forward. "She's not gimpy, and she's not a chick. So yeah, dude." He poked the boy in the chest. "Harm." He poked the boy again. "Foul."

The subway pitched and braked. The boy lost his balance. He grabbed for the pole but his fingers slipped and he landed on his denim-clad ass. The car exploded with laughter and applause. One of his friends helped him to his feet. "C'mon Nick. Just drop it."

Nick jerked his chin at the man. "Another time, old man."

The man laughed. "Bring it, shit-for-brains."

When the doors opened, the boy and his crew scrambled out and ran down the platform. Passengers that filed past the tall, broad man patted his shoulder, gave him a thumbs up, mumbled "way to go" and "atta boy" before disappearing out the open maw of the subway car.

Billie smiled up at the man. "Thank you." Her cheeks warmed at the sight of his crooked nose and rugged chin, darkened by the shadow of afternoon beard scruff.

"You're welcome. If you don't stand up to the little bastards, they'll walk all over you. Or worse." He trundled away, plopped his bulky frame into the seat he'd risen from, picked up his own newspaper, and shook the crease from it. He caught her eye and winked, the corners of his mouth upturned.

Billie looked at her lap. That's exactly how that story should read. She wouldn't edit a thing. Except maybe her own fear. Not of the boys, of their insults and their callous mocking. She was used to high school bullies. No, she'd strikeout her fear of holding the man's gaze. Her fear of what might happen if she found the nerve to speak to him. Fear of rejection, of being tossed aside like damaged goods. She cut her eyes to his face.

He was absorbed in the paper, ignoring her angst.

She folded her newspaper and read the headline. Another horrific crime. Another criminal off on a technicality. Cops didn't get a proper warrant before searching a vehicle. Her father was probably rolling over in his grave. And the useless public servant prosecutors rushed through the trial, didn't do their due diligence on behalf of the victims. She mentally edited the piece, at best, a piss-poor excuse for journalism. It read like it was written for a grade four language class. Must they pander to the lowest common denominator?

She huffed a breath at the misspelling of informant, dug in her purse and pulled out a red pen. She filled the article with proofreading marks, deleted unnecessary words, corrected spelling, undangled participles, and closed compound words. What newspaper reporter worth their salt spells it "news paper?"

Once the proofing was complete, she went back to the beginning. She edited for content. For plot. It seemed unreasonable, unlikely — or at least a damn sight unfair — that the depraved clowns who had raped an eleven-year-old boy in the back of a van, then tossed him out like so much trash on Tuesday morning, should get away with it. And in this case, "clowns" was literal. Two schmucks dressed in full pancake makeup, neon-wigged, oversized red-shoe regalia. They abducted the boy from the corner after they'd performed at a four-year-old's birthday party just up the street.

Goddamn clowns. Nothing sucked more than clowns. Except maybe Batman.

She struck out an entire paragraph, wrote her own conclusion in the margins. A gruesome form of justice meted out to the most deserving of pedophilic scum.

"Yeah, I didn't like how that one ended either."

She started and looked up into the face of tall, dark, and stalwart. She blinked. Her tongue refused to cooperate with her brain and just sat there, mute and dry. A witty retort died on her lips. Just as well. It was probably lame. He would have laughed at her.

He sat beside her and scanned the paper. His eyes moved side to side when he read, like there was a tennis match being played out on the page. He poked out his lower lip and nodded. "I like what you've done with it." He tapped the paragraph she'd rewritten. "Incarceration is too good for them. So is death. Public castration, now that's creative." He grinned and held out his hand. "Bruce."

Her eyelids fluttered. Maybe she could edit his name. Randall. Or Dennis. Even Chester. Anything but Bruce. What was his surname, Wayne?

Her cheeks warmed and she looked at the paper. She held her hand toward his. "Billie."

He shook her hand. "Billie? Isn't that more of a guy's name?"

She willed the heat in her cheeks to subside but failed miserably. "Short for Wilhelmina."

"Ah." He nodded. "Yeah, Billie's better."

The subway jerked to a halt. Bruce slid on the hard plastic seat. His thigh brushed against hers. A heat she wasn't accustomed to burned where their clothing met.

"Well, my stop. Stay safe, Billie. Edit a few more endings and make those bad guys pay." He winked, stood, and was gone from her life in a single beat of her heart.

2001

LEAVES RUSTLED OVER BILLIE'S HEAD. THE COOL breeze of early fall cleared her brain and let her creative juices flow. She'd sat on her favourite bench under her favourite oak for more than an hour, engrossed in the third edit of the fourth short story she'd written that month. It wasn't even extra credit work. She wrote them for fun. For release. For companionship. She was well on her way to completing her bachelor's degree in English in almost half the time her fellow students would take. Then onto a master's. Perhaps a PhD was in her future. She was devoted to her studies, to her writing. Especially to editing. Editing was the best part. That's where she truly shined.

The bench shook with the weight of an intruder who dared to plop down beside her. Billie ignored whoever was encroaching on her space, invading her privacy. Trying to muscle in on her loneliness.

"What are you writing?"

She shot a sideways glance at the poacher and rolled her eyes. George something. He always sat near her, tried to make small talk. He came off as thick as a redwood's trunk and just as dense. Her constant rebuffs failed to deter him. Like spilled coffee on a Scotchgarded sofa, her rejection didn't sink in, just rolled off him. And he came back for more almost every day.

She pulled her binder cover half-closed so he couldn't read the pages. "Short story."

"We're supposed to write a story?" He dropped his books on the bench.

She threw him a scowl. "Not for any class I'm in. It's just for me."

"You do extra work for nothing?" He leaned back on the bench and draped his arms across the backrest, his right hand resting against her shoulder.

Billie sat up and his arm slid down her back. She glared at him. "Hands off."

"Shit, sorry. Man, you're jumpy." He withdrew his arm and bounced one knee up and down. "Can I ask you something?"

She sighed, closed her binder, half-turned in her seat, and tried to stab him with her best piercing stare. "What?" Despite his intrusive behaviour, his average grades, and his rather large proboscis, she had to admit he was kind of cute.

He licked his lips. "I wondered if maybe, sometime, you and me could grab a coffee or something."

She gritted her teeth. "You and I."

"Yeah. Us. Coffee."

"No, I mean… Never mind."

He squished his lips together and raised his eyebrows. "Is that a no?"

"Yeah. It's a no."

"Can I ask why? You already have a boyfriend?"

She huffed. "Are you trying to be funny?"

His brows descended and furrowed. "I don't understand."

"Haven't you heard? I'm a freak." She yanked up her pant leg and flicked her prosthesis with her middle finger.

"I know about your leg. How does that make you a freak?" He tugged her pant leg down.

"See? You can't even look at it. You think I'm a freak too. Just like everyone else."

"Billie, it doesn't bother me. It's just that you're being kind of loud and people are staring."

"So let them stare."

"Fine, you want to make an ass of yourself, be my guest." He gathered his books and stood. "You need to chill out. Maybe let somebody past that iron wall you've built around yourself."

"Screw you."

He shook his head. "It's a shame too. You're so smart. Pretty behind that angry scowl you wear. Cute but crazy. And I don't need the crazy." He walked away and didn't look back.

And he never bothered her again.

TUESDAY EVENING

BILLIE SAT IN FRONT OF HER LAPTOP, INTERLACED her fingers, flipped her hands until her palms faced out, and straightened her arms. The crack of knuckles in the quiet apartment left a satisfied grin on her face. She twisted her neck until it snapped to attention, straightened her teacup so the handle was at just the right angle for easy access when the desperate need for a shot of sweet warmth jumped up and bit her, then opened Annabelle Wright's — her first client's — manuscript. All four authors she'd approached for references had sent glowing reviews, and Annabelle happily accepted the offered rate. Perhaps Billie should have come in higher? No matter, it was a start. And a start meant everything.

Step one, format the document. She adjusted the margins, modified normal style to be double-spaced with Times New Roman twelve-point font. She went on a search and destroy mission for the dreaded double space after periods and replaced them with singles.

With that finished, she set Word to track changes and launched into the work. It was a historical romance with dystopian elements. Not exactly Billie's cup of Earl Grey, but it was a paycheque. Three pages in and the author's crutch words were jumping off the page. *Just. Smile.* The objectionable overuse of *that*. And ellipses. What makes a writer think *dot dot dot* more than once on a page is a good idea? Heck, twice in a chapter, maybe. Five times in the whole manuscript, tops.

Seven pages in and Peg Leg decided it was time for a break. He mewled at her until she bundled him onto her lap. He crawled onto

51

the countertop and made a move for her keyboard. "Peg Leg, no!" He got one paw on it before she snatched him up and dropped him back to the floor. "Darn, look what you did." She hit undo until his less-than-professional edits disappeared and she was back where she left off. She saved the document, something she hadn't done since she opened it, and closed the lid.

He mewed at her from the floor, his tail swishing side to side.

She sighed and scratched his head. "You're right. Time to stop." Her mental red pen drew a fourth leg on his sleek body. If only it were that easy. She'd draw herself a new leg too. And a new life.

Billie awoke to the clink of coins. She scanned the sidewalk to either side of her, panic rising in her throat. She ran her hands over her nightgown and found loonies, toonies, and quarters in her lap. Her eyes darted about and landed on her sneaker-clad foot and her bare at-home prosthesis.

Her gut hollowed and she swallowed the urge to vomit. What time was it? And where the hell was she?

She gathered the coins and inched her way up, her back against a brick wall. She took a mental inventory of her body parts and ran her hands over what she could without looking perverted. Why was she wearing workout shorts under pyjamas?

At the corner, a cab turned right and headed her way.

Her head down, avoiding the gaze of passersby, she held her nightgown close to her chest and bolted for the curb. She held up one hand and whistled.

The cab veered across two lanes of traffic and screeched to a stop beside her.

She climbed in and gave him her address. She watched the unfamiliar buildings slide by the window. She tapped on the Plexiglas barrier. "How far a drive is that?"

He eyed her in the rear-view. "Don't you know where you are, lady?"

She shook her head. "Is this Wednesday?"

He nodded.

"The twenty-seventh?"

"Yeah. You okay? You need a hospital or something?"

"No, I just need to go home." And to get out of this disgusting car. Her bare prosthesis crunched against dirt and her sneaker stuck to the car mat. "How long?"

"About half an hour."

The blood drained from her face and she nodded. A half hour by car. How long had she walked? Or perhaps she needed a midnight jog. In her sleep? Without her blade?

If the cabbie knew all she had was about ten bucks in change to pay the fare, he'd boot her out right there in the middle of God-knows-where. She shrunk down in her seat and held her stomach.

"Lady you don't look so good. You puke in my cab and I'll have to charge you extra."

"I'm fine," she snapped. "Just hurry up."

Ten minutes later, familiar landmarks popped into view. They crossed Sixty-Seventh Avenue just a few miles from Grandmother's old house. When the taxi pulled up in front of her apartment, she hopped from the back seat and approached his open window. "Here, take this, it's all I have."

He counted it, then looked up at her, his cheeks afire and his eyes bulging. "That's about twenty short lady. You get me the rest or there'll be cops on your ass in two minutes."

She held her palms up. "Give me five and I'll be right down with the rest."

"You trying to rip me off?" He snatched his radio from its dash-mounted holder.

"No! I would never, ever, do that. I'll be back right away. I promise." She bolted into the building and raced up the stairs, past Mrs. Rogerson, who gaped at Billie with her mouth hanging open.

At the door to her apartment, Billie slowed. The morning sun slivered into the hall from an inch-wide crack between the door and the jamb. "Well, at least I didn't crawl down the fire escape."

She eased the door open. At the creak of hinges, she cringed. She slid inside, her nerves on high alert, her eyes ping-ponging about her apartment. Her purse sat on the floor under the breakfast nook where she'd left it. Peg Leg lay on the window ledge in the sunshine, his eyes locked on her every movement, his tail doing its usual metronome swish.

She did a quick recon. The apartment was in order, nothing missing. And no one inside. Except for the cat.

She retrieved her wallet and keys, locked the door, and went to pay the irate cabbie.

1993

"GOODY TWO SHOES! GOODY TWO SHOES!"
Billie cowered behind the trunk of the ancient maple and covered her crying eyes. Three boys and two girls, including Justine who had been her best friend until grade three, when fashion choices and religious leanings meant nothing, circled around the tree and taunted her with mangled lyrics to that song she hated so much. She shifted her hands to her ears to block their off-key voices. Why would she drink or smoke? She was only ten years old. Just because Justine let Ronald kiss her and touch her places his hands had no business being. Just because they stole their parents' cigarettes and lit them behind the garbage bins at recess instead of playing soccer or hanging from the monkey bars like normal children, why did she have to follow suit? Why did that make her the target of their cruelty?

Ronald smacked at her head on his way by, then yanked the pile of books and extra-credit work out from under her arm. Texts and paper landed in the dirt and strew across the grass. He grabbed the small ivory leather-bound book she kept with her at all times. "What's this?" He flipped it over. At the sight of the cross on the cover, his eyes lit up. "Oh man, what are you, one of those Gee-hova's witnesses or something?"

Billie tried to snatch her bible back but he pulled it away.

"No wonder you dress like that." Another boy yanked on her plaid, pleated skirt. It was long and grey, with forest green stripes, not the red tartan mini that her former friend sported. Billie wore her hair long and drawn into a low ponytail. She had no bangs to curl over her forehead and glue into place with hairspray like Justine, and all the little clones who followed her around, did. Billie was all buttoned up in her thrift-store hand-me-downs, knee-socked, and penny-loafered. Cheap comfort and common sense. Justine was show, flash, colour. And money. Their friendship hadn't survived the summer break before grade four started in the fall.

Ronald held the bible above his head. "My dad says all you bible thumpers are a pain in the ass. You should keep your religion at church where it belongs."

She jumped for her bible, came down on a tree root and twisted her ankle. She landed on her knees in the dirt. Pain shot up her legs. With her hands on the ground, she stared at his red high-top Converse All Stars. "I do keep my religion at church." She looked up, past his skinny jeans and neon, lime green T-shirt — all the new fashions her parents couldn't afford to buy her. And she would never ask for anyway. "And I see you there every Sunday."

His face turned crimson. "I'm no bible thumper." He brought the book down and hit her on the head with it.

Justine grabbed his hand. "Stop it, Ronald. Teasing her is one thing. But no hitting." She held out the bible. "Sorry, Billie."

Maybe some of the old Justine was still in there somewhere. Billie smiled up at her and reached for the book.

Justine snatched it away. "Psych!" She held it above her head and laughed.

The end-of-recess bell rang. Its sharp tone echoed off the surrounding homes and bounced back into Billie's ears. Ronald grabbed the bible from Justine and ran toward the school. He tossed it into the air.

Billie watched the sunlight catch the silver cross stamped on the cover. The book landed in a mangled heap in a puddle. She glared up at Justine.

Justine bent down as if to help Billie get up, but instead waved her hand in Billie's face and smirked. "Bye-bye, goody two shoes." Justine turned and raced back to the school.

Billie pushed herself up and sat with her back against the tree trunk. She wiped tears from her dusty cheeks and slapped dirt from her scraped knees. When she was certain all the kids had returned to class, she retrieved her books and papers. She plucked the bible from the puddle and wiped it on her skirt, tried to flatten the wet and stained pages. Tears dripped onto them, thwarting her efforts. She ran three blocks to home. She eased the door open and sneaked inside so she wouldn't wake her father, who was on a night shift rotation.

At four in the morning, she would hear the click of the door against the jamb, the clank of bullets emptying from his service revolver into the box of ammo, the scratch of his key in the lock of his gun safe. She never slept until he was home safe, tucked into his own bed.

She peered into her parent's bedroom. He was snoring under the covers. His badge and empty holster sat on the dresser next to the little wooden bowl he emptied his pockets into. She loved the sound of change and keys jangling with every step he took. The sound of the handcuffs tinkling against each other at his lower back where they were clipped, ready to snap on the wrists of evil people who dared commit crimes in his precinct.

She closed her eyes and imagined cuffing Ronald and Justine together, their arms around that tree, faces smooshed into the ragged bark. She took her father's gun and made them pay for how they treated her. They were evil to the core. She held the gun to Ronald's temple until he peed his pants and cried like a baby, begging for his pitiful life. But she wouldn't give him what he wanted. The weight of his dead body after one efficient shot to the brain dragged Justine to the ground with him. She deserved no mercy either. Three well-placed bullets to the abdomen made her bleed out slowly. Billie squatted and watched the life drain from Justine's eyes. When she was gone and her stare was as blank as the space between her ears, Billie smiled on the inside.

Her father snorted sleep from his nose and rolled onto his back. She pulled the door closed with a quiet click and tiptoed to the bathroom. She fetched a dry washcloth from the cupboard, opened her bible, and wiped dirt and water from each soiled page. She hummed and sang to herself.

Jesus loves me! This I know,
For the bible tells me so;
Little ones to Him belong;
They are weak, but He is strong.

She paused, the washcloth poised over Leviticus 24:20. She was weak. She needed Jesus to hold her up. To show her the way.

Eye for eye. Tooth for tooth.

The words jumped from the page. That was God's plan then, wasn't it? Justice. Swift and in-kind.

If only she were strong enough to deliver it.

BAT HEAD

NICK FRASER STOOD BETWEEN HIS COURT-appointed attorney and Todd's court-appointed attorney.

The old hag of a judge droned on and on about the impact of their little shoplifting spree. It was no big deal, just a few grab-and-runs in the mall. A victimless crime, a dare. Normal teenage bullshit. But apparently, bullshit was a criminal offense. Didn't help that the old bat kept eyeing up their tats. Bitch was probably jealous. No one would want to see body ink on her flabby ass.

His fucking old man wouldn't even pop for a real lawyer. It's not like he didn't have the cash, he was a stock market trader for fuck's sake. No, daddy had to teach his wayward son a lesson. What lesson was that, exactly? That his father was a cheap-ass bastard who would rather let his son go to jail than home?

"I realize this is a first offense for these …" the judge looked at them over the rim of her reading glasses … "gentlemen." She smirked and looked at the docket. "But I get a vibe that if we don't nip their activities in the bud, soon they'll be back in my courtroom for more serious offenses. So, as a message to you and your peers, I sentence Nick Fraser and Todd Williams to one month in juvenile detention."

A month in juvey? For a few bucks worth of smokes and couple of leather wrist cuffs?

Nick jerked his head at her. "We got no fucking peers, lady."

"You stupid little shit." His father's baritone boomed from behind him.

Nick turned and smirked at his old man.

He took a swing at his son. Nick bobbed and weaved, just like the old fart had shown him. Just like he did when he got arrested and his father went for his throat. He got the "no kid of mine" speech, and the "how do you think this makes your mother feel" talk. When Nick dismissed it all with a flip of his middle finger, his father laid hands on him.

It hadn't been the first time.

The judge slammed her gavel down. "That's enough." She pointed her scraggly finger at Nick. "You just made it six weeks, young man." She shook her head. "The apple clearly doesn't fall far from the tree."

Thursday the Twenty-eighth

BILLIE SHIFTED HER BUTT ON THE HARD PLASTIC subway seat. She scratched her red pen across the newspaper article, fixed poor grammar, corrected spelling. And altered the ending to ensure the bad guys got away with nothing and the legal system was on the ball for a change.

This had become her new routine, her latest obsession. With each article she edited, each wrong she righted, each scumbag who got their not-so-happy ending, her mind wandered to Bruce. He didn't only share Batman's real name, he'd also swooped in when she needed him, then disappeared into the bustle of the city like the Dark Knight himself. She hadn't seen him on the subway since their first encounter a few days before. Not because he didn't ride the subway, she concluded. But because she hadn't needed him.

She didn't need him to rescue her. Not in the damsel-in-distress kind of way. But she did long for rescue from her daily life. For some sanity and order in her world. Would his presence bring that? Could anyone bring her that?

Every day she scanned the faces in the crowded cars, hoping to catch a glimpse of Bruce's imperfect face and swarthy bulk. Even if he never spoke to her again, it didn't matter. She could edit that part in. If only she could see him, verify his existence and prove he had spoken to her. Touched her. Prove he wasn't a figment of her mental red pen.

She flipped the newspaper page. Some underage petty thieves got away almost scot-free. First offense. Rich parents. Good lawyers.

Only six weeks in juvenile detention.

She tapped her pen against her lips. Sounded familiar. Like a certain band of high school thugs who rode the subway. Thugs who were nowhere to be seen the past couple of days.

She scratched her pen across the page, sent the future crime bosses to adult prison, and made their parents pay fines. Hefty bloody fines.

"Yeah, get 'em before they go rogue for good."

She froze at the sound of the throaty bass, shifted her eyes until they focused on the black pants and shiny, fancy shoes. She drew her brows together. Those shoes didn't match the rest of him. She raised her eyes. It was Bruce, all right.

He sat beside her, nudged her with his shoulder. "You missed one."

"I — I'm sorry?"

He pointed at the page. "Shouldn't that be 'further?'"

She smiled. He was so cute, in a rough-and-tumble, don't-mess-with-me kind of way. And so clueless. "It's distance, so it's 'farther.' If it was about time, or doing something to a greater degree, then it would be 'further.'"

He nodded. "Yeah, that's why I have an assistant. She can fix all that stuff." He bit his top lip with his bottom teeth. "Are you an editor? Like, for a living I mean?"

She opened her mouth to say no, just a proofreader, but stopped. She had one client. A real one. She was an editor now, damn it. "Yes. Yes, I am. How about you? Assistants and fancy shoes? I figured you for more an outdoorsy type. Fireman maybe."

"Fireman was the dream. Or policeman. But then, you know, I hit puberty and all." His laugh filled the subway car. "I worked construction for years, started as a labourer when I was just a kid in high school. Worked my way up the ladder, so to speak. Now I'm construction management. Traded in my steel toes for wing tips, my safety vest for a suit jacket. Not bad for a guy who barely scraped his way through high school and doesn't know when farther is further. Or further is farther."

His smile was enormous. And the ease with which he threw it around enviable. She normally hid her smile behind her hand, behind a book. Or behind her mouth, more often smiling on the inside, unwilling to share her happiness, what little of it there was, with the big, ugly world. But his smile wasn't a shield. It wasn't a salve to be thinly spread or meted out in measured doses. It was just him. No pretense. No shame. No fear.

What did that feel like?

"So who do you edit? Any famous authors? Stephen King maybe? You do have a flair for gruesome justice."

Her cheeks burned. "I freelance. Only one client so far. An independent author."

"Freelance? You just ride the train for fun? Feed your desperate need for other people's B.O. and the less-than-gentle nudging of asshole high school bullies?"

"I work as a proofreader for a publishing house. I hope to be an editor there one day, but until that happens, the freelance thing seems like a good idea." Katherine's flesh would have to be dripping from her bones in the fires of hell before Billie ever got a shot at promotion. She drew the outline of horns on Katherine's floating image and filled them in with red ink. And grinned on the inside.

"You always sit in the same seat, in the same car, at the same time. Creature of habit?"

"I'm not always in the same seat." Her weak protest faded as she spoke it. The only time she sat elsewhere was when someone beat her to it.

"Sorry, that wasn't an insult."

Then why did it feel like he'd slapped her?

He touched the skirt at her knee. "I find it comfortable. I like predictability. If I need you, I'll always know where to find you."

The subway did its usual jerk and spasm. Bruce stood. "This is me. Meeting on the construction site." He tipped his imaginary hat. "Catch ya on the flip side, Billie the editor."

Billie scribbled a red fedora on his head before he turned and the living zombies on the platform swallowed him whole. She rubbed her knee where his hand had been. He'd always know where to find her. Why would he want to do that?

THURSDAY, JUNE 4TH

"WHEN ARE YOU HAPPIEST?" DOC KROFT DID THAT thing where she bored into Billie's brain with her laser eyes and tried to extract truths that even Billie didn't know existed.

Billie grabbed a throw cushion and squeezed it into her belly. "When I'm running. Or editing. Or with Peg Leg."

"What about when you're with other people?"

"Not so much." Bruce popped, uninvited, into Billie's head.

Doc pursed her lips. If she had a selfie stick, it would have been a perfect narcissistic pic for Facebook or Instagram. But, like Billie, Doc probably didn't waste her time on so-called social media. What was the point of virtual friendships? Sounded more lonely and pitiful than no friends at all.

"We need to fix that. You have to make some connections. Someone outside of your head doctor and the trainers at the gym."

"Oh, no worries there. I don't talk to any of them."

Doc sighed.

Billie stared at the purple paisley pillow, ran her fingers over the nap of the velvet, short and soft like little boxes that gold crosses come in. "There is someone. Sort of."

"Oh?" The doc leaned forward. "Tell me."

"A man I met on the subway."

Doc leaned back again, a satisfied grin on her face like she'd just finished a turkey dinner. "A man. Interesting."

Billie's cheeks warmed. "Not that interesting. We've only spoken twice. I doubt he wants anything more than that."

"His name?"

"Bruce."

Doc scrunched her face. "That's unfortunate."

Billie smiled. "It's all right. He's no Batman. For one thing, he's real. And I bet his parents weren't murdered when he was a kid. And he doesn't live over a cave or dress in tights in his off hours." At least, she didn't think he did.

Doc let an uncharacteristic laugh escape. "So, you only have his name?"

"And what he does for a living. Construction management. He didn't write his number on my palm or anything."

Doc nodded. "And what if he had?"

Billie stared at the pillow. What if, indeed?

Billie sauntered through the lobby of Doc Kroft's office building, her mind affixed on Bruce's face and sturdy frame. She imagined her hand against his cheek. His skin, like the finest tanned leather, soft yet thick, supple, and virile.

She slowed as she neared the door. Her thoughts toyed with an erotic scenario that she'd never be able to complete. Lack of context. Zero experience. And two men on the sidewalk, standing beside a white minivan, distracted her.

One of them wore polka dot pants and massive red shoes. The other was fitting a wig of spun neon-orange fibres over his balding head.

Her vision blurred and then focused on the face of the tall one who was donning a rainbow wig. The pedophile clowns who, thanks to overzealous cops with no search warrant, got away with raping a young boy. The ones she punished with an edited sentence of penile dismemberment.

She wanted to scream, call the cops. Do something, anything to put them away. To prevent them from ruining another child's life. But she was riveted to the floor. All she could do was stab them in the crotch with an imaginary red pen, powerless to complete the act in real life.

The rainbow-wigged one slapped the other on the back and laughed. They climbed into the van and pulled into traffic.

Billie ran to the bathroom, pushed open a stall door, fell to her knees, and vomited her chicken Caesar wrap into the toilet. She called silently to God and apologized for her murderous intentions. She was going way over their unspoken agreed-to allotment of dark thoughts.

As usual, God ignored her.

Maybe it was time to update that agreement. After all, she wasn't a frightened little girl anymore. She was a chicken-shit woman.

ROGER THE CLOWN

"I AM SO SICK OF FUCKING TODDLERS. MAN, I NEED A beer." Roger yanked his rainbow wig from his head and scratched his bald scalp.

"Maybe birthday clown wasn't your best career choice, you stupid fuck."

Roger kicked Colin in the butt of his oversized polka dot pants. "Shut yer trap." Roger lit a cigarette and watched a group of four boys ride by on their bikes. "The work sucks, but you can't beat the side benefits." He tapped Colin with the back of his hand and pointed half a block up the street. "Ready?"

"Always ready."

Roger dropped his cigarette to the pavement and ground it out with the toe of his giant, red shoe. He set his wig back on and tugged it over his ears, his eyes trained on a fifth boy, a straggler who kept falling farther back from his friends.

"Come on, Alan, pedal faster." The volume of the boys' calls dropped with each block of distance they put between them and the slowpoke.

Roger grinned. There was always one left behind. The weakest member of the pack. Easy pickings. No marines, these kids.

Semper fucking fi.

Roger scanned the street. It was long past suppertime, the sunlight waning. Families were inside prepping for lights out. The neighbourhood was quiet, almost in stasis. The perfect hunting time. No one to hear the muffled screams of the sole weak link.

He stepped into the road and tossed a glance over his shoulder. Where the hell did Colin disappear to? And why wasn't the van door open and ready? "Colin," he hissed. "Haul ass." He ran his hands down the apple pattern that dotted his pants and strutted his wide-legged clown walk diagonally down the street toward the boy.

The kid had dismounted his bike and was walking it up the inclined sidewalk. Ten yards away, he stopped and smiled at Roger. Then he smirked. "Nice wig."

Little shit. Mocking the clown. He'd soon learn.

Never. Mock. The clown.

A guttural moan cut through the silence, then a dull thud. Roger eyed the boy, his groin throbbed and ached. He looked back at the van. Through the passenger window, Colin's rubber baldhead and polyester spun hair hit the windshield. A scream split the night.

"Colin!" Roger turned back to the boy and mentally groped his untouched, soft, naïve flesh. "Damn it."

The kid's smile had melted into a look of wide-eyed horror, his eyes pinned on the van. He put his feet on his pedals and found the adrenaline-fueled strength to speed his bike up the sidewalk.

Roger grabbed his wig with both hands and ripped it from his head, watched his victim put too much distance between them to catch up. He couldn't race after him. Not in clown shoes. "Shit!" Kid was right there, a sitting duck. So close he could taste him. Fucking Colin, probably just a clap scream. Another painful piss.

Roger spun around. "Damn it, Colin." Roger lifted his knees high and managed a comical jog. He stopped short at the front of the van. Colin's wig was on the ground, red stains marred the pavement. Man, that was a bad case of gonorrhea. He needed to get to a doctor.

The van jostled and rocked. Roger slid the door open. Colin was inside the darkness of the windowless van, face down. His checkered pants looked like they were soaking wet. The idiot had pissed himself.

Roger kneeled on the van floor, rolled his partner over and slapped his cheek. "Colin, what the hell, man? We had the kid. He was right there."

Colin's head lolled to the other side.

Roger sat back sharply and gasped. He returned his eyes to his partner's pants. It wasn't piss, it was blood. His pants were cut, and —

Roger opened his mouth to scream. Nothing came out but a gurgle.

Pain shot through his back. His body convulsed and flopped like a fish on the boat deck before it gets nailed in the head with a hammer. He fell on top of Colin's legs, his face in Colin's crotch. The coppery blood that soaked his clown pants filled Roger's nostrils with the smell of welds he spent his working days burning onto pipes under strangers sinks and behind their piss-stained toilets.

A hand grasped his shoulder and rolled him over. An imposing figure loomed above him. Heavy set, broad shouldered, hunched like the guy had seen his share of time in the boxing ring. He pulled a knife from his coat and brandished it in the dusk. He held it above his head. The sunset glinted off the edge as he swung it at Roger's pants.

Roger screamed like a little girl afraid of clowns and tried to cover his dick.

The knife cut through his hands and stuck in his crotch. He screeched and cursed and kicked at the guy's leg.

The man didn't flinch.

Roger rolled over and tried to drag himself further into the van. It was like some lame-ass movie, a crappy slow-motion scene. All he could hear was his heartbeat thrumming in his ears. All he could smell was sweat and blood. Pain ripped through his ass. He screamed, his voice gaining volume. Why didn't anyone hear him? Why wasn't anyone trying to save him?

He dug his fingers into the van's smooth, metal floor. His pants were hot and wet but his legs like ice. His eyes lost focus and his head felt like a balloon floating above him. Blackness descended.

Roger blinked against the glaring fluorescent light. The stink of antiseptic and anaesthetic with the underlying sulphur of stale urine seeped into his consciousness. He tried to sit up. Metal clanked against metal. He tugged on his right arm, opened his eyes wide. The room was stark white. He lay in a bed with little-kid bars. What, were they afraid he'd fall out like a fucking baby? He scanned his body. Bandages covered his hands, his wrists handcuffed to the bars. Blinding pain seared between his temples and ached between his legs.

At the end of the bed stood a uniformed cop, one hand on his sidearm, the holster unclipped. The cop smirked, turned to the door. "Hey. He's up." He turned back and sneered at Roger, one side of his upper lip lifted and quivered. Elvis would have been proud. "Or should I say awake. You'll never be *up* again."

The blood drained from Roger's head. "What the hell does that mean?"

The cop jerked his head at Roger's crotch. "It means your days of sodomizing little boys are over, you sick fuck. He castrated you. Hell, he did one better. He lopped your entire package off."

"What?" Roger craned his neck and stared at his groin. All he saw were bed sheets. "You're full of shit." He dropped his head to the pillow.

A tall reed of a man swept into the room, a white polyester coat open and flapping behind him. He lifted a chart from a hook on the end of the bed and came to a stop near Roger's cuffed wrist. "Mr.

Roger Graves?"

"Yeah, that's me."

"You lost a lot of blood. We cleaned up the wound and closed." He flipped a page up. "We couldn't. Couldn't —" The doctor kept his eyes on the chart.

"Couldn't what, for fuck's sake?"

The doctor shifted his gaze and looked directly into Roger's eyes. "Couldn't reattach your penis or testicles."

The room spun. The bed opened up and swallowed Roger's body whole. "No, that's crap. You're just fucking with me."

The doctor smirked too. "Well, fucking isn't something you need to be concerned with anymore." He snapped the paper back down and tossed the chart onto a side table. It landed with a crack. "Whoever did the honours of castrating you and excising your, shall we call it 'manhood,' didn't leave the offending pieces behind."

"Must have kept 'em as a souvenir," the cop said. "Personally, I'd have chosen a postcard."

The doctor huffed a short laugh out his nose.

Roger shot his eyes between the smug, bastard cop and the holier-than-thou doctor. "You think this is fucking funny? I'm mutilated. Maimed. Did they catch the guy?" He jangled the metal bracelet against the bar. "And why the fuck am I cuffed?"

"A, nobody is looking for the guy." The cop shifted his feet and fingered his trigger. "And B, your partner is dead. Bled out in your van of horrors. We searched it. You know, for evidence in the attack of two clowns. And guess what we found, you moron?"

Roger swallowed. He knew what they'd found.

"Yeah, your little Polaroid collection. Not the one we already have, the one that got thrown out of court. No search warrant, what a joke." The cop's face got redder as he spoke. "No, this is a new batch. Fourteen shots. Two boys. You dumb fuck." He came around the other side of the bed. Bent down until his face was just inches from Roger's. "We canvassed the neighbourhood. Another little kid identified you as the clown who was approaching him while he rode his bike. Whoever attacked you, well I'd say he got there just in the nick of time." He stood at attention. "Right, Doc?"

"Not my area. But I must agree." He strode toward the door. "He's yours anytime you want to lock him up, officer."

Roger glared at the cop. "Don't you want my statement? A description of the prick that, that ..."

"Cut off your prick?" The cop threw his head back and laughed. "Yeah, sure. Tell me all about it."

Roger swallowed. "He wasn't that tall, but he was big. Or at least, his clothes were big. Had a hoodie, like he was wearing his dad's clothes. He was all in black. With giant pants. Like he was a clown too, but a mafia clown or something."

The cop nodded. "Is that it?"

"Aren't you gonna write any of it down?"

"Got it all up here." The cop tapped his temple.

"Sure. Sure you do." Roger turned his head and looked out the window. Like hell would he let this ass-wipe see him cry. "He hid behind the hood, I never got a clear look at his face. He didn't say anything. Not one fucking word." He squinted. "One other thing. And it's weird."

"What?"

Roger turned and looked at the cop. "He smelled nice."

TUESDAY, JUNE 9TH

BILLIE SLAPPED THE SNOOZE BUTTON FOR THE fifth time. She opened one eye and glared at the red digits. Almost six o'clock. Time to get out of bed already.

She sat up and stretched. An ache shot through her shoulder and down her back. She arched her spine and turned side to side. A lovely crack eased some tension. She rubbed at her eyes. They just didn't want to open fully. It was as if she hadn't slept at all.

She reached for Peg Leg but he wasn't in his usual place. She swung her legs over the side of the bed, grabbed the horse-head cane that rested against the wall next to her headboard, and stood. She yawned, her mouth so wide open that her jaw cracked too.

Coffee. That would fix her.

Her foot caught on something and she pitched forward, flailed the cane in front of her and grasped the edge of the dresser. She righted herself and inspected the floor, which should be spotless. She never left anything out that she could trip on.

The carpet was littered with clothes. She prodded a mound of black material speckled with cat hair with the brass tip of the cane. She snagged one of the garments and lifted it in the air.

It was her father's hoodie. She gasped, dropped the cane and sat on the carpet. She gathered his favourite hoodie, the one with his alma mater emblazoned on the back, into her arms and cradled it next to her cheek. She inhaled and squeezed her eyes shut. That hoodie used to keep her warm at night, but the remnants of his scent, British Sterling cologne and Irish Spring soap, had been overtaken by her own cocoa butter body lotion and vanilla bean deodorant. She'd tucked his things safely in the bottom of her closet hoping to make the smell last forever. Even after it had disappeared, she couldn't bring herself to throw them away. It would be like burying him all over again.

She turned to the cat. "Peg Leg, you naughty boy. Spent the night digging in the closet, eh?" Maybe she should have put them up high and out of reach of three-legged cats that can't do vertical jumps. "His clothes smell like cat litter. And something else." She sniffed again, scratched at a dried stain on the sleeve. Probably cat spit or snot. "Maybe I should wash them." She bit her lip and stroked the hoodie. If she did that, would every bit of him be gone? Eliminated? He'd been eliminated once too often.

She wagged a finger at Peg Leg. "You stay out of my closet, young man." He purred and ran his body against her stump. She sighed and rubbed between his ears. It was impossible to be mad at him. He was the only one who stayed with her, alive and in the flesh. He hadn't meant any harm. And she and the Lord knew the cat had no boundaries.

She ran a lint roller over the clothes and folded them into a neat pile. She tucked them on the top shelf of the closet and went to find caffeine.

New members at the gym always stopped and stared. Billie was so over it. She used to look away, blush, explain her circumstance so they'd stop looking at her. Now they could just flap in the confused wind. Maybe they weren't confused. Perhaps they were totally freaked out. Whatever. They weren't the first. And they wouldn't be the last.

She wiped sweat from her brow before it dripped into her eyes. Her reward for marathon gym sessions was the saline trail of her own exertion that dangled from her chin before dropping into her cleavage to tickle her breasts. The puddles of perspiration that soaked her underarms and dampened her crotch. Sweat was her gold medal in long-distance running. Proof that her heart still beat. But getting that salty liquid in her eyes burned like hellfire. The one time she wore a headband to prevent it, the regulars teased her about listening to Olivia Newton John and doing the Jane Fonda workout. The vague eighties references barely registered. She knew what they were talking about, but she was only a baby in that decade. Far more involved with Rainbow Brite and Teddy Ruxpin than leotards and aerobics.

It was oddly comforting to be chided, as if she were one of the gang. She couldn't remember the last time she'd felt part of a group. She secreted her pleasure at being teased for something other than missing a foot, for being stared at for wearing a headband instead of a running blade. At least she had control over her wardrobe. Though she never wore the headband again. Even gentle teasing from people that had grown accustomed to her presence shone too bright a spotlight on her. She'd rather be as invisible as possible in baggy, grey athletic gear, her hair in a ponytail high and wrapped into a bun so it didn't bounce between her shoulder blades. Sweat-soaked hair became as sharp as a leather whip at seven miles per hour.

Her shoulders ached through the run, her back tight. She almost didn't bother. But it was Tuesday, and that meant she went to the gym before facing the subway, the office, the weasel, and the witch. That damn six-hundred-page behemoth of shit had already screwed with her schedule. Cost her four workouts and ruined the first Sunday sermon she'd attended in months. She had to get back on track. Back to ordinary. For Billie, ordinary meant strict adherence to the plan. To her daily outline. Her story and plot. She knew the narrative of her life. She knew the outcome. And vampire dreck and distractions like Bruce What's-his-name didn't fit. Freelancing. That was the new plot. Freedom from the manacles of Katherine's employ and undesirables on the subway. That was her happily ever after.

Her earbuds slid against the sweat that pooled at the entrance to her ear canals. She wiped the sweat, poked the buds back in, and flipped through the early morning gym-TV choices. She'd loved the day the gym popped for new machines with personal screens. No more satellite soaps or being forced to watch Dr. Phil. She scanned through national news, music channels, and old sitcoms — too old — before finding a local news broadcast. She didn't need the big, wide world. She wanted to know what was going on right here. Right now.

A picture of two clowns popped up behind the newscaster. The two who had raped that little boy. The ones from the newspaper article. The same guys she saw outside Doc Kroft's office.

Billie turned up the volume and slowed her pace.

"Colin Jenkins was murdered. Roger Graves, with the rainbow wig, was castrated." The news anchor cleared his throat.

Billie turned the treadmill off and stared at the tiny screen.

"Police are looking for a man wearing a dark hoodie and dark, oversized pants." The man seemed to be struggling to keep his serious newsman face on. "If you have any information, please call the tip line at the bottom of your screen."

A lump in Billie's throat refused to go down no matter how many times she swallowed. She ran to the locker room, raced to remove her running blade, and hastily returned her flat-shoe prosthesis to her stump. She tossed her gym gear into her locker, snapped the lock over it, and ran out, hurrying up the block to her apartment.

Once inside, she pulled the recycling container from the

pantry. She ripped empty takeout containers, all washed and dried and stacked neatly, out of the bin and tossed them on the table, followed by a wine bottle and the flattened and stacked empty boxes her favourite chai tea came in.

Peg Leg mewed at the mess, backed away, and slinked under the couch.

About halfway down she found the newspapers. She flipped through them until she came across the one she was looking for. She ran her fingers over her red-ink edits.

Jesus, Mary, and Joseph.

The anchor's story matched her edited version of what happened. Though not castration. Full on penile excision. But no one was supposed to die. She fell back onto a kitchen chair and ran her hand over her damp hair. Nausea rolled up her body. She dashed to the kitchen sink and vomited, her hands gripping the counter's edge. She ripped a section of paper towel free from its roll and wiped her mouth. She rinsed the sink, stared at the chunks of her breakfast swirling in a vortex of puke-water and disappearing down the drain.

She wiped the sink dry, gathered the newspaper, ripped it into tiny bits and tossed it into the stainless-steel tub. Matches. Where were the matches? With the emergency candles in the cupboard over the microwave. She found two packs, lit one match after another after another and threw them on the paper. She watched the evidence of her imagined justice burn. Flames danced and black smoke curled into the air until each red mark was devoured and turned to char.

The smoke alarm screeched above her head. She covered her ears. "Damn it all to hell." She turned on the cold water, stepped her good leg on the chair to boost herself up and twisted the smoke alarm off its base. She ripped the battery from its gut and pitched it onto the counter, raced to the window and threw it open. She leaned out into the fresh morning air, her heart hammering and her legs unsteady.

Bruce's face jumped into her mind, layered overtop the description the news anchor gave of the castrator. Could he be behind this? Was he living up to his namesake. Was he … Batman?

Laughter shook Billie's breasts. She wiped her brow with trembling fingers and shook her head.

Get a grip. Editing the news for proper justice was one thing. But maybe she'd better stay in the shallow end of the fantasy pool, not dive into the deep end and drown.

WEDNESDAY

THE SUBWAY CAR CAME TO A JERKING HALT. BILLIE scanned the platform for high school thugs, but not a one darkened the station. Perhaps they chose to walk to avoid running into Bruce. She grinned at the image of him in her head. Her own personal hero. Even if he did only save her once. And he would have done it for anyone. It wasn't as if he liked her or anything. How could he? Plain, boring, dismembered Billie. She'd probably never even see him again.

She pulled the newspaper into her lap and stared at the headline, read the article about the fate of those damn clowns for the eighth time. Her fingers itched to pull out her pen and fix the sloppy writing, elevate the grade level. But the outcome, the ending, this time, was like Baby Bear's bed. It was just right. Those clowns would never harm another child.

The plastic seat jolted and creaked with the weight of another passenger's butt. All those empty seats and the idiot has to sit right beside her?

"Hey, I read that this morning." A thick finger poked at her newspaper.

She held her breath at the rumble of bass vocals and did something she always tried to avoid. Made eye contact.

"Morning, Billie." Bruce's wide grin exposed a mostly-gleaming set of teeth with some evidence of years of smoking — evidence she could smell in his clothes. The crowded ivories on the bottom of his mouth were crooked. Perhaps his parents could never afford dental work. She ran a tongue over her own cramped teeth.

"Good morning." She looked at her lap, unable to hold his blatant stare, to return his gregarious smile.

He tapped the paper. "A little crazy, hey?"

She shrugged. "How so?"

He leaned his head next to hers, his wiry curls brushing against the smooth surface of the hair at her temple, pulled tight into a bun and sprayed smooth. She sniffed a slow, deep breath. His subtle cologne found its way past the cigarette smoke and filled her head. Was that ... British Sterling? No, her mind was playing tricks on her. Did they even make that anymore?

His warm breath kissed her cheek. "Because they were castrated," he whispered.

Her knees went cold and her stomach hollowed.

"It's just like you wrote. Like your edits. Wild, right?" He sat up straight and extended an arm across the back of her seat. The warm pocket of air he'd created between them cooled.

"I guess it's a little wild." She'd never described anything she'd done as wild before. "But," she dropped her chin and twisted her head to look back at him. "Just coincidence." She focused on his face, on any cues to his involvement. Any twitch of his eye or clench of his jaw. "Right? Just coincidence?"

He let out a guffaw. "Well yeah, unless by night you're some editing vigilante, righting wrongs that the justice system couldn't. Fixing the cops' fuck-ups." He put his other hand over his mouth. "Sorry. That was rude."

She grinned. Her, a vigilante. That's a stretch. But at least he didn't seem to know about it. Just a coincidence. But a damn freaky one.

"So, I was wondering." Bruce leaned forward and put his forearms on his thighs, rocked on his toes. "Maybe one night, you and me." He leaned back and looked at her out of the corner of his eye. "Maybe we could go to dinner or something. Maybe a movie?"

Billie stared at him. What kind of mean joke was this? "Why?" She didn't know what else to say.

He scrunched his brows and snorted. "Well, because I kind of like you. You're cute behind those old-lady spectacles, and all that librarian-chic clothing."

She squinted. "Was that supposed to be a compliment?"

He put one of his big paws over his face and shook his head. "Shit. I'm sorry. I'm not very good at this sort of thing."

"What sort of thing?"

"You know. Dating. Relationships." He looked around the subway, his lips pursed. "I get it if you don't want to. Hell, you hardly know me."

"No."

"Okay. I won't bother you again. No hard feelings." He stood.

"No." She reached out and touched his hand. She expected his skin to be rough, dry. As weathered as his face. But it was as soft as Peg Leg's fur. "I mean. Yes." Her face was on fire and she couldn't meet his eyes. But the only other place to look was right at the zipper of his pants.

Look at him, Billie. Just damn well look at him.

She raised her chin. "I'd like that. To go out, I mean." She looked away, a small giggle escaping her lips. A giggle. Of all things. "Clearly, I'm not very good at this either."

He dropped back into the seat beside her. "How about a movie? Then maybe a coffee or two." He took a stray strand of her hair that had sprung free from its incarceration in her bun and tucked it behind her ear.

An inkling of warmth twitched down her spine and her breath caught in her chest. Her head bounced in a shallow, if not too vigorous nod. "Yes. That would be lovely."

"How about Friday? Pick you up at seven?"

She shook her head and tore a strip of newsprint off the front page, fished her red pen from her purse, and scratched out her name and phone number. "I can meet you. Just let me know which theatre." She handed him the paper.

"You're a smart one, Billie. And sensible. See, that's one of your charms." He beamed. "Your many, many charms." He tipped his imaginary red fedora and skipped out of the subway car.

She stared at the closed door and smiled on the inside. Her many charms. Just what did he see that she couldn't?

1998

B ILLIE SCRATCHED THE POINTED TIP OF THE RED marker across her short story. She shifted in her metal seat, permanently welded to the tiny desk in the middle row, and shook the pen, urging the ink to make it through just four more paragraphs.

Serves her right for pilfering the antique writing implement from her grandmother's old pencil cup. So many pens, pencils, pencil crayons, heck even a few wax crayons that looked like they'd been gathering dust since Billie was in kindergarten and used to sit at her grandmother's kitchen table and draw while Billie's mother bitched about Billie's father to his very own mother.

Billie's ears rang with her grandmother's patented *"tsk tsk."* She'd been right to tell her daughter-in-law that she couldn't do better. That Billie's father was the best her mother would ever find. But to Billie's mother, better meant more money. Lots of it.

Grandmother, like Billie, didn't give a damn about money. It corrupted people. Even people who didn't have any, but always yearned for more.

Her father was never like that. He'd been above reproach. Incorruptible. Incontrovertibly honest and good.

He was perfect.

Her mother would have dropped them both in a beat of her gold-digging heart if a wealthy man had given her a second look. It wasn't that she wasn't pretty. Old pictures proved she was. Billie could understand why her father fell for her when they were so young, still in high school. But Billie's memories of her had faded to the smell of booze and cigarettes, the vertical lines on her lips that blossomed from sucking on her beloved menthols, and the pinch in her forehead every time Billie's father opened his mouth.

How long had it taken her mother's dreams to come crashing to the ground? Was it when her father decided to become a cop instead of a lawyer? Or when the recession hit a couple of years before Billie was born and they lost their house? Billie recalled many drunken rants where her mother droned on about mortgage rates and the damn government.

Billie finished marking her story with red ink, correcting spelling and fixing grammar. The editing process brought a sense of peace. An understanding that she was making things right. Righting wrongs. Or perhaps righting writes. She glanced at the clock, pulled fresh foolscap from her binder, and began to write out a good copy of her story in blue ink. The Rollerball grated against the page like tinfoil against gold teeth. She shook the pen up and down and tried again. It was as dead as a cop in an alley.

She shut her eyes and took a mental red pen to her thought. She scratched out "cop in an alley" and wrote in "doornail." She pitched the dead pen into her pencil case and pulled out a brand new one. Grandmother bought blue pens in ten-packs, Billie went through them so fast. Now if only she'd stock up on the red ones. Or better yet, buy her a computer. They'd save a bundle on pens.

The classroom door opened with a hollow click. The room buzzed with whispers and chair legs screeched against linoleum. Billie looked up to see a new kid standing at the teacher's desk, his back to the class. Great. Another one to add to the fold of bullies and abusers.

She sat straighter and pulled her skirt over her knee, covered what she could of her prosthetic leg. May as well delay the onslaught of taunts and jibes.

"Class, pay attention, please." The teacher tapped her ruler on her desk. "We have a new student. I expect you to make him feel welcome." She smiled at the boy. "This is Gregory."

The boy turned and nodded, gave a royal wave to the room.

Billie stared at his eyes, blue like she imagined the ocean looked at its most shallow points, with perfect white sand under the surface. A smattering of freckles dotted his nose and his blond hair hung to his shoulders in loose waves. He was the most beautiful thing she'd ever seen.

"There's an empty desk in the middle row." The teacher pointed in Billie's direction.

Gregory followed the teacher's pointed finger, but hesitated when his eyes met Billie's. He smiled at her, and meandered to the desk behind her.

When he'd passed, Billie closed her eyes and let out the breath she hadn't realized she'd been holding. The smell of apples and Juicy Fruit swirled about her head, and the squeak of his sneakers filled her ears. She imagined them standing in a field, a ring of flowers in her hair, their hands entwined. A priest pronounced them married, and Gregory leaned in to kiss her.

"All right, everyone."

The clap of the teacher's hands shook Billie from one of the best life-edits she'd imagined yet. She opened her eyes to reality. A reality that would include a cute boyfriend when amputee pigs could fly.

"Ten more minutes, then hand in your stories."

Billie sighed and kept transcribing her edited story. At the bell, she gathered the pages and tapped them against the desk to tidy them into a proper pile. The other kids streamed past her and dropped their papers on the teacher's desk, racing out the door as fast as possible. It was last bell on a Friday, after all. They had places to go loiter, people to tease, beer to steal, cancer sticks to smoke.

Gregory passed her desk. Billie wanted to take a bite out of his

Golden Delicious cheek. She watched him chat with the teacher. The woman handed him the assignment he'd just missed, asked him to work on it over the weekend and hand it in next week. She touched his arm, let her fingers linger there.

Billie understood. He was perfect. Her mental red pen drew an aura around his head. Not that he needed help to look angelic.

"Come on, Billie, move along now."

Billie focused her red pen on the teacher and stabbed it into her heart. "Yes, Ms. H." Billie wanted Gregory to leave first. She wasn't ready for him to see her awkward escape from the too-short desk. But his eyes were glued on her.

She slipped her good leg into the aisle, put both palms on the desk, and dragged her prosthetic leg out from the confines. Why didn't they have any left-handed desks in this damn school? Not that she was left-handed. But at least then she could make a graceful exit.

A sweat broke out on her brow and her cheeks warmed. She gathered her books with trembling hands, picked up her assignment, and turned. One step up the aisle under the scrutiny of his piercing gaze and she dropped her story. The pages scattered on the floor.

He rushed toward her and gathered the papers. He plucked the last one from the floor at her feet and stopped dead. "Whoa. You got a wooden leg." He stood, the mess of her story in his hands, the pages out of order, upside down and wrong side up.

You have, you moron. Why did the beautiful ones always need to be left behind a grade or two?

"Technically," she cringed at the squeak and crack in her voice. "Titanium. Lighter than wood. Stronger too."

She couldn't gauge his reaction. He looked almost impressed. Maybe even … Interested? That would be a first. But she would happily forgive his terrible grammar and syntax if he wanted to ask her out. Or even just not be mean to her.

He shoved her story at her. "That's freaky." He turned and left the classroom.

Freaky. Yep, that was about right. Why would she expect him to be any different than any other boy in school just because he could live the rest of his life on his looks and never have to open his pretty, dumb, luscious mouth?

She sighed, stared at the pages of her story, spotted a misspelled word on one of the upside down sheets and took her mental red pen to it. Too late to make a real correction. Dang, that was one lost mark.

It wasn't enough that God tested her mettle by allowing her parents to die and then strapping her with the titanium albatross where her leg used to be. Nope, Billie had to compound the torture of her peers by being smart. By peppering her schedule with advanced placement classes and maintaining a perfect four-point-oh grade point average. Because nothing screams nerd louder than perfect grades and perfect attendance and sailing through junior high in less than two years. She would graduate high school a full year ahead of kids her own age. Kids that knew her before the amputation. The only group among which she thought she still had a friend or two. Now there were none. But at least she had her books and stories. Her journals and her imagination.

She handed the story to the teacher on the way by and walked out.

AGATHA FRIESEN

AGATHA FRIESEN TWISTED THE CRIMSON CONE out of its silo. She raised one eyebrow and ran the oily colour across her lips. Every time she touched up her lipstick she imagined Jeremy's dick in her mouth. Except his dick wasn't red. And it was huge.

A rush of moisture wet her underpants. If she had time she'd masturbate right here in the courthouse bathroom. A final eff-you to the justice system. But the cameras waited, and she'd rather let Jeremy get her rocks off in the limo. And the pool. And the kitchen.

She squished her lips together then smacked them, ran her tongue across her teeth. She leaned into the mirror and dabbed the tip of her pinkie under each eye. Not bad for a broad in her fifties. Of course, regular Botox injections didn't hurt.

She squinted and examined her chin. Damn, she was getting that big-pored fatty chin of her mother's. She pitched the lipstick in her purse, poked at the crepe-like skin of her neck, and smoothed the front of her dress over her augmented breasts. There was only so much of God's work she could fix before she'd start to look like a caricature of herself. Better to age gracefully, with only the tiniest of help from modern science. And a huge boost of libido from her twenty-something paramour.

She swung the door wide and made a grand entrance into the marble-floored hallway. She was met with silence, only her lawyer and Jeremy there to appreciate her. She eyeballed Jeremy's frame, imagined the hard muscle under the silk suit she had custom-tailored for his tight body. More moisture flushed from her crotch. At this rate she'd need Depends just to prevent her love juice from staining her dress. Either that or trade her young buck in on an older, flabby lover.

Jeremy flashed a grin at her and held out his hooked arm. She entwined her arm in his.

Depends it was. No way was she giving up that gorgeous face. Women half her age envied her, and not just for her money. They could all suck it. She glanced down at the ever-present lump in Jeremy's pants. No, she'd suck it. The rest of them could just go straight to hell with her husband.

"Just hold your head high and ignore any questions." Her lawyer puffed out his barrel chest, his hand on the push bar of the exit door. "You're innocent. The jury said so. That's all you need to say."

She smirked. Even if they'd found her guilty, he'd say she was innocent. That's what she paid him for.

He pushed the door open and walked into the limelight in front of Agatha.

"There she is!" The media swarmed, like wasps on a discarded hunk of sausage. They thrust microphones in her face, dangled them overhead from long handles. "Mrs. Friesen, what do you say to the people who believe you killed your husband?"

She jutted out her old-lady chin and jerked her head to flick a small strand of stray hair from her forehead. Damn wind ruined her 'do. "I say I am innocent. And the court agreed."

A shrimp ball of female reporter jostled her taller peers. "With double jeopardy attached, you can't be retried even if you confessed. So tell us, Agatha. Did you kill your husband?"

Jeremy reached over Agatha's shoulder and shoved the microphone away. Her lawyer held up his hands. "Mrs. Friesen has no other comments. Please, let us through."

The lawyer dove into the mosh pit of reporters with Agatha in his considerable wake. Jeremy fell in behind to protect her from the rear. Every few steps his pants-bulge bumped into her ass. She struggled to maintain a straight face, but couldn't prevent the heat from rising in her cheeks. At the curb, a black limousine idled. The lawyer opened the door. Agatha climbed in, then Jeremy clamoured over top of her. The lawyer put his foot in the car.

Agatha thrust her arm out and peered up at him. "Oh no you don't. You take a cab." She reached for Jeremy with her other hand and cupped his bulge. "We've got some private celebrating to do." She pushed the lawyer and yanked the door shut.

JUNE 12TH - FRIDAY

THE EYELINER PENCIL SAILED THROUGH THE AIR, landed on the floor and rolled behind the toilet. Hands on hips, Billie glared at her reflection in the mirror.

Gosh darn, dang it, damn, shit, fuck.

She plucked two Kleenex from their cheerful sunflower-clad box, dripped baby oil onto them, and wiped her third attempt at makeup from her eyes.

How did women do this every day? She glared at the mirror before glancing at the reflected digits of the alarm clock on her nightstand. Six-ten. Only fifty more minutes. Her first date.

Ever.

She closed her eyes, grasped the sink's edge, and swallowed a bit of vomit. No way. Not happening. She would not let herself screw this up.

Her stomach calmed and she opened her eyes. Should she tell him it's her first real date? Would the world's oldest virgin scare him off? She raised one eyebrow. Surely there were bigger losers in the world than she. More outcasts and scaredy cats among the billions on this planet.

She glanced at the eyeliner on the floor, examined the brown line of it on the side of her nose. She wiped it off, heaved a huge sigh, and picked up the shadow.

She coaxed a small amount of taupe powder onto the brush and blew on it with a gentle exhale. So far so good. She closed her eyes and pulled up the memory of the woman at the cosmetics counter who'd sold her this glop all those years back. Her one attempt to be pretty, an unexpected and unwelcome desire that reached up and grabbed her by the throat. She'd never cared about pretty before. She'd only strived for normal. But the disaster with the kitten-heeled prosthetic the night she found Peg Leg was so disheartening, had so effectively underscored her utter failure, that she hadn't even opened the bag. Hadn't practiced what the woman with the painted lips and penciled brow and glued-on lashes, like so many spider legs screaming for emancipation from her purple-lined eyelids, had shown her. The makeup sat at the back of the bathroom drawer where she'd pitched it.

She eyed the brush. Does makeup have a best-before date?

Too late to worry about that. She feathered the brush across her right eyelid, dragged the subtle shade up toward the end of her brow. Not too shabby. She repeated the procedure on the left side. An avowed righty, she struggled to match the path of the shadow. Not horrible. Not perfect. But close enough.

She picked up the dreaded eyelash curler and brought it to her face, her hand trembling. She managed to straddle her lash line with the open implement, then squeeze it shut. "Holy shit!" She snapped the wretched thing open and pulled it from her face, certain it had ripped all of her lashes out by the root. She eyed the foam between the curved metal bits. Only two lashes sacrificed to the jaws of beauty.

She shook her head. One more time, other side. Her hand shook when she brought the miniature torture device closer to her eye. She fumbled, it flipped into the air, ricocheted off the mirror and crash-landed in the sink.

Lashes would remain uncurled.

She coated her lashes with a fine layer of brown mascara. The painted sales clerk tried to convince her to go with sparkly amethyst shadow and blacker-than-black eyeliner and lash goo to "bring out the lovely green flecks in her eyes." Oh, brother. Taupe and brown were as far as Billie was willing to go.

She picked up the lipstick tube and twisted the rocket of greasy pink out of its faux gold case. She sniffed it and recoiled. It smelled of her mother. The Saturday nights out, the two-in-the-morning bed checks when her breath was sweet with too much alcohol. She'd awaken Billie, sit on the edge of her bed, tell her how much she loved her, and kiss her with red lipsticked lips. The smell of it, the chemical taste, the stain of it on Billie's own lips, brought all the feelings rushing back. Embarrassment in the privacy of her own bedroom. Confusion at how different her mother was in the middle of the night after too many Manhattans, too sappy, too maudlin, too stinky. Billie preferred the Wednesday morning mother, bright and cheerful and fueled with black coffee, flipper of flapjacks, and giver of hugs in the sunshine of the breakfast nook. Until black coffee came with a splash of whiskey. Then all love was lost.

Billie returned the offending pink grease to its cave, capped it, and tossed the whole thing into the trash. A thin layer of petroleum jelly was all she ever needed. Lips were already pink, after all.

She surveyed the result, turned her head side to side and pursed her lips. She didn't look like the hookers on third, nor like the old ladies who couldn't see just how blue and thick their eye shadow was. Billie looked like herself. With a tiny improvement.

Baby steps.

She dragged a brush across her scalp, along the length of her brown hair to the ends that hovered just above her waistline. Her mother said it was like flowing gravy. The most delicious *au jus*. Billie just saw dog shit and a river of dried muck. But when it wasn't tethered into a high ponytail and wrapped into a constricted bun, it did catch the light in a lovely way.

She gathered her hair in her fist, yanked it behind her head, and reached for the elastic next to the collection of bobby pins. She hesitated for a second, then let the tresses go. They framed her face and draped across her breasts. Maybe, for once, it was time to let them run free.

She slid on her glasses and eyed her look. Beige cardigan over a black blouse tucked into a brown skirt that hung just past the knee. Nothing clinging, nothing tight. Not much to prove she was even a woman. She sighed. It would have to do. It was her best outfit.

Lined up on her bed were all of her prosthetics. Well, the date-worthy ones. She certainly had no need for a running blade. She ran a finger along the toes of each one, her fist in front of her mouth. Should she dare the kitten heel? Stick to the flat foot her stump was already snug inside of?

She bent over and looked at her bare feet, wiggled the toes that would wiggle. She balanced on tiptoes of her real foot, the fake one hanging there, ninety degrees to the carpet, like a sledgehammer. Or an anchor. Dynamic response or not, the damn thing wasn't real.

She imagined the heel on her prosthetic foot caught in a sidewalk grate, Bruce to her rescue, yanking on her fake leg, his arm around her waist, her hand on his shoulder for balance. Kind of romantic. Until her red pen appeared and scribbled a word bubble over Bruce's head. "If you'd just watch where you're going." A word bubble appeared above hers. "Shut up and yank it out already." She struck out romantic and wrote in comedic.

There it was, her life in edits. Ludicrous. Farcical. Painful.

Her hair swung in front of her face and she inhaled a strand into her nostril. She sneezed and lost her balance, stepped flat on the floor. The hair tickled her nose and she swiped it away. Not ready for heels. Not ready for hair freedom. She was going to need a lot of practice.

She tied her hair into a low side ponytail, split the difference between control and whimsy. It was out of her face, but securely tethered. Only tickling the edge of freedom and hugging her curves.

Or at least, hugging the clothing that did a fine job of hiding those curves.

Billie pulled her best flats from the closet, the patent black ones with a silver buckle and satin bow through them. She fit her prosthetic foot into the right one, and slid the other shoe onto her real foot. She hooked her purse over her shoulder, tugged her skirt straight, and smoothed her hair.

A date. With a real man. Not one borne of her imagination. Not one she edited into her life on the subway, or in line at the grocery store. Not one drawn from red ink, improved by red ink, made taller, more handsome, and wittier than is possible in real life. No, Bruce was an honest-to-goodness man. At least, that's what she hoped he was. Honest and good.

Billie stood at the corner and waited for the walk light to turn.

Bruce was on the other side of the street in front of the theatre, his hands in his pockets. The evening sun cast him in a golden glow. He checked his watch, wiped sweat from this brow.

Was he nervous? Or was it just the heat?

He buried his paws in the pockets again, and scanned the street. His gaze passed right over her. On his second sweep, he passed her by again, twitched, and snapped his head back around. His lips parted and his teeth gleamed through. Without taking his eyes off her, he pushed the walk button repeatedly, as if that would make the light change faster.

When the little white walking man lit up, Billie stepped into the crosswalk with a small swarm of humanity. One guy bumped her and rushed past, not even bothering to apologize. Strikethrough humanity with the sweep of imaginary red ink. It was a small swarm of two-legged carbon life forms. And one one-legged one.

Bruce grasped the arm of the bumping man on the other side of the street and growled something in his ear. The man turned, his face crimson, his eyes darting in all directions. "I — I'm sorry miss. Didn't see you there."

Bruce let his arm go and held his hand out to Billie. "How can you miss someone this lovely? Time to look up, sir."

Billie's cheeks warmed. She took Bruce's hand and nodded at the bumping man.

Bruce opened the door for her and ushered her inside.

"Thanks for that." Billie urged the blood to drain from her face. "But you don't need to rescue me. I've done all right so far."

"Don't need to." He put his hand inside hers without asking. "But I want to. As long as you're not offended by it."

She'd never been so unoffended in her whole life.

He bought her popcorn and soda. Held the theatre door open for her. Allowed her to go ahead of him into the aisle. He never treated her like a cripple. Didn't suggest they stick to the first level and avoid the stairs. He was all the best parts of any man she'd met all rolled into one. If only he didn't smoke, he'd be perfect.

During the movie, he rested his arm on the back of her chair. He never tried to kiss her, to grope her. Not that anyone else had ever tried before. Her red pen appeared and dragged his hand onto her shoulder, moved the popcorn bucket to his lap so she'd have to reach over and dig in. The pen turned his head and leaned it in. A "Kiss me" word bubble popped up.

He turned and looked at her. "Everything okay?"

She glanced around, her mouth parted, her heart pounding in her chest. She swallowed. "Yeah, fine. I was going to make a comment on the movie, but I forget what it was."

He leaned in. "We can dissect it over coffee." He turned back to the screen, picked the popcorn bucket up from her lap, took a handful, and set it back down.

All she'd ever wanted was a gentleman. Now it appeared that she had one. So why did she want so badly for him to be a little less gentle?

Bruce opened the door of the coffee shop. A bell jangled to announce their arrival. A lone barista looked up and smiled. "Welcome! What can I get you?"

Billie asked for black coffee, Bruce got some kind of vanilla-flavoured milky girly drink. He offered for her to choose a pastry, but she declined. He insisted they at least share one. She couldn't decide and wouldn't be so bold as to choose. So he did. A thick slice of lemon loaf.

Bruce gathered up their late-evening snacks and led Billie to a spot in the corner. He set the cups down on the table, his on the side with his back against the wall.

Bruce made small talk, where you from, favourite colour, what's your sign. All the clichéd banter that Billie had assumed was more urban legend than actual dating practice. An awkward silence descended between them. He rubbed the back of his neck with one hand, glanced out the window. Billie mostly looked at her coffee cup.

"Billie what?" The sonorous tones of his hardy voice broke the silence.

She raised her eyeballs and furrowed her brows. "Pardon?"

"I don't know your last name."

"Oh." She cleared her throat. "Fullalove."

He pursed his lips. "Wilhelmina Fullalove. That's quite a

mouthful. What's your middle name, Supercalliffragilistic?"

She giggled, rolled her eyes, and covered her mouth to make it stop. "It's Angelina. My dad used to call me Billie Angel."

His face contorted as if laughter was forthcoming. Or tears. "Wilhelmina Angelina Fullalove? Man, I thought I had it bad."

She faux-slapped his hand. "How about you? Bruce what?"

"Montoya."

She cocked her head, her mouth askew. "What's your middle name, Inigo?"

Bruce grimaced. "Yeah, I get that a lot. But no, just Bruce Adam Montoya."

The awkwardness descended once again. Bruce eyeballed the scenery outside the window. Billie drew invisible patterns on the handle of her coffee cup.

He put his palms on the table and pushed himself part way to his feet. "I'm going to grab a paper. I didn't have time for it this morning. There's still a couple left." He left a swirl of smoky cologne-filled air in his wake.

He wanted to read a newspaper? In the middle of a date? Billie slid down in her seat. First date ever and she was killing it. Not in that good, slang, "killin' it, baby" kind of way. No, she was letting it die a slow, painful death right before her eyes. She drew a knife with her mental red pen, brought it down on the table until the blade penetrated the cutesy wannabe-Greek-bistro tiles. It was the sword in the dating stone. But she didn't have the magical powers to pull it free and rule the dating land.

A newspaper landed atop her imaginary knife, which evanesced into the dark-roast-scented ether.

"You got your red pen?" His eyebrows bounced up and down.

"Sorry?"

"I figure we could edit a few endings. Thanks to you, I can't read any article the way it was written. I'm imagining a red pen in my hand, editing out the crap and adding the ending I want. A good ending. A just ending, if you know what I mean."

One side of her mouth curled up. A just ending. Yes, she understood him exactly. "Really?"

He nodded.

She fished two red pens from her purse. Her heart pattered about her chest cavity, bounding with excitement. She bordered on gleeful. Not only was he rugged and strong, sturdy and ruddy, he was of like mind. How rare that must be, to find someone just as off, just as touched.

Just as normal.

"Do you fix grammar and spelling?" She handed him a pen.

He roared a giant laugh. His breath was sweet with vanilla. "I'll leave that to the professionals." He took the pen with one hand and placed his other hand over hers. "I'm having a wonderful time with you, Billie." He crunched his face up and shut his eyes. "Wow, how lame did that sound?" His easy laugh bellowed from deep inside him.

She added her other hand to the knot of knuckles in the middle of the table. "Not lame. I'm having a wonderful time with you, too."

Bruce squeezed and leaned his body toward her. A tiny gesture, but a lean all the same. He held her in his gaze for longer than she had ever felt comfortable before, squeezed again and released her hands. "Okay, what dastardly crimes against justice can we put right tonight?" He spread the newspaper open. "Maybe you need to come closer. You know, so one of us doesn't have to read upside down." A tinge of pink crept into his face.

Billie nodded. "Yes, upside down is so annoying." She dragged her chair to the other side of the table and sat. A shock of static sparked between them when her skirt brushed his pants. Billie jumped. Bruce laughed. She settled into her chair and allowed her thigh to rub against his. The tiny chairs did nothing to reign in his girth. Warmth spread from that point of connection, crawled down her right leg and pooled in her stump. Her fingers faltered and the pen flipped in the air and landed on the page. She giggled.

Where had this giggle come from? Before she met Bruce, she hadn't giggled since she was ten.

Bruce put his right arm around the back of her chair and picked up the pen. He was a lefty. She hadn't noticed that before. They scanned the headlines, flipped the pages. It would appear that Thursday had been a slow news day. Then there it was, deep in the society page. Murder. Or the appearance of it. The whisper of it. Only rumours and unproven suspicions. The justice system had put the widow, Agatha Friesen, on trial for conspiracy to commit murder. The jury hung. At a second trial, a new group of her peers found her not guilty. Perhaps that was the problem with the justice system. Peers. Peer pressure. Too much emphasis on the rights of the accused at the utter denial and expense of any rights for the victim.

With double jeopardy firmly attached, the widow was free to take up with a younger man — one the prosecution had claimed was in on the conspiracy. She was free to spend her inheritance and the life insurance money, since her husband was the last living member of his family and there was no one to challenge the will.

Billie put her red pen to the page. Time to fix that.

With the widow's proper fate carefully etched in red ink, the date ended with a promise to go out again the following Friday.

"It could be our regular thing," he said. "If you want it to be."

Her cheeks warmed and she glanced at her feet. "I'd like that." She tried not to sound too eager, but probably failed at that too, with her head bobbing yes faster than her mouth could demurely concur. Of course she wanted it to be a regular thing. Recurring human contact. The pleasant kind. Not that Peg Leg wasn't good company. And maybe if he spoke actual words and said all of the things that her mental red pen said for him, that would be enough.

No. No it wouldn't.

Bruce held her hand in his strong grip. She felt safe with him, but free at the same time. Like a leash she could take off whenever she needed to.

He walked her to her building, kissed her cheek under the streetlight, and waited until she waved from her third floor walk-up before lumbering up the street to the nearest subway station.

She sat at the window, her forehead against the cool pane, and watched until the last tendril of his lengthy shadow disappeared from her view.

MONDAY

BILLIE SLID HER CHROME-PLATED LETTER OPENER under the flap, all sealed shut with some stranger's spit. She used to use her finger until the day she sliced the tip open with that spitty sliver of transformed tree, ripe with foreign DNA. What kind of disease had she introduced into her bloodstream?

Some schmuck in the office was whistling a disagreeably catchy tune. She slipped a letter from the envelope, unfolded the sheet and hesitated, the page held mid-air, her lips pursed.

It was her. She was the whistling schmuck. She smiled, nodded, and resumed her rendition of *Happy* by Pharrell Williams, amping up the volume.

Her weekend had been filled with editing Annabelle's manuscript, treadmill running, and weight training. And shopping. She bought a new dress, new shoes. Even a pair of boot cut jeans, tight in the butt with legroom for her prosthesis. Her ass looked great in them. And she bought a cookbook. She spent Sunday teaching herself the fine art of roasting chicken and mashing potatoes. It wasn't great, burned skin and dry meat and lumpy potatoes. But it was a start.

"You're awfully cheery this morning."

She shut her eyes. The happy whistle died on her lips. "What do you want, pest?"

"Why are you always so mean to me?" The whine of his voice made her ears ache.

She cracked her neck and turned to the little weasel. "You're kidding me, right?" A red knife sliced through the air and stabbed Jeffrey in the eye. Ink blood spewed from the wound and his mouth became a surprised O. Her inner bitch smiled. "You are never nice to me. You poke fun at my prosthesis. You annoy the snot out of me constantly. And you never miss an opportunity to rat me out to Katherine, even when there's nothing to rat on." The pen added whiskers and a pointy nose to his already mousy face.

"Well, I can't help it. That — thing — is always there, staring at me." He scratched his whiskers. "It's icky."

"Icky?" She swiveled her chair and yanked up her skirt. "It's my leg, you dolt." She knocked on the prosthesis. "Just metal and rubber and plastic. How is that icky?"

"Not the fake part. The real part. Underneath." He shifted on his feet and scanned the room.

"You can't see that part. And don't worry, I'll keep it under wraps in the office. Don't want to harm your delicate sensibilities. Give you more fodder to stoke Katherine's obvious hatred of me."

Jeffrey snorted. "Hatred? You idiot, she doesn't hate you."

Billie squinted. "What are you talking about?"

He leaned in. "She doesn't hate you. I mean, she doesn't *like* you. But mostly, she's afraid of you."

Billie crossed her arms over her chest. "Give me a break. Afraid of what?"

"All that affirmative action crap head office is spewing. They want to make a show of how progressive they are. They want to move some handicaps up the ladder."

Billie looked askance at his rodent face. "Well, there's the problem."

Jeffrey cocked his head and raised his eyebrows.

She shoved her skirt down. "I'm not handicapped." She swiveled the chair and faced her computer.

"Suit yourself. But you're missing an opportunity. That

vampire writer, the typing guy, he liked your edits." He bent over and put his pointed nose near her face. "And so did the editor," he whispered.

Billie's heart hammered. They liked her work? Katherine was stonewalling her. That bitch. She squinted. "Why are you telling me this?"

"Maybe one day you can repay the favour." He leaned in. "And I like to stir the pot." He tossed his head back and spewed a whiny, wimpy snicker.

Taffy's squeaking yip was like an air raid siren. Warning, Katherine incoming! Duck and cover! Any other day, Billie would have crawled under the desk until the danger had passed. But today she was pissed. She donned her best glare and eyed Katherine's daily catwalk. A red pen jumped up and drew a leg jutting out from Jeffrey's hole. Katherine's four-inch Christian Louboutins, the disgusting cowhide stilettos with actual cow's hair still attached and dyed to look like an executed zebra, caught on the leg and she landed on her red-ink ass on the Berber.

Katherine strode by with her practiced model's gait. She ignored Billie except for one fleeting flick of her azure-contact-lensed eyes. A whiff of Chanel N°5 tickled the tip of Billie's nose. When Katherine passed, a red butcher's knife protruded from between her shoulder blades.

Billie boiled in her seat. If the editor liked her work, the author liked her work, and head office was looking for poor, needy, handicapped folk to promote, then Billie was going to damn well get promoted. She just had to figure out how to get past the gatekeeper. How to slay the corporate Cerberus and lop off all three of her two-faced heads.

THURSDAY THE 18TH

I HAD A DATE."

Doc Frost raised both eyebrows. That was a first. Billie had surprised and impressed her in one four-word sentence. "A date? With subway Batman?"

Billie snorted. "With Bruce, yes."

"Well," Doc leaned back and donned the practiced finger-tented pose, "that's progress. How was it?"

"It was lovely. Quiet. A movie and coffee. He's a perfect gentleman." Billie couldn't meet Doc's eyes. Didn't want to blurt out all the private thoughts she'd been having, all the times she'd copulated with Bruce in her mind. Of course, in those life-edits, she had two real legs. Doc might think she was even more bat-guano crazy.

"So?" Doc spread her palms wide and plastered a question mark on her face. "Will there be more?"

Billie nodded, her cheeks warm. "Tomorrow night. Dinner."

"Excellent!"

Billie's laughter spurt from her mouth like the bark of a trained seal. Doc had never been so loud, so exuberant. "So glad you're pleased."

"Well, I am. This is a huge step, Billie. Huge."

Billie grabbed the pillow into her lap and hugged it to her belly. "No pressure or anything."

"Sorry. How about church? Have you been since our last meeting?"

"Both Sundays." Though she could barely sit through an entire service and skipped the weekly glad-handing in the foyer.

"Also excellent. Have you had any more instances of dissociative fugue? Wake up anywhere unexpected?"

"Not a once." Well, how easy had that lie been? Billie had considered telling Doc of the morning panhandling scene. But she was certain it was an anomaly. Like the near-jump from the fire escape. Coincidence. Like the clowns.

Doc nodded. "That's good news. Maybe we can hold off on the meds then. Keep up with therapy. But I am worried about your safety. It would be nice if you had a roommate to keep an eye on you."

"Well, I only have Peg Leg and that's not about to change anytime soon. I'm fine, Doc. It was just a little sleepwalking." She nodded as if trying to convince herself.

Doc looked skeptical. "Let's hope so."

FRIDAY

B ILLIE TUGGED ON THE BRASS KNOB AND TURNED the key in the deadbolt at the same time. The trick to getting the door open — pull and turn. If she didn't do it just right, the bolt wouldn't slide all the way and she'd have to do it repeatedly. Wintertime was the worst, when the drafts in the hall dropped the temperature to five degrees and the door warped, its frozen front and its toasty back at odds with the jamb. But this was a warm spring. The bolt slid into place.

She stood with her hand on the knob. The steady flow of Bruce's breath became loud in her ear. Was he nervous too? She shot a look over her shoulder. "I haven't had anyone up in quite a while."

He put one hand around her waist and turned her to face him. "If you'd like to take a rain check, I'm cool with that." His fingers brushed hair from her cheek.

For their second Friday date, he'd taken her to dinner. Thai, her favourite. Though he hadn't known that. Some little hole in the wall in the 'burbs he discovered a couple years back when overseeing construction of a residential development. He picked her up in his black Tahoc. Clean as a whistle in the cab. Construction nightmare of hard hats, clipboards, rolls of blue prints, and a mass of empty takeout containers in the back.

She shook her head. "No, I'd like you to come in. I might have some wine." She smiled, reached behind her back, and turned the knob.

Inside, she slipped off her one shoe, bent, and pried the other from her prosthetic foot. Bruce took his shoes off with the toe of one shoe against the heel of the other. That explained the scuff marks on the backs.

"Have a seat." Billie opened the fridge and pulled out a bottle of wine. "Do you like Riesling?"

"I like anything."

She turned to find Bruce reclining on her sofa, his feet on her coffee table. Peg Leg was sprawled across his lap, tummy in the air. Bruce petted and rubbed the cat, cooed at him. Peg Leg licked his fingers. Any ill ease or jitters she'd had about him being in her home dissolved at the sight of her best friend's eyes, just slits of pleasure. Her red pen popped up but she tossed it aside. This was a rare perfect moment and she didn't want to mess with it.

She placed two glasses of chilled wine on the coffee table and eased onto the other end of the sofa. Peg Leg stretched his inky bulk and tugged at her skirt with one paw. She reached over and stroked the soft fur between his ears.

"He's a great cat. What's his name?"

"Peg Leg."

Bruce snorted, scratched under Peg Leg's armpits, ran his hands over the cat's hind leg, then rubbed his stump. "How'd it happen?"

"I don't know." She patted the knee of her amputated leg. "This is how we found each other."

Bruce grinned, his gaze locked on Peg Leg. "Kismet. You were meant to be together."

She couldn't take her eyes from his rough-hewn face, from the scars that others might think marred him, lessened his ruddy handsomeness. To Billie, every scar enhanced his uniqueness. Made him stand out. Added to his charm.

His many, many charms.

She reached out and ran one finger along the longest mark.

His face relaxed and a grin crept up on his lips. He kept his eyes on the cat.

The scar started under his left eye, ran the length of his cheekbone and disappeared into his hairline at the temple. It wasn't deep or even easily visible. Just a wisp of a white line, a cobweb of a scar. She wanted to kiss every millimetre of it. "What happened?"

"Just one of far too many fights. Guy cut me with a razor." He took her fingers from his face and kissed them. "I used to be an asshole, Billie. A big one."

"How so?"

He sighed and slid down in the seat. "Those thugs on the subway? The high school boys? That was me. I did too many drugs, pushed my luck one too many times. And ended up in the hoosegow for my juvenile delinquent efforts."

"What charge?"

He cut his eyes to her face. "Public intoxication. Drunk and disorderly. Possession. And the cherry on top of the idiot-sundae — I took a swing at a cop. A solid uppercut to the jaw. His partner took me to the ground and laid the boots to me good."

"They aren't allowed to do that."

"What they are supposed to do and what they actually do are usually not connected. But shit, I deserved it. I was high and had a knife in my pocket. If he hadn't stopped me, hell, I might have stuck the guy."

"Do you think so?"

He shifted and turned to face her. "Like I said, big fat asshole." He rubbed his fingers on the sleeve of her cardigan. "I'd understand if you didn't want to hang around with me anymore."

"Because of the you who doesn't exist anymore? You seem pretty decent now." She wanted to wrap him in her arms, stroke his head and tell him how wonderful he was. Instead she took his hand in hers. "I think you should forgive yourself. Seems that we wouldn't need to edit this story if we'd found it in the newspaper. You paid for your crime. Maybe even a couple you didn't get charged with. And you turned your life around." She raised one eyebrow and pursed her lips. "You did turn it around, right? No more drugs, no more concealed weapons or pokes at the po-po?"

Bruce let his laughter fill her apartment. "No more of that shit. I'm older. Wiser." He shook his head. "I can't believe you just said po-po."

She clamped her lips together but couldn't keep the laughter in. It snorted from her mouth and her nose at the same time. Bruce's body shook with amusement. Peg Leg hissed and jumped from the sofa, curled up on his bed beside the radiator and glared at them for interrupting his stump rub.

Bruce slid across the thick, black denim of her sofa. He put his hand behind her waist and leaned his face toward hers.

Her heart nearly stopped dead. Sweat broke out on her palms and she fought the urge to push him away and flee. She'd been waiting for this moment. Craved the chance to kiss him. She held her breath and closed her eyes.

The first, tentative touch of his lips against hers sent a thunderbolt aching through her chest. She could hear the pounding of her heart and feel the blood thump through her veins. Heat spread through her body and pooled in her lap. Pressure built in her bladder.

She put her hand against his chest and drew away. "I need to pee." She jumped up and bolted to the bathroom, closed the door, and leaned her back against it. She put her hands to her face. "Damn, damn, damn." She looked in the mirror. "Did I just say pee?"

What the hell was wrong with her? She should have crushed her lips to his. Stuck her tongue in his mouth. Ran her hands all over him and held him against her body. But she just couldn't bring herself to do it.

That sealed it. She was a total chicken shit.

"Billie?" A light tap at the door. "Are you okay? I pushed my luck, didn't I?"

She wiped her sweaty palms on her skirt. "I'm fine. I'll be right out." Her eyes darted around the room. She flushed the empty toilet, wiped flakes of mascara from under her eyes. She splashed cool water on her cheeks and washed her hands, put her hand on the knob, took a deep breath, and opened the door.

Bruce waited on the other side, his face flushed, his gaze at his feet. "Look, I'm sorry. I'll just leave." He looked up and took a step toward her. "I like you, Billie. A lot. You're very ... unusual. In a wonderful way. And I don't want to lose your friendship." He rubbed the back of his neck. "I'll let myself out." He turned away.

"Wait. Don't go." She took his hand. "I have to confess something."

"Confess?" He raised an eyebrow. "You're not like, half guy or anything are you? Not that there's anything wrong with that, just not my thing." One side of his mouth curled up. "Then again, for you, I could give it a try."

She shook her head and grinned on the inside. "Nothing like that." She led him to the sofa. "I'm sorry for running away. I got scared." She couldn't meet his eyes. Had no clue where to look, so she fell into old habits and stared at her lap. "I've never really been kissed before." She closed her eyes and waited for the taunting jibes to fly.

"Never?" He cupped her chin in his hand and lifted her head until she looked him in the eye. "Billie, have you never been with a man?"

Tears sprang to her eyes and she sniffed. She shook her head.

He slumped back into the sofa. His lips clamped together and his cheeks bulged. His breath expelled from his mouth like someone had popped his cheek balloons. He rubbed his palm over the top of his head. "Wow. That's huge. I had no idea, really. If I had," he sat up straight and took her hand, "I would never have been so damn presumptuous."

"You don't want to run screaming from the building?" She searched his eyes for the truth.

"Run? Hell no. Like I said, I like you. A lot. A whole freaking lot." He took her hands and lifted them to his mouth, kissed her fingertips. An easy gesture, and one she was fast growing comfortable with. Why did his lips on hers scare her so much? He looked so wide-eyed and vulnerable. Shields down. Open to attack.

She put one hand to his cheek and stroked his pocked skin. She swallowed, inched her body closer to him, and brought her face just an inch from his. "I'm ready. I am. I just panicked." She swallowed three times. "Can I kiss you?" she whispered.

He smiled and his eyes softened. "You bet you can."

He didn't make a move, just sat there like a stone. He let her take charge, go at her pace. Were all men like this? So kind and understanding? She doubted it. Hell, she knew for a fact they weren't.

She placed her palm flat on his chest and neared his lips, their warmth touching hers before their skin met. The wine on his breath made her stomach lurch but the beat of his heart under her hand calmed her. She closed her eyes. When their lips came together, a smaller thunderbolt raced through her. She rested there, in kissing stasis. A contact coma.

And still, he waited for her.

She opened her eyes to find his open and staring. That was the moment, the catalyst. The sign. She parted her lips and tilted her head as she'd watched other women do, on television, in the movies, on the street corner.

Bruce moved his lips, gently and tenderly, never forcing her to do more. His arm found its way around her waist and tugged her closer.

She didn't resist. Didn't want to run away. Her chest ached, her heartbeat staccato, disjointed from the pulse in her ears. She dropped her hand from his chest and placed it behind his neck, her other arm under his, around his body. She moved closer until their chests were snug against one another.

They remained there, locked in a sweet, slow kiss for more seconds than she dared to count.

She broke the spell, released her embrace, and dropped her chin to her chest. She smiled.

He stroked her hair. "We will take this as slowly as you want, Billie. Like a glacier. Like continental drift." He kissed her forehead. "You set the pace. I'm in no rush."

JANIS JONES

JANIS JONES LIT ANOTHER CIGARETTE AND BLEW THE smoke at the window. She picked tobacco from her lip and flicked it at the glass. Well, she flicked it at the media scum trampling her lawn. The glass just got in the way. Every time she showed herself they scrambled around like dice in a game of Pop-O-Matic Trouble. Trouble, trouble, that's the name. But she didn't want to send these media game pegs back. Even if they were ruining her roses. Leaving the house was out of the question. They'd rip her to pieces, and not just in a metaphorical, thrown-to-the-lions kind of way.

She refused to flinch, to give them what they wanted. For her to fall apart. To show weakness. To confess.

Screw 'em. Screw 'em all.

The horizontal blinds crashed against the windowsill. She let the nylon string trail between her fingers and dangle from the valance. She stubbed out her cigarette in a tin ashtray. They could suck on that until the next curtain call, until her next award-winning performance. If they insisted on sticking around, at least she could toy with them. Squeeze every ounce of exposure from her fifteen minutes.

Her third husband put his hands on her shoulders and began to knead the tension from them. She closed her eyes and dropped her chin to her chest. "Oh, bless you."

He kissed her cheek. "I don't know why you won't let me chase them off."

She shook him off her. He didn't understand her at all.

"They're insatiable. They'd just come back."

He sighed and held up his palms. "Fine. Personally, I'd like them off my property. It's just a moment-by-moment reminder that Ryan is gone. They just won't let him die."

"Well, he is dead." She spat the words at him.

His eyes filled with tears and he balled his fists. "Why'd you leave him in the bathtub alone? How could you turn your back on him? He was only nine months old." Tears streamed down his pathetic cheeks.

"What are you accusing me of?" She drew back her arm and slapped his face.

He closed his eyes and rubbed his jaw.

She lit another cigarette. "And I told you, the phone rang. I was only gone a few seconds."

"We have voice mail. You could have let it go to voice mail." He broke down and sobbed, holding his face in both hands.

She rolled her eyes and checked her watch.

He wiped his nose and shook his head. "You don't even cry anymore. Hell, you barely cried at all."

She blinked and pinched herself as hard as she could under her armpit until tears welled up in her eyes. "I've cried! You bastard, how dare you?" She stood straighter and jutted out her chin, her indignation growing. "Maybe if you hadn't marooned us out here in the boonies, it wouldn't have taken so long for the paramedics to get here. Maybe they could have saved him." She crossed her arms and smirked. "Maybe it's your fault he's dead."

She looked at him, his dead gaze getting deader by the moment. He was just like the others. No grit. No balls. No fight. Couldn't handle their evil spawn dying. Like they think part of them died too. They should all just grow the hell up.

He strolled to the bar and poured himself a scotch. Didn't even offer her anything. Chivalry truly was dead.

"I need a shower." He turned and headed for the stairs.

Bastards were all the same. They woo her, fawn over her, give her everything her beautiful heart desires. She patted her perfectly coifed hair and blotted her shimmering lips together. She gave them each a child and they adored her even more. Until they held the baby. Then she was just part of the furniture. And as soon as those children were gone, they all went cold.

Is that all she was good for? Fucking and making babies? Being a mommy and a nanny and a nursemaid to those mewling, screaming, bundles of mucous and spew?

She ran a hand over her less-than-taut tummy. She used to have definition. Tone. Now she had stretch marks, love handles, saddlebags. She should have gotten herself fixed. Avoided the whole damn mess. But then they would have left her because she couldn't pop out their pitiful progeny.

Men. They all sucked.

She parted the blinds with her fingers and peeked out. One of the reporters was having his makeup touched up, a white cloth tucked into his collar to save it from the flesh-coloured powder. He was even more handsome in person than on the screen. She must be huge news if they sent out the big talent.

He glanced at the house and caught her eye.

She raised the blinds, smiled and licked her lips, sucked hard on the end of her cigarette and winked at him.

He grinned, ripped the cloth from his collar and threw it on her lawn, motioned for his cameraman and ran toward the window. "Mrs. Jones!" His voice was just as deep and resonating as on television, even filtered through her double-pane picture window. He stood under the window, stretched the microphone up toward her. "Do you have any comment about the new allegations that you may have murdered your first two children?"

Her eyes became slits and her flirtation withered like trampled roses. She yanked on the cord and let the curtain of blinds come down.

Yep. Bastards were all the same.

TUESDAY, JUNE 30TH

B ILLIE WALKED IN A FOG FROM THE SUBWAY TO the office. Since meeting Bruce, she'd lost focus on her daily life. Her schedule was muddled, missing the occasional gym day, or going on a Monday thinking it was Tuesday. Her head filled with the touch of his lips to hers, the soft caress of his sturdy hands. The vision of him lounging with Peg Leg kept popping up and blurring the rest of her world. No red ink, just a real vision. A perfect moment. One she wanted to crawl into and stop time so she could live there forever. Without work, without pain, without the torment of other human beings.

And without the possibility of moving her relationship with Bruce into a sexual realm. A realm she yearned for, yet feared.

She was a coward. And ridiculous to boot, wanting to stop time to prevent potential joy, love, promise. Perhaps even ecstasy. Something she'd like to know just once before she died. Pure, unadulterated ecstasy. And not in pill form, thank you very much.

She fantasized about it, but had no real-life frame of reference. Her red ink-marred version of sex soon morphed into a bad movie sex scene. Watching actors fake it onscreen didn't provide sufficient data. She needed to feel it. Experience it. Live it.

If only she could strip off the damn chicken suit.

The crash of a tin garbage can tipping over shook her from her sexual pondering. She stopped and turned to face the alley, darkened by the shadow of the forty-story building that housed her office. In the dimness, two men towered over a smaller man. One of them held him by the scruff of his collar and jabbed a pointed finger into his chest.

The surroundings closed in around her, her vision focused on the centre, the periphery spinning in a kaleidoscope of light and dark. She was staring down a familiar tube. Dark alley. Angry men. Pain pending.

The thug holding the little guy pushed him to the ground and kicked him in the stomach.

Billie snapped out of her kaleidoscope. It was Jeffrey.

She dug her hand into her purse and dropped her briefcase onto a bag of garbage.

The second thug kneeled on the grimy asphalt and punched Jeffrey in the eye.

"Stop!" She ran toward them, her cell phone in one hand. She'd already dialled and held the phone to her ear. Her other hand fingered the can of pepper spray she kept hidden in her pocket.

"Nine-one-one, where is your emergency?"

The men stopped and turned to her. They both stood.

"Alley between Perry Tower and the Dilly Deli on sixth. Gay bashing."

Jeffrey cowered against the building, his arms shielding his head, his knees drawn up under his chin.

"She called the cops." One of the men bolted down the alley away from her.

The other ran at her. When he was five feet away, she pulled the can from her pocket, her index finger already on the trigger. She held it up at arm's length and sprayed a stream of pepper into his face.

He screamed and dropped to the ground. Billie, her heartbeat in her ears, her legs flush with adrenaline, stood over him.

He swiped at his eyes. "You fucking bitch, you blinded me."

"That was the point." She put the phone to her ear. "Is

someone coming?"

"Yes ma'am, units are en route. Are the attackers still there?"

"One of them. I've got him subdued." Billie placed the foot of her prosthetic leg on his crotch.

He squirmed. "No, don't do it."

"That foot has titanium bones. You move, and I crush your sorry balls like robin's eggs. You hear me?" She applied enough pressure to make her point.

"All right, all right, just — just stop." He held one hand over his face. His cheeks blossomed in pepper burns. Tears streamed from his eyes and dripped onto the pavement.

"Yeah, you bastard." Jeffrey had come out of his cocoon and stood beside Billie. He kicked the man in the ribs. The man groaned.

"Jeffrey." Billie put her hand on his arm. "Don't. Don't be like them." She touched his swollen cheek. "That eye's going to be a mess."

"Thank you, Billie." He rested his forehead on her shoulder and wept.

The man on the ground took his hand away from his face and blinked.

She leaned forward. "One move and I spray you again." Blood and adrenaline coursed through her. Even her absent shin and foot were alive with power. Justice palpitated her heart. Billie stood a little straighter, shifted her shoulders back, and stuck out her chest. All that was missing were tights and a cape.

"Where the hell have you two been?" Katherine stood, arms crossed, waxed legs shoulder-width apart, stilettos stabbing the carpet.

Jeffrey pointed to his eye.

Katherine's face contorted, turned crimson, and then softened. "Jeffrey. What happened?" She strode toward him and cupped his chin in her manicured talon, eyed his shiner and the bandage the EMT had taped over an open wound.

"I got jumped in an alley. We had to give statements to the cops. And a totally hot paramedic cleaned me up and disinfected me."

"That's horrible!" She turned to Billie. "What's your excuse? Where's your mortal wound?"

"Billie saved me. She was amazing. She maced the guy and nearly crushed his man parts under her awesome titanium foot. It was the best thing ever." Jeffrey reached out and took Billie's hand. "If it weren't for her, I might be dead."

Katherine crossed her arms again. Shields up. "Really? Well, isn't that … surprising." She turned to Jeffrey. "Go home for the day. Get some rest."

He shook his head. "No thanks, I'm not ready for the big, ugly world yet. Can I stay for a while?"

"Of course." Katherine patted his hand. She turned to Billie. "You've got deadlines." She jerked her head at Billie's desk, turned, and retreated to her lair.

Jeffrey headed for the kitchenette. "I'm going to get your coffee," he said over his shoulder.

"You don't need to do that."

He stopped and spun around. "Oh, yes I do." He flashed a toothy grin and disappeared behind the divider.

Billie set her briefcase on her desk and stared out the window. Score one for the good guys.

Throughout the morning, Jeffrey topped up Billie's coffee four times. Between the afterglow of superhero adrenaline, added caffeine, and his heavy hand with the sugar shaker, her heart was pulsating out of her chest. But she just couldn't tell him to stop. He even took her to lunch. Not ready to step into the mean streets, as teeming with cutthroat ruffians as he envisioned they were, they stuck to the tiny sandwich shop in the lobby and noshed on soggy tuna salad on rye and limp pickles.

Back at her desk, Billie popped a breath mint into her mouth and shook her mouse until her screen came to life.

A stilted laugh filled the office. Not a genuine laugh, more the kind you allow yourself when you have to laugh even when whatever was said is not the least bit funny. Billie poked her head out of her hole to see the editor of Dreckula with her hand on Katherine's doorknob.

The woman clicked the door shut and wended her way through the cubicle maze to the exit. She caught Billie watching her, paused and rapped her knuckles on the metal frame of a short divider. "Hey, nice job on those edits."

The heat rose in Billie's cheeks. "Thanks. And sorry. I know I'm only a proofreader."

The woman snorted. "Hell, don't apologize. Made my job easier. You've got quite an eye for fiction. Ever thought of applying to be an editor?"

"As soon as a job comes open, I'll be all over it."

"Well, one's open now." The woman's forehead crinkled like a normal person's. "Didn't Katherine post it?"

Over the woman's shoulder, a machine gun appeared and sprayed Katherine's door with red bullets. "No, she hadn't mentioned it."

"Well," the woman rested her hand on Billie's shoulder, "I'll send you the post." She slid a business card from her jacket pocket, dropped it on the desk and tapped it with one fingertip. "Use me as a reference. You're a shoo-in." She winked, turned, and headed for the exit.

The second the door clicked shut, Jeffrey's head popped out from his hole. He rolled his chair backward, leapt from it, and bolted to Billie's side. "Did that just happen?"

Billie nodded. "Yeah. I think it did."

He faux-punched her arm. "A shoo-in, she said." He giggled and tapped his fingertips together in silent applause. "Are you going for it?"

She glared at the door to Katherine's den. "I've got nothing to lose."

He punched the air. "Yes! That'll show her. You should go confront her. Give her what-for."

Billie nodded. Wisps of mightiness from her morning brush with heroism still pumped through her veins and buoyed her bravado. She pushed away from her desk and stood, patted Jeffrey on the shoulder. "I think I will." She stormed into Katherine's office and slammed the door.

Billie stood over Katherine, her fists on the desk, her resolve set. "I want a shot at that promotion."

Katherine looked at her with the usual disdain. "What promotion?"

Billie slapped the desk. "The one you're keeping from me. What's wrong, Katherine, afraid I'll eclipse you? Afraid I'm better than you? That maybe, one day, I'll be *your* boss and treat *you* like the muck I scrape off the bottom of *my* shoe?"

Katherine huffed. "Like that could ever happen." She leaned her elbows on her desk. "I didn't bother telling you because you're not ready yet. They'd just toss your application in the slush pile and move on."

"That's my choice, not yours."

Katherine picked up a pencil and leaned back in her chair, tapped the eraser against her cheek. "Fine. You want to embarrass yourself?" She snapped her chair erect and shuffled through a stack of files, pulled a document out and tossed it across the desk. It spun through the air, floated to the floor and landed at Billie's feet. "Knock yourself out. But here's the deal. If you don't get it, you're fired."

Billie stooped and retrieved the document. "You can't fire me for that. I'll take it to HR if you try." She shook the pages at her. "But I'm not worried. Because I'm qualified for this job. And I darn well deserve it."

She straightened her skirt, spun on her good foot, and left Katherine's office with quiet dignity, pulling the door shut with a click. She did deserve it. Was qualified for it. But if she didn't make the cut, could she be fired? Her heart hammered in her throat.

How could she take down a six-foot cretin in an alley and fight for justice one minute, then be scared to death of the plastic gorgon in the corner office the next?

FRIDAY

BRUCE PULLED A BOTTLE OF PINOT GRIGIO FROM the ice bucket, wiped the bottle with his linen napkin, and filled Billie's glass.

"You trying to get me drunk, mister?" She picked up the crystal stem and swirled the citrusy elixir before taking a generous sip.

Bruce filled his own glass. "You've discovered my devious plan."

She giggled, the wine fuzzing her brain, her cheeks warm. Maybe he was a bad influence on her. She'd drank more wine since she met him than in the entire year before he'd taken one giant step into her life.

"So," he said, his eyes on his wine. "What happened to you, Billie?"

Her eyelids fluttered. "What do you mean?"

He found her gaze. "I mean your leg. Sorry for being so bold, but I've been curious. And there's no subtle way to bring it up."

"Dessert?"

Bruce started at the intrusion. He threw the waiter a withering look.

The waiter slid a leather-bound slab of menu in front of each of them. "I recommend the beignet. Or the crème brûlée, it's a big seller." He smiled at Billie and poised his pencil over his notepad.

Bruce cleared his throat. "Maybe give us a few moments."

The young man's cheeks pinked. "Oh. Of course, sir." He slipped away.

Bruce relinquished his wine glass and reached across the table, taking one of Billie's hands. "So, your leg. Will you tell me?" He raised her hand and kissed her fingertips.

She rarely told anyone the whole story. Most people didn't ask. Maybe didn't care. Or perhaps they couldn't handle the pure and utter sadness of it all.

"It was my eleventh birthday." Her voice came out like a squeak. She willed it free from her throat but held it back all the same. She told him about the restaurant. About the roast chicken and garlic mashed potatoes. The asparagus with hollandaise. "I hated that. Smelled like when I'd fart under the covers then wave them." She pulled her hand away from his and covered her mouth. She could feel the blush race through her body until sweat pooled under her breasts. "I can't believe I just told you that." She moved her hand to cover her eyes.

Bruce held his stomach with both hands, his belly-laugh drawing stares and hushes from other diners.

"Don't sweat it," he said. "I used to try to light mine on fire."

She peered at him through her fingers. "Did it work?"

"Nah. That's one of those stupid urban legends. Or old wives' tales. Or something." He waved the waiter over. "You like crème brûlée?"

"I'd rather have the pie."

"Excellent." He turned to the young man. "Two pieces of apple pie, with all the à la mode and cheese and everything you got." He handed the waiter the menus and watched him hustle away. Bruce turned back to her. "So, chicken, potatoes, farty asparagus. Then what?"

"Apple pie." She smiled. "A la mode and cheese and all." Déjà vu all over again. "After dinner we walked along the strip. It was all lit up, the store windows full of wonderful things. Nothing we could afford. I was young, but not stupid. I knew we were poor." Tears sprang to her eyes. "We took a shortcut down an alley to where the car was parked. There were three men in the shadows. I was never told what they were doing, but I'd guess it was drugs. They were counting out money. Dad flashed his badge. He was off duty, didn't have his gun. No radio." She wiped her cheek. "Stupid, eh?"

"I don't know. Sounds like the right thing to do."

"Except they weren't impressed. One of them ran away. One pulled a knife and cut my dad's arm. The other brought a huge gun out from under his coat. He shot my father in the chest. Mom tried to pull him away, tried to stop the bleeding. She told me to run. But I just stood there."

"Did your dad die?"

"Right there on the pavement. Then the man shot my mother. She died too. Then," she tapped her prosthesis with her knuckles and closed her eyes, "he shot me. But I didn't die. I remember sirens in the distance. Then an ambulance. I woke up the next day without the bottom part of my leg or any parents."

She opened her eyes. Bruce was in tears, his ruddy cheeks ruddier than usual. He wiped his nose with the back of his hand. "Shit, Billie. I had no idea. I figured maybe you were born that way. Or some childhood disease or something." He shook his head. "Did they catch the bastards?"

"One of them. Not the shooter. I couldn't identify him, all I saw was the barrel of his gun. But I remembered the other guy. His bandana. His weird teeth."

"So you helped put one of them away, good for you."

"Mostly he did that to himself. He dropped his knife. Had his fingerprints in Dad's blood on it. But he wouldn't give up his partner."

"No wonder you edit the news. Reality sucks."

"And blows."

The waiter slid a plate in front of her. Steam wafted from a thick slab of pie. A generous scoop of ice cream — the good kind with actual flecks of real vanilla bean — melted beside it. A slice of orange cheddar wilted over the crust. Cinnamon and apples filled her senses. Saliva filled her mouth. She grabbed her fork and cut off a huge chunk with a corner of cheese, dragged it through melting ice cream, and brought it to her mouth.

She focused on the memory at the end of her fork, but was aware of Bruce's eyes on her. She raised her eyes to his face. It had a new look to it. A softer, warmer look. Maybe she'd edited that in, added his empathy for her tale of sorrow. But there were no red pen marks scratched on him, just his gentle smile. She lifted her fork. "Cheers." The whole bite went into her mouth, ice cream dripped down her lip and tickled her chin. She chewed and flashed her eyebrows at him.

He tossed his head back and laughed.

1993

BILLIE STOOD ON THE BLUE MAT, HER HANDS gripping the wood on either side of her. She imagined herself in gymnastics class, swinging between the parallel bars, balancing upside down in a handstand and then letting her legs fly through the air until she was airborne. She performed a triple flip and landed with precision and perfect form onto the mat. The judges flashed scorecards. Tens across the board.

Reality stood before her in the form of a physical therapist clad in pink polyester.

"Way to go, Billie. One step at a time." Suzanne clapped like Billie had just won a gold medal at the Olympics. Or had caught a bright rainbow-striped beach ball on the end of her trained-seal nose.

She looked down at her temporary prosthesis. Just a pole stuck in what looked like an upside down toilet plunger and a chunk of wood for a foot. It would be weeks before she'd be healed enough, before the swelling subsided enough, to be fitted for her first leg.

No matter how many socks they layered over her stump, it hurt to put on that plunger. Pain shot through her, from the toes to her calf to the thigh, around her back and up into her shoulders. Except there were no toes. No calf. Nothing but stump below the knee. How did nothing hurt so much?

Stump. That was a word she needed to get used to. It used to mean what remained after her father cut down the diseased tree in the front yard. Now it was what remained of her leg. She would lie in her bed and stare at it, draw limbs and branches and leaves growing from it. Change it from a dead stump to a living thing.

"Billie, darling. It'll be all right. When you get your own leg, you'll be back to normal in no time."

Grandmother meant well, and Billie loved her for it. The woman hadn't been ready to take Billie on full-time and raise her. But she was here, every day. Willing to see Billie through puberty and into adulthood. Help her through the pain, adjustment, therapy, and grief. That's a lot to ask of an old lady. But what other choice was there? Billie had no aunts or uncles. Her other grandparents were all gone. No other family. Dead parents. Missing leg.

She was adrift in a sea of emptiness. Her grandmother was the only thing left to hold onto.

Yes, Billie loved her. But, God damn it, she said some stupid stuff. *When you get your own leg.* Seriously? Last Billie checked, her own leg was gone, just stains on the alley floor, bits of her flesh and bone hauled away by rats and fed to their young. Billie bones. Billie rinds. Billie snacks.

Billie's arms shook against the bars. She'd begun to take her Lord's name in vain. Had taken her grandmother's kindness for granted and inwardly shamed her for her awkwardness. God wouldn't like that. But Billie was certain He would forgive her for the terrible thoughts she kept bottled up inside, as long as she didn't let them out. Sure that He'd forgive her brutal and bloody fantasies of appropriate justice that would be handed down to the men who murdered her parents. Who left her an orphan and a cripple.

She'd planned their demise through many sleepless nights. Envisioned firing squads or public hangings. She shoved so much crack cocaine up their noses and down their throats that they foamed at the mouth and convulsed on the alley floor until they died in pools of cat piss.

As much satisfaction as those thoughts brought, they also smothered her with guilt. Thou shalt not kill. That's what the bible said. But it also said an eye for an eye, tooth for a tooth. If you aren't to kill, but you can take a life in retribution for a life stolen, then where are you? What is the right answer?

She'd talked to God more than ever these past weeks. Almost every minute of every day. He didn't answer. Maybe he was bored of her whining. Sick of her sorrow. Or maybe others needed him more and he was just too busy. Perhaps his silence was his answer. If he spoke, maybe she wouldn't like what he'd have to say.

"I can't do anymore." Tears spilled down her cheeks. One wrist buckled under her weight and exhaustion and her good leg went out from under her.

Suzanne caught Billie and helped her to the wheelchair. Grandmother jumped to her feet, wrung her hands and danced on her toes like she needed to pee.

"It takes time. You'll get stronger." Suzanne kneeled beside the chair and dismantled the various parts of the peg leg. She patted Billie's real leg and looked up into her face. "I promise. One day, you'll be running down the street, playing with your friends." The woman smiled as if that would solve everything.

Chin up, buck up, smile and wave.

What a load of crap.

"We'll see you tomorrow." Suzanne wheeled her out to the hall before relinquishing the chair to Billie's grandmother. "You both have a good night," she said, a huge smile plastered on her face.

Billie wanted to sew her happy mouth shut.

Her grandmother nodded and allowed the woman a thin smile. Not even a smile really. More of a grimace with the ends curled up. It was the best she could muster. Billie understood. Smiling was something she couldn't make herself do on the outside. She was a Judas if she even smiled on the inside. Would happiness mean she didn't love her father? Billie even missed her mother, evil witch that she was. Missed the way she was before whiskey became her best buddy and she reeked of cigarette smoke. Or maybe she'd always been that way and Billie only began to notice when she grew up. When she smelled that smell on Justine and Ronald, where that smell just didn't belong.

Grandmother pushed the wheelchair toward the exit.

Billie grabbed the rubber wheels and forced the chair to stop. "I can do it myself." She cringed at the anger in her voice. She grasped the push rings and grunted. The chair lurched forward, veered a bit to the right. She corrected and tried again.

She hadn't meant to snap at Grandmother, but Billie had to figure out how to fend for herself. Grandmother wouldn't live forever. Heck, she might die that very day. Billie too. Because apparently God didn't give His own damn who got shot.

SATURDAY AND SUNDAY

It WAS THE BEST WINE SHE'D EVER TASTED, CRISP and light with orange and lemon undertones and perfectly chilled. Billie sipped at the last of her second glass of chardonnay and stared westward. The sun hovered above the mountains on the horizon, getting ready to set and end another day. The remaining spring snow capping the peaks glowed purple in the waning evening light, the downtown lights of high-rises twinkling in the dusk. A twinge of envy pecked at her heart. The view from her apartment sucked compared to this.

The pop of a cork pulled her attentions away from the floor-to-ceiling window. She looked over her shoulder, scanned the leather sofa and original paintings hanging on each wall. It bordered on opulent. She expected a butler to appear from the Batcave and offer her a gin fizz. Her gaze found Bruce in the kitchen, visible from the waist up in the open-floor concept, standing behind a granite island, pouring two more glasses of wine. He came out from behind it, his apron still wrapped around his waist, his skin aromatic with garlic and shallots and thyme from the wonderful pan sauce he'd whipped up to top the spatchcock chicken he'd fed her.

He handed her a fresh glass of wine, took the empty and placed it on the coffee table, slipped one arm around her waist, and stood behind her, his chin on her shoulder. "It looks so beautiful from up here, so shiny and clean."

His breath, thick with chardonnay, warmed her cheek. She had the same feeling she got every time he stood close — heat between her legs and aching warmth in her belly. He was an adrenaline shot to the heart. She leaned her head against his shoulder. "Too bad it's so dirty when you're down at ground level."

He swayed her body to silent music and rested his cheek against hers. "How about we watch a movie? There's bound to be something on Netflix."

She sipped her wine, ran her tongue across her teeth. It felt a little thick. "Maybe I should head home. If I finish this wine, I won't be able to walk to the subway. And you've had too much to drink to drive me."

He tugged on her hand and led her to the sofa. "It's Saturday night. Can't you stay?" He pointed to the sofa. "I can sleep on the couch. You can take my bed. No funny business, I promise." He kissed her. "I'm just not ready to let you go yet."

She touched her hand to his cheek.

Sleep overnight? At a man's house? At this rate, she might just quality for full-fledged adulthood. "But what about church?"

"I'll get you up early. Take you home to change and shower. You'll get to the church on time."

"You don't even know what time that is, do you?"

"Not a clue."

She smirked. "Okay. I'll stay. As long as you get me home by nine."

"Nine?" He checked his watch. "I guess I can always catch a nap while you're off praying." He gave her a gentle poke in the ribs.

She grabbed his hand and squeezed. "And as long as we watch anything but Batman."

"It's a deal. Though I'm surprised you're not a fan. Since you pretty much have the same story."

"Except he was rich."

"True. And a man."

"And he dresses up like a bat and beats the crap out of bad

guys."

Bruce pulled one bobby pin from her bun and set it on the side table.

Her breath caught in her throat and her heart bounced about her chest. "And he had both of his legs." Her syllables slurred together.

"Well, maybe you're not Batman, but I'd love to see you in a leather suit and cape." He tugged another bobby pin free, then a third. Her hair fell onto her shoulder. "And you right wrongs in your own, weird and wonderful way. With your magic red pen." He untangled the elastic from her ponytail. When he freed her hair, he ran his fingers through it, from the base of her neck to the ends near her waist. "And you're way better looking than him." He grabbed her with both hands and tickled her abdomen.

She squealed like a little girl and wrested free of his grip. "Very funny." She settled onto the sofa next to him, his arm around her shoulder. "Why don't you have any pets?"

He pointed the remote at the television and clicked buttons. "I'm not home enough."

"Is that why you're not married?"

He looked at her out of the corner of his eye. "Nope." He sighed. "I was married. Been divorced for five years or so."

She traced random patterns on his buttoned-down shirt with one finger. "What happened?"

"Remember what I said about being a big asshole?"

She nodded. "In the past."

"Well, my ex put up with a lot of that assholedness through our marriage. Even as I began to grow up, it was too late. It was like a bad taste in her mouth, you know? None of my new found ...." He pursed his lips and rocked his head back and forth, searching for the right words. "Goodness, I guess, cleansed her palette. She just fell out of love with me." He slugged back the rest of his wine. "That's life in the big city, right?"

"I'm sorry."

"Not your fault. Besides, it was for the best. She remarried, had a kid. She's happy now. She deserves to be happy. And," he kissed Billie's cheek, "I found you. So I'd say it's a win-win."

He'd found her. The gimpy chick who was a thirty-three-year-old virgin and afraid to let him fully in. Lucky guy. He deserved to be happy too. Deserved so much more than she'd been able to give him.

"I think you should get a cat."

He laughed. "Well, I sure like Peg Leg. Never been a cat guy before. Maybe. Would make this place a little less lonely." He scrolled through movie titles. "Have you seen *Hancock*?"

She grinned. "An alcoholic superhero. How romantic."

"Hah, sorry. I'm not the romantic comedy type."

"Me neither." She settled in beside him and rested her head on his shoulder.

They watched the movie in silence, save for a few guffaws and snickers. Billie hadn't had her prosthesis off all day. Her stump was carping at her to air it out, lotion it up, give it a bloody break already. She shifted and squirmed, tried to scratch without Bruce noticing.

"Does it get itchy a lot?" He leaned forward, slid her skirt up a few inches and eyed the works of her prosthetic leg.

Her cheeks warmed and she tugged the skirt down.

"Oh, shit, sorry. I didn't mean anything. Just, you know." His entire head turned red and sweat broke out on his brow. "Just curious." He wiped his mouth. "Sorry."

"You can stop saying that, you know."

"What?"

"Sorry. You say it all the time." She sighed and pulled her skirt up at bit. "I'm just not used to people being genuinely interested. Usually they're staring or pointing, but not for any good reason." She glanced at him. "You want to see?"

He looked at her with such sweetness. No rubbernecker eyes, just kindness and empathy. Something she hadn't seen in another's eyes since Grandmother passed.

He swallowed. "If you're okay with it. I do."

Each bit of her prosthesis she removed, each layer of sock unrolled, was a strip tease. The most intimate moment of her life. It bordered on sexy. So why did her stomach churn and leap? She was about to reveal something few were allowed to see, except doctors and therapists and her grandmother. And the office staff, but damn, she had to take the thing off occasionally. After so many years working in close quarters, she felt an odd familiarity with those jackasses. And sometimes, she just liked to gross them out.

She pulled off the prosthetic leg and rolled the socks away. There it was, her naked stump. She watched his face for signs of disgust, for the fight-or-flight response. Though, where could he flee to? He was already where he belonged.

But she didn't see any of that. He looked as curious as he said he was. He eyeballed her stump, ran his gaze along the scars and stretch marks from the growth spurts she had through her teens. If he hesitated on the ugly nubbin of scar tissue, it was probably all in her mind. He showed no indication of any negative emotion. She smiled on the inside and parked her red pen for the night.

"How does your leg stay on?"

"It just does."

"You don't even limp. Can you run?"

She grinned. "Why don't you come to the gym with me and see?"

His face broke out in a big smile. He looked ten years younger when he was smiling. Better than any face lift, any Botox injection. "It's a date."

Billie stretched and reached for Peg Leg. The pillow was cool to her touch and empty of her furry companion. Her eyes flew open and she bolted upright.

Was that bacon?

Sun streamed in through the gauzy curtains of Bruce's large bedroom. She found the clock radio. Eight-fifteen.

"Good morning, Billie sunshine." Bruce came into the room, freshly showered, his short curls damp. He wore only boxers and a grey T-shirt. He was laden with a tray, the Sunday paper tucked under one arm, his biceps prominent, the veins in his forearms bulging.

She pushed herself against the pillows, wiped her fingers under her eyes, and tried to pat down her morning hair.

He sat on the bed and placed the tray between them. The newspaper fell onto the comforter. He leaned over it and planted a kiss on her morning-breath mouth.

Oh, God, why didn't she carry a spare toothbrush in her purse?

He settled onto the bed and lifted a napkin from the tray with a magician's flair. Ta-da! Underneath the napkin was a large plate with a mound of scrambled eggs, cheddar melting on top, a pile of buttered toast, jam on the side in a little bowl with a tiny spoon. And bacon. Lots and lots of crispy bacon. Could he read her thoughts? She must have told him how much she loved bacon.

"You cooked breakfast?" The tray held two cups of steaming coffee.

"Of course. It's Sunday. That's always a big breakfast day for me." He picked up one of the forks and handed it to her. A red pen rolled out from beneath the rim of the plate.

She picked it up. "Are we editing justice gone awry this

morning?"

He fit half a strip of bacon into his mouth. "Or doing the Sunday crossword." He swallowed. "Or both. Or neither." He flashed his eyebrows at her.

She squinted. "Well, I'm starved. And there's just enough time to eat and maybe start the crossword before you have to get me home by nine, as promised."

"Right. God awaits your presence in His house." He didn't even try to mask his sarcasm.

"You're not a believer, are you?"

"I'm not sure anymore. I used to be, when I was a kid. There's just too much that can't be explained. Too much bad that, if there really were a God, He'd prevent." Bruce ran his hand over the blanket that covered her amputated leg. "Just too many good people are dealt shitty hands to think He can be up there watching out for them."

She shoved a forkful of eggs into her mouth and stared at him while she chewed and swallowed. "I don't think His purpose is to keep everything right."

Bruce's eyebrows popped up in surprise. "Then what is it?"

"It's to give those who are dealt a shitty hand something to hold onto. Something to prevent themselves from drifting out into a bitter sea and drowning in their own self-pity. He gives strength to get up every day and face the crappy truth about life." She snapped off a bite of bacon between her teeth. At least the salt and nitrates would camouflage her hangover wine breath. She chased it with a gulp of sweet, creamy, perfect coffee. "Will you show me how you make your coffee? Mine sucks."

He took the cup from her hand and set it on the nightstand, moved the tray to a long dresser with a mirror hanging above it.

Billie caught a glimpse of her reflection. Hair matted, pillow seams denting her face. And what little mascara she'd worn the night before now rested under her eyes and on her cheeks.

Bruce kneeled on the bed and put his fists on the mattress on either side of her hips. He brought his face an inch from hers. "You, Ms. Wilhelmina Fullalove, are the most interesting person I've ever met."

Heat rushed to her face. "I doubt that."

"Believe it." He kissed her.

She closed her eyes and let the heat spread through her chest, into her abdomen, and pool in her groin.

He shifted forward and took her into his strong embrace. He lifted her from the bed and brought her into his lap. The massive T-shirt he let her wear as a nightgown bunched around her waist.

Her arms floated until they were around his neck. One of his hands slipped under her T-shirt and ran up the length of her spine, leaving a trail of gooseflesh in its wake. He held her with one big paw, explored her skin with the other.

When his fingers grazed the side of her left breast, she gasped and opened her eyes. He was staring at her, his eyes soft but anxious. She rested her forehead against his and drew her lips away, gulping for breath and commanding her heart to stop pounding.

He ran his lips over her neck, suckled an earlobe. "Tell me to stop." His voice rasped in her ear.

She swallowed and looked at the clock. If she was going to make church she'd have to cry uncle now.

He pulled the neckline of the T-shirt away from her skin and kissed along her collarbone until he got to the edge of her shoulder and the end of the skin the taut material allowed him access to.

Uncle. Uncle. Come on you chicken shit, you're not ready. Cry. Uncle.

"Billie." His other hand found its way inside the T-shirt. "Tell me." He pulled away and looked into her eyes, his hands on the bare skin of her waist. "Tell me now."

She closed her eyes and felt the lump in his boxers against her wet panties. The red pen struck through her fear, slayed the chicken, murdered uncle. She shook her head, clamped her lips shut, and stripped off the T-shirt. She counted three hippopotamuses, swallowed, and opened her eyes.

His gaze was fixed on her face. He yanked his shirt over his head and tossed it on the floor. He let his eyes drift over her body and swallowed hard. "My God, Billie. You're perfect."

She cast her eyes to the end of her right leg. Her mental red pen inked in the rest of her calf and a perfectly manicured foot.

Bruce wrapped his arms around her, pulling her bare bosom to his hairy chest. He eased her to the bed and licked her lips, kissed her with an open mouth, and darted his tongue in and out.

She responded in kind, with hot, wet kisses, their hearts throbbing against each other's.

He slid down her body, kissed her neck, her collarbone, the tender strip of skin between her breasts. His tongue left a wet trail along the curve of her right breast until his mouth found her nipple. He took it in, suckled and nibbled.

She arched her back and moaned. His breath cooled his saliva and her skin bubbled with pleasure. Shivers rocked her body.

He slipped further down, lapped at the fine hairs of her belly at the edges of her white cotton underpants. He hooked one finger under the elastic waistband and inched them down, his tongue chasing behind. He slid his tongue into the space her grandmother always said was Billie's private place.

Billie's eyes flew open. Her red pen scratched the vision of her gray-haired pseudo-mother from her consciousness. She covered her eyes with one hand and dug the fingernails of her other hand into Bruce's shoulder. "Oh, my fucking God," spurt from her mouth.

To hell with church.

Bruce pulled away and cool air rushed in where his head had

been. "Well. That was a long time coming."

Billie was afraid to look at him, her hand firmly over her eyes. She giggled at the double entendre, whether he'd intended it or not. "Only a decade and a half or so." She split her fingers and peered at him. He kneeled on the mattress between her legs and smiled at her, his grin lopsided and filled with satisfaction. She glanced between his legs. He'd stripped off his boxers. At the sight of his erection, something she'd only ever seen in artsy photos or Google image results, her legs liquefied. "So." She gulped. "Can you make me do that one more time?"

He threw his head back and roared, his face heavenward. "Oh, sweet Billie. I can do better than that."

TUESDAY MORNING

BILLIE EXITED THE CHANGING ROOM IN HER usual workout gear: long, loose, grey sweat shorts and an oversized grey T-shirt doing its one and only job — hiding her sports bra and her curves.

Bruce sat on a bench along the mirrored wall and laced his shoes. He looked up when she approached. His eyes lit up and he whistled.

She held her hands out and dipped in a shallow curtsy before sitting next to him.

"That is spectacular." He pulled the leg of her shorts up and inspected the blade. "It's not long like those Olympian guys wear."

"Not for the gym. I'd like one, do some track running. But they cost a fortune, so one will have to do."

"Well, let's see it in action." He got to his feet and held his hand out. She took it and stood. He kissed her nose and led her to the rows of treadmills. "You have a preference?"

Her usual machine stood empty. But to hell with usual. "Nope. Any will do."

They chose the closest two and each stepped onto a machine, side by side. Billie pressed the buttons she always pressed, chose the pre-programmed route that took her up hills, down vales, had her jogging, walking, sprinting in random patterns. She would often listen to music, shove the earbuds in and block out the world, imagine she was running through the hills of Italy, or perhaps Greece. But today she didn't feel the need to imagine. There was no desire to edit reality. Today she simply wanted to be in her own life, in that moment, with Bruce at her side.

The belt began to roll and she warmed up with a walking pace. Within a couple of minutes, she was jogging at a six-percent incline and a speed of five. The same feeling overcame her that did every time she ran. Confidence. Power. Freedom. Control. Even with the rubberneckers on the machines nearby watching, her blade hit the belt with precision and without any perceivable limp. They were probably on standby, waiting for her to stumble, to fly off the end of the treadmill and land in a broken heap on the rubber mat. But running was her comfort zone. It was when she took it up in her teens that her agility improved and her limp disappeared. Running was what took her from frightened mouse cowering in the corner of life to independent woman poking her nose out of her hidey-hole and living it. Even if it was a life lived safely. A life barely lived at all.

The program cranked everything up a notch and she was running at full tilt: speed, seven-point-three; incline, nine. The thud of her feet against the treadmill and the *shoosh* of the spinning belt lulled her into a familiar and comforting rhythm. She was in the zone, her face hot, sweat beading and dripping from her brow, her neck, her armpits, and her breasts. Should she be self-conscious that the first man to see her naked, to touch her and taste her and make love to her, was on the next machine watching her turn into a stinking bag of sweat? Because she wasn't.

She cut her eyes to his face. He was just watching her, barely even walking.

"Hey, you're supposed to be running."

"Have to take it slow. My running days were a few years back when the running was mostly from the cops." He beeped his treadmill off, leaned against the handrail, and crossed his arms. "Holy shit, can you move."

"It's kind of my thing."

"I thought editing was your thing."

"Then I guess I have two things." On the outside, one side of her mouth curled slightly. But on the inside, the clouds parted and streams of heavenly light poured forth and shined upon her. And she kept on running.

When the treadmill slowed after her final ascent, she wiped her face and neck with the towel she brought from home. She glanced at Bruce. "So, that's the running blade in action."

He was a little pink-faced. In the forty-minute workout, Billie had run for about thirty. Bruce had maybe got through ten at a slow trot, the rest a walk. "Pretty damned impressive. Better than most folks with original equipment intact." He stepped off the machine. "I need to practice to catch up with you. In the meantime, how about I show you my thing?"

"I've already seen your thing." The blush of the century crawled up from her five toes and steam exploded out her ears. Did she just say that out loud?

His head rolled back with the force of his laughter. He put his hands on either side of her waist and shimmied her body against his. "Yes, you have. And I hope it wasn't for the last time." He stepped onto the belt of her treadmill and kissed her right there in the gym, gave the rubberneckers something new to gawk at.

Oh no, it wouldn't be the last time. She wanted to see his thing as often as possible.

Bruce took her upstairs to the weight training area. It wasn't the first time she'd used it, but normally she just did push-ups and chin-ups and avoided the over-stuffed men — and a couple of women — who looked like they ate steroids for breakfast. Had Bruce been one of the regulars at her gym, she'd have likely avoided him, too. Assumed him to be like all the others — self-absorbed, egomaniacs who looked down on anyone who wasn't as pumped up as they were. But Bruce was nothing like that. Who knows? Maybe the other guys and gals on the second floor weren't like that either. Of all people, Billie ought to know that appearances don't mean a damn thing. That what's on the inside and what the eye can see on the outside rarely match up.

He showed her proper form for squats and presses, different methods of curls that worked more than just that lump of biceps that, when flexed, made mere mortals swoon. She impressed him when she performed seven chin-ups without the assistance/resistance machine, and, blade and all, dropped and pumped out thirty push-ups. Not the 'on the knees' lady push-ups, but full-fledged military style.

"Look out world, don't mess with Billie. She'll fuck you up." He faux-punched her arm.

Even his profanity was growing on her. His comfort with just saying out loud what she would only whisper in her head. But that was her deal with God, only in her head. Oh, how she longed to unleash onto the world some of what she kept bottled up, kept prisoner in her brain. But she wasn't sure she had the strength for it.

FRIDAY, JULY 10TH

YOU DON'T THINK IT'S KIND OF GROSS?"

Bruce furrowed his bushy brow. "Gross? There's nothing gross about you."

"But it's all stretched and discoloured and, and … gnarly. It doesn't turn you off?"

He ran his fingers over her lips, down her chin, between the cleft of her breasts, and across her belly. He stared into her eyes and let his hand draw a map across her body, ending at the base of her stump. He cupped it in his hand and massaged it, while his mouth nibbled on her ear. "Billie," he whispered, "every part of you turns me on."

She closed her eyes and let the touch of his skin, the heat of his tongue, and warmth of his breath awaken feelings in her that she had never known. "You are so weird," she said on a breathy exhale.

"I sure hope so," he said into her neck. He rolled onto his back and dragged her with him until she straddled his legs. "You are so beautiful, Billie."

Heat spread from her thighs and shot to her cheeks. "Stop it."

"Nope. Don't want to. It's the God's honest truth. I just wish you'd believe it." He lay there and stared at her, his eyes like hot lasers burning every inch of her. "Nobody is perfect. Who'd want to be? Too much work. Too much to live up to." He ran his fingers along her thighs. "What about me? Anything about me that grosses you out?"

She bit her lip and nodded.

155

One of his eyebrows shot up. "There is? Is it this weird bellybutton dent where they fixed the hernia?" He poked at his stomach.

She grinned and shook her head.

"How about the crooked nose. One too many left jabs that I was too drunk to block. Gross, right?" He smiled through every word.

She shook her head. "Nope. Keep guessing."

"Well, shit, there are just so many things to choose from. Acne scars? Thirty pounds of extra weight? Too-curly hair for a grown man?"

She shook her head with vehemence through his whole list and that wretched giggle found its way out of her mouth again. Perhaps not so wretched. It was starting to grow on her. She'd even stopped editing it out. "No, no, and no."

He jiggled her side to side. "Well come on, Billie Sunshine. Do tell."

"Well, first of all, I love every one of your scars and marks and crooked parts."

He raised both eyebrows until they wrinkled his forehead. A slight grin graced his lips. "Love?"

Her cheeks burned and she looked away. "It's not the way you look. It's one thing that you do that grosses me out."

His hand touched her cheek and turned her face to look at him. "Tell me what it is. I'll change it."

She cocked her head. "That simple, huh?"

"Anything for you."

She took a deep breath. "It's the smoking."

His brow furrowed. "I've never smoked in front of you."

"You don't have to. I can smell it in your clothes. Your hair. On your breath. And no amount of breath mints hide it." Didn't work for her mother, wouldn't work for Bruce.

"Well I'll be damned, I thought I was being so stealthy." He pressed his lips together and cut his eyes to the left. He bit his bottom lip and nodded. "Okay, I'll quit."

"Really?"

"Really. I mean, I'll try my damnedest. I've been smoking since I was a kid. Tried to give it up but one hard day and my first stop is the corner store for a carton."

"Better than drugs I guess."

He laughed. "Shit yeah. But according to my doc, not so good for my heart and lungs. He's told me to stop or I'll be dead on the floor before I'm forty-five. Cigarettes are killing the muscle, slowly but surely. You'd think that would be motivation enough."

She slid up his legs and lay on his chest, slipped her arms under his wide body, and pressed her ear against his beating heart. "Sometimes you need a little push. I'll push you. If you want me to."

He wrapped his arms around her and rolled her onto her back. He propped up on one elbow and traced the contours of her face with one finger. "I want you to," he whispered. His eyes met hers. "You're my motivation, Billie. I never gave a shit if the smokes killed me. I screwed up my marriage. Never had any kids. Same old routine day in and day out. And for what? Just to put in time until I croak." He swallowed, brushed hair from her forehead, and gave her a gentle kiss. "I'll give it my best effort."

"Is doing it for me enough motivation?" She stared at his lips.

He smiled. "I'm doing it for me. I'm not just punching the earth clock anymore. I don't want to miss one single moment with you."

Her eyes softened. For the first time since her father died, she felt safe. Not only physically — he protected her from bullies, from rude people, from gawkers and assholes and finger pointers and snickerers — no, she was safe in every way. It was a new feeling, one she had grappled to define this past month. She wanted to grab onto

157

it and hold on tight. Hold on forever.

She ran her hands through his too-curly hair and down his too-crooked nose. "Love."

He squinted at her and cocked his head. "Love?"

Her hands circled the back of his neck and she pulled herself up until their lips met. She lingered in his kiss, lived there for that moment before lying back down. "Definitely love."

AGATHA FRIESEN

AGATHA FRIESEN DIPPED HER TOE INTO THE shallow end of the pool. She licked one finger and ran it around the edge of her crystal martini glass until the vibrations sent music into the late afternoon heat.

"You should slow down. Shit, you've barely been acquitted and you've spent most of the insurance money already."

She did a slow turn and laid a laser glare on Jeremy. Poor, sweet, Jeremy. So young. So stupid. But hot damn, could he fill out those swim trunks. She eyed his tanned form, the bulge of muscles at his shoulder, his biceps. The bulge of her favourite muscle in his pants. He lounged by the pool, drank the booze, and ate the caviar while bitching at her about buying it all.

"You have no idea how much money there is to spend, you gorgeous simpleton. And I'm innocent, remember? I can spend as I please. They can't touch me." But a jury of his peers hadn't tried him. He'd better watch his hypocritical forked tongue.

"All's I'm saying is, people are talking." He popped a giant shrimp in his mouth.

"Let them talk." She raised her arms and looked around her property. "I'm innocent," she yelled at the cotoneaster that bordered her yard.

"Keep your damn voice down," Jeremy hissed. "The neighbours might hear you."

"Fuck the neighbours." She set down her appletini and leered at him, reached back and tugged the strap of her bikini bra free. "Or better yet. Fuck me." She stripped off her top and dived into the pool.

Jeremy jumped in after her. They surfaced simultaneously. He ran his hands over his wet hair, long, wavy, and sun-kissed, and pushed it from his face. He grabbed her by the waist and yanked her against his hard body. "Come here, you old broad."

She smacked his arm. "I am not old."

He buried his mouth in her neck. "Older than me," he said into her skin.

His hot breath sent shockwaves through her body. She swallowed and closed her eyes. "But not as old as my poor, dead husband."

Jeremy laughed. "Nobody is as old as that coot. You're way better off with me. I can fill your every insatiable desire."

"As long as I have money."

He shrugged. "Good thing you have a shitload of it." He grinned and grabbed her ass in both hands. His hard prick pressed against her crotch.

She slid her hands into his swim trunks. "Just shut up and do me. As long as you can keep it up, you can stick around."

The tinkle of shattering crystal startled her. "What the hell?" She crossed her arms in front of her naked breasts. "Who's there?" She spun around.

Jeremy climbed from the pool and kneeled beside the broken martini glass. "Chill out, Ag. The wind knocked your drink over." He stood and turned to face her. "I don't know how you can drink this green crap. It's like apple-flavoured anti-freeze."

The sun glistened off his wet skin, his dick still hard and poking at his trunks like a boy scout's tent pole. She licked her lips. "It cuts through the aftertaste of your spunk. Now hurry up and get back in here before that thing goes to waste."

He shed his trunks and dove headfirst into the pool. He swam between her legs, stripped her bottoms off, and surfaced in front of her. He kissed her, lifted her up, and brought her down on top of him.

She loved fucking in the pool. The threat of being seen. Well, maybe not a threat, she'd love it if that prissy bitch next door got an eyeful of Jeremy's prime, grade-A meat slamming Agatha until she screamed.

The sun beat down on them, sparkled off the water and flashed light in her eyes. Damn she was glad she'd had her tubes tied all those years ago. Anything to prevent getting pregnant by her codger of a husband. She only wanted his millions, not his pitiful offspring. Not that he could keep it up long enough to fill that void in his life. And nothing beat Jeremy riding her bareback. Not that twenty years with that old fart hadn't put her past prime childbearing years. Nature was taking too damn long to kill him. Agatha had needed to give her an assist.

Jeremy groaned and shuddered.

"Damn it, Jeremy, I wasn't done yet." Agatha's bikini top hovered on the water. She slipped it back on and fished the bottoms out of the pool. She swam to the edge and grabbed his trunks, turned, and tossed them at his face. "Float me a raft and get me another drink."

He put his trunks on under the water, sent an inflatable chaise lounge her way, and crawled out of the pool.

She climbed onto the raft and lay on her back, one knee in the air. She closed her eyes. Something cool tapped against her shoulder. She squinted into the sun and looked up into Jeremy's handsome young face. Hard to stay mad at him for rushing his own orgasm. He'd be ready for more in ten minutes if she wanted another go. She took the offered appletini. "Thanks, love. I'm a little sleepy."

He smirked. "So take a nap. Build up your energy. We can go again before dinner." He grabbed his limp dick over his trunks and bobbed it up and down. It was hard in seconds.

She shook her head. "You are such a little boy."

"Yeah, and that's why you want me."

She couldn't argue with that. She downed her drink in two gulps and handed him the glass, settled into the chaise, the sun warming her skin, the water cooling her back and ass, and drifted off to sleep.

A splash shook her from her slumber. Her raft bounced against the side of the pool. She rubbed her eyes. "Jeremy?"

He was a few feet away, bobbing in the water.

"Shit, I was sleeping. Couldn't you wait for a swim?" She propped up on her elbows.

He was floating, face down, the water around him stained pink, like someone had dumped Kool-Aid in the pool. "Jeremy, you jerk. Quit with the infantile pranks." She dipped a cupped hand into the pool and splashed him. He didn't move. Just lay in the water, arms out, face down, legs dangling below him. A burp of air bubbled from beneath him. His body shifted and slid below the surface, leaving a pink swirl in his wake.

Agatha tried to scream, but her open mouth produced nothing but silence. A shadow crossed her body. She looked up to find a man in a black hoodie and baggy black pants standing over her, his face shaded by the hood and blocked by the sun behind him.

He covered her face with his black-leather-gloved paw and pushed her under. She clawed at his arm, but her fingernails found nothing but fleece. She slipped off the chaise and bicycled her legs for purchase on the bottom of the deep end. Her hair tangled in his leather glove and pulled at her scalp.

Agatha batted at the man's arm, but her arms barely broke the surface. Lights exploded in front of her open eyes. She opened her mouth and gasped for breath. She swallowed water, metallic from Jeremy's blood, bleachy from chlorine. Her vision faded. She closed her eyes and took one final gulp.

SUNDAY

BILLIE JERKED AWAKE, TREMBLING AND BATHED in sweat. The remnants of a crazy dream, justice revisited, edited and corrected, had come alive in her head and gone horribly awry. She rubbed her eyes and blinked. Sun streamed in through the vertical blinds.

She tossed the covers aside and eyed the alarm clock. Nine forty-three. She put both hands over her eyes and moaned. The gym would be packed by now, her usual treadmill probably four deep in line. And she'd slept through her editing time. At this rate, she'd never get Annabelle's novel finished. Good start to freelancing, Billie. Lose your first client.

How on earth had she slept so long? She picked her phone up from the nightstand and poked in her password.

Three text messages from Bruce.

She flopped back against her pillow, unable to keep her smiles on the inside anymore.

Hey, movie's starting. Did you miss the subway? I knew I should have picked you up.

Movie? That was tonight. Man, he needed a break. He must be stressed. She scrolled to the second message.

Knock, knock. Billie, where are you? Is everything ok? I'm calling you.

The furrow of her brow deepened. She switched screens. Four missed calls? How did she not hear her phone? She listened to the messages, each from Bruce, the panic in his voice a bit edgier with each subsequent recording. In the final message, he said he

165

understood. They'd been seeing too much of each other. He was moving too fast. He'd leave her alone for a while.

Leave her alone? Too fast? She bolted upright.

No, God damn it, no. She was screwing everything up. Total, epic failure. As usual.

Her phone buzzed in her hand.

I know I said I'd leave you alone. Just can't. Missed you last night. Be a good girl at church. Call me later?

Church? She switched screens and checked the date. Sunday, July Twelfth?

The cat lay at the end of her bed, his tail swatting side to side like a furry whip. "Peg Leg, tell me what day it is. What the hell, did I sleep through Saturday?" She tossed her phone on the bed and buried her eyes behind the heels of both hands. She breathed long and steady, urged her heart to calm down and beat slower.

She was supposed to go to the movies with Bruce tonight. Or, last night. She searched her memory for yesterday and came up empty. A flash of water, breaking glass. Damn it all to hell. Doc Kroft's red glasses floated by. Dissociative fog. Or whatever. Billie dismissed that notion, and the doc's spectacles, with a wave of her hand.

Sunday. Church. She should go to church. Meet God in His own house and ask for His guidance. Or at the very least, shed a little holy light on just what the hell was happening.

She sent Bruce an apology text. Vowed to call him and explain later. If she could just figure out what the explanation was.

She hopped toward the bathroom. Her father's clothes lay in a heap in the middle of the floor. She stooped. The hoodie sleeve was damp. She sniffed and recoiled. Bleach. Or chlorine. How the hell?

But she'd put them out of Peg Leg's reach. No way could he get up that high. And they weren't there when she went to bed last night. What time was that? She closed her eyes and searched for any other remnants of Saturday.

Everything came up blank.

She tossed her father's clothes into the laundry bag. She'd have to wash them now, just to get the stink out. Eradicate the remnants of his beautiful scent from her life. Forever.

She pulled the hoodie out and buried her face in it, inhaled as deep as she could. There was nothing but chlorine. She broke down and cried, let her tears soak into the fleece.

After a long shower, she put on her church clothes. She glanced at the clock on the stove. She'd be late for services, would miss some of the Scripture uttered by the luscious lips of the beautiful Reverend Keene. Not that she was particularly smitten with him any longer. He was too smooth. Too pretty. Too perfect. Nary one bit of gravel in his voice, no scars or marks or imperfections to his skin. Had he lived life at all? Or just hidden out in the sanctuary of his church, ministering to those who'd seen it, done it, survived it. Officiating at the funerals of those who'd died from it.

Billie stood outside the door and put her ear to the crack. The service was well underway. She pushed the massive slab of antique mahogany open. Billie winced at the creak of its elderly and rarely oiled hinges. She slipped inside and moved with stealth behind the last pew. Before she sat, the door slammed shut with the thundering sound that only heavy wood on heavy wood can accomplish. It echoed in the huge, hollow space. Sunday-best clothes rustled as the congregation turned to glare at the intrusion.

"Good morning, Billie." Reverend Keene singled her out for public humiliation. "Glad you could join us."

She nodded and threw him a brief smile.

"Shall we all wait for Billie to find a seat?" He raised his eyebrows and drew his lips into a thin line.

Her pen drew a red halo above his head, then ripped it out and threw it to the ground. A match lit and the halo burst into flames.

Billie glanced at the ceiling and apologized to God. Burning religious symbols wasn't part of their deal.

She tried to pay attention to the Reverend's sermon, but her pen insisted on defacing him. His true colours shone through, as if the heavens had opened up and focused a laser beam of self-righteous light on him. Just another bully hiding behind the folds of his Christian cloth. How had she not seen it before? She'd always been so goody-goody when he called out other members of the church. Always on his side. Maybe God was allowing her these edits because He knew she was right. Maybe He had a plan of his own for the reverend. A way of outing him, as it were.

Billie squirmed in her seat, the pew like a sack of rocks against her rump. She held her hands in her lap, checked her watch, eyeballed the panes of stained glass. Her pen skittered across her thoughts, editing the events of the past few days. But the chlorine-stinking mystery pile of her father's clothes cluttered her mind. The possibility of that fog thing the doc kept yammering on about was becoming too real to ignore.

After service, the nave emptied in its usual fashion — front rows first. In the past, Billie would have been heading toward home by now. She used to love the front row, close to the Reverend, close to God. First out the door and never stuck in the crowd of Sunday Christians and their gossip and the stench of their Saturday hangovers. But this Sunday she didn't feel as close to God as usual. Not within the confines of the church. And not because she was in the back row. She was closer to God on the subway. In the movie theatre. At her laptop in the sunny slice of her breakfast nook. She was closest to God in Bruce's arms. In his lap. In his bed.

She waited for the last of the full congregation to file past her. Before Reverend Keene, the pews were sparsely filled. Now it was hard to find an empty spot. She'd never noticed the man/woman ratio before. It was heavy on the woman. Were they here just for the reverend's pretty face? He brought in more souls looking for salvation. And they risked damnation for their lusty thoughts.

Many of those women tossed her looks alternating between pity for her sad past and deformed body and disdain for interrupting the service with her rude lateness. Screw them. Screw them all. Each received an edit on the way by — a devil's tail, a forked tongue, a crown of thorns.

In the foyer, a crowd milled about, an evangelical mosh pit. Billie jostled her way through it. Bits of their voices, slices of their opinions, their observations, drifted into her ears. "… floating in the pool …" "… half-naked …" "… served her right, the whore …"

Billie froze amidst the chatter and listened. Mrs. Hanabaker, gossip of grotesque proportions, sweet on Sundays, evil bitch every other day of the week, stood nearby. Billie touched the old biddy's arm. "What's happened?"

Mrs. Hanabaker's face lit up at the prospect of a new audience. "It's that awful black widow, Agatha Friesen." She nodded, her eyes wide and bright.

Billie remembered the name. The woman who was tried and found not guilty of killing her husband. The one she and Bruce drowned in her pool with their red pens of justice. A just end for a woman who drowned her feeble husband in the bathtub, hastened his pending death so she could get at the money sooner than later.

Billie's pulse quickened. "What about her? What happened?"

"Her and that young man she was … well, you know. I don't want to repeat it."

Billie drew a thought bubble above the old biddy's head and wrote, "She was fucking him, the lucky bitch." Billie kept her satisfaction internal and nodded. "No need, I get the gist."

"Well they found them both dead in her pool. He had his throat cut. She was drowned. Dead as her husband." She nodded and pursed her lips. "That's justice if you ask me. The jury certainly didn't do right by him. Seems like maybe God set it straight."

Billie clenched her fists. "God isn't in the business of revenge, Mrs. Hanabaker." Billie turned and stormed out of the church. No, that wasn't God's agenda. But Jesus, Mary, and Joseph, whose was it? How many articles had she and Bruce edited? Five? Six? And two of them had come true. Not word-for-word perfect, but so close that it made her stomach knot. Was someone spying on them? Waiting to find out the appropriate end and exacting that justice laid out in the scripts they wrote?

She raced to the corner. As she approached, the walk light extinguished and the amber signal flashed at her. "Run, run, run," her father would always chant, as if that were the right thing to do when commanded to "don't walk." If he were here with her, she'd take his hand and sprint to the other side. Instead, she paced on the street corner and waited to be told when to cross.

Two of the endings she and Bruce edited had come true. Or maybe only one. The clown edits were hers and hers alone. But Bruce read them. She balled up her fists and released them several times, as if she were gripping the stress ball at work. The one she'd drawn a mouse face on in red pen.

Bruce didn't seem to have first-hand knowledge about the demise of the clowns. Maybe he was a great actor. But no, she knew him now. He wouldn't harm anyone without a personal reason.

Would he?

She fished her cell phone from her purse and found his number, tapped her thumbs over the keyboard.

Did you hear?

The walk light lit and Billie rushed across the street and up the sidewalk toward her apartment. She checked her phone every few steps. Why didn't he answer?

She rushed up the stairs of her apartment building. Her prosthetic foot caught under the lip of the riser and she tripped, grabbed the railing for balance. Her blood coursed through her veins, her whole body atremble. It wreaked havoc with her coordination. She slowed her breathing and her pace, rested on the landing of the second floor for ten hippopotamuses before continuing.

Inside her apartment, she threw the keys on the floor and raced for the television. Channel after channel of sports and religion. Too early for news on a Sunday. She clicked on her laptop, chewed at her thumbnail, and bounced her good leg up and down while the computer booted up. She found a local news website and scanned the headlines. There it was. Couple found dead in pool.

She read the article. Except for the man, the drowning part was just as she and Bruce had written it. She checked her phone. No reply from him. Could he be involved? Would he exact revenge on behalf of someone he'd never even met?

Glimpses of blood, of a swimming pool, the water shimmering in the bright afternoon sun, and a broken martini glass flashed through her mind. She closed her eyes. Stop imagining it, for Christ's sake.

Her eyes flew open. Shattered glass? She re-read the article. It didn't mention anything about broken glass. She couldn't recall including that in their edits. Man, she needed a drink.

She looked around the apartment. Peg Leg perched in his sunshine square, his eyes glued to her, nothing moving but the tips of his whiskers. He mewed and blinked. He wouldn't care if she drank. Hell, he didn't even know it was Sunday.

She opened a new bottle of Sauvignon blanc that Bruce had brought, warm off the counter. She tossed ice cubes in a tumbler and filled it with wine. Half of it was gone before her phone buzzed.

Are you home? Can I come over?

Her thumbs sailed across the keyboard. *Yes and yes. I'm freaking out.*

Chill, Billie Sunshine. Just another coincidence. I'll bring lunch.

As if she could eat anything.

Billie paced the small strip of carpet in front of the window and sipped at her wine. "Coincidence, my butt," she mumbled. "Once, maybe. But twice?" She shook her head. "Right, Peg Leg? Twice is too much." She rubbed the cat's ears. "You agree with me, right?"

The door handle jiggled. Billie jumped, sloshing wine onto the carpet. She set the tumbler down on the table beside the sofa, didn't bother with a coaster.

"Billie?" Bruce called through the door and rapped his knuckles on the wood.

She ran to the door, unclasped the chain, and unlocked the deadbolt. She threw the door open and leaped into his arms.

He dropped a bag onto the floor and engulfed her in his arms. She laid her head on his chest and took solace in the pounding of his heart, still thumping from his race up the stairs. "Hey, you're trembling. Come on, let's be bold and have a morning drink."

"Already way ahead of you." She pulled away, stooped to pick up the bag, and peered inside. Her worries about being unable to eat were drowned out by the grumbling in her stomach. "Tacos? I'm starved." She took his hand and led him to the kitchen. "So, you saw the news?"

"Yes. Like I texted, coincidence."

"Once. Twice is not coincidence. Peg Leg agrees with me."

Bruce raised one eyebrow. "Sure he does." He ripped the bag open and set tacos on the counter, fished out packets of hot sauce and little plastic cups of sour cream.

Billie handed him a plate, grabbed three tacos and covered them with sauce. "It was just like we wrote it. Drowned in her own pool. Or her dead husband's pool."

"It wasn't exactly the same. We didn't write that her lover would die. Or even be there. And hers was an accident. We didn't write murder." He watched her shove a third of a taco in her mouth and snap off the crunchy shell. "God, I love the way you eat."

She covered her mouth with one hand. "How do I eat?" Hot sauce dripped down her chin.

"Like a man." He shoved a taco in his mouth and gave her a thumbs up.

She giggled through meat and cheese and crushed corn tortillas. How did he do that? His very presence put her at ease and let her paranoia melt away. She poured them both a glass of wine and clinked her glass to his.

Yes, she was being paranoid. That was all there was to it. Please, God? Just paranoia.

THURSDAY THE 16TH

BILLIE LAY ON DOC KROFT'S CHAISE AND STARED at the tin ceiling. Her eyes followed the swirls stamped into the metal, round and round and round they go. Like a labyrinth with no walls, a maze with nothing but exits. Annoying in its planned randomness. Flecks of peeling paint drooped from the smooth finish, poked holes in perfection.

"I just can't find any focus, Doc. Church isn't helping. I think I might be losing my mind."

"What about your boyfriend?"

Billie sat up. "What about him?"

Doc cocked her head. "Any ..." the fingers tented in front of her chin. "Progress? In the relationship I mean."

"Do you mean am I still the oldest virgin on record? No, I'm not."

Doc's eyes came alight with repressed mischief. "I see. And how does that make you feel?" She looked as though she was going to spew spittle-fueled laughter through her psychobabble façade.

Billie poked her tongue into her cheek and grinned a sideways grin. "Oh, like running through a field of wildflowers? No, wait, that's when my tampons are absorbent." She shook her head. "What do you think? It makes me feel like a grownup. Like a full-fledged woman. I can't believe I waited so long." But she hadn't waited. She'd just never been offered the chance.

"So maybe that's what's pulling your focus?"

"Maybe. Or because I'm waiting on a promotion and they start interviewing next week. Or because I'm having weird —" She scratched at an imaginary spot on the seat, "dreams, I guess. Sort of."

Doc shifted and put on her serious face. "What kind of dreams?"

Billie leaned back and put the heels of her hands over her eyes. "Okay, not dreams." She dropped her arms to her sides and looked at Doc. "There's some privilege thing between us, right? Confidentiality?"

Doc squinted. "Yes. Why?"

"So if I tell you something that I might have done." Billie held her palm toward the Doc. "Just might. Theoretically. Something not legal. You have to keep that between us, right? Like a priest?"

"Billie." Doc Kroft set her notepad aside and sat forward. "Tell me."

Billie stared at her lap, picked at a scab on her forearm. "That dissociative fog thing. It's real, right?"

"Not fog. Fugue. F-you-g. And yes, it's real. Rare, but real. Have you had another incident?"

"I'm not sure. Sometimes I wake up sore and achy. One morning I woke up on an unfamiliar street corner." The scab fell off and a drop of blood oozed from her skin. "I don't even remember last Saturday. I stood Bruce up. Missed a date." Her eyes pinched and her throat ached with held-back sobs. "And some stuff has happened," she wiped a rogue tear from her cheek, "that I can't explain."

"Try." Doc picked up her notepad and poised her pen above it.

Billie opened the flap of her purse and slid a red-marked newspaper from it. She tossed it on the coffee table. "I edit the news. When the bad guys get away with it, I make them pay."

Doc picked up the paper and scanned the edits. "Nothing weird about that. You used to do the same with storybooks. Changed the endings so that nobody died."

"Huh. I'd forgotten about that." A vision of *Bambi*, covered in crayon edits, came to mind.

Doc placed the newspaper on the coffee table. "So why is this different? What are you worried about?"

"Well," Billie cleared her throat. "Two of the edits have come true. Sort of."

Doc's chin dropped to her chest and she looked at Billie over the rim of her glasses. "Come true how?"

Billie explained about the clowns and the widow's drowning. She told Doc of the pile of her father's clothes in the middle of the floor after each event. She hadn't connected it to the clowns, and the first time she could explain it away as Peg Leg being a brat. The second, not so much.

When Billie was done, she lay back on the chaise.

Doc didn't say a word, just tapped her pen against lilac paper and pursed her lips. "Well, that's interesting."

Billie huffed. "No kidding."

"How many people do you think read the newspaper each day?"

Billie shrugged. "I don't know. Thousands?"

"In a city of two million? I'd bet around two hundred-thousand or more. And how many of them do you think are unsatisfied with the justice system? Pissed off at what criminals and murderers and pedophiles get away with?"

"A few."

"Yeah." Doc tossed her notepad aside and picked up the paper. "I bet, red pen notwithstanding, thousands of people want proper justice. Any one of them could have done this." She smacked the newsprint with the back of her fingers. "Or it could be a complete coincidence."

"Kind of a strange one though, don't you think?"

"Perhaps." Doc ripped the paper into shreds, crunched the bits inside her fists, made a tight ball from them, and lobbed it into the garbage can.

Nothing but net.

"But most coincidences are."

FRIDAY

BILLIE SCURRIED ALONG THE SIDEWALK, HER HEAD down. Every passerby eyeballed her like the murderous sinner that she was beginning to think she was. Coincidence, maybe. Strange, definitely. Possible? The jury was still out.

She stared at her shoes and counted each time they hit the pavement. At the limits of her vision, glimpses of the world passed her by. A garbage can. A border collie balancing on three legs, peeing on a fire hydrant and all over his leash. Wingtips, sneakers, flip-flops, patent leather pumps. The shoes of humanity, whose accusing stares she was desperate to avoid. A homeless man with a gold tooth.

Billie froze in the middle of the walkway. Someone slammed into her from behind and her body lurched forward.

She spun around to face a balding man straightening his glasses.

He set his mouth in a thin line and glared at her. "Shit, lady, keep moving or step aside." He brushed past, jostled her arm and stormed off, in a hurry to get nowhere fast.

Billie shuffled to the side and stood against the building. She inched toward the homeless man, a lump of rags and stink and dirt on the sidewalk. He held out a paper cup and grinned at anyone who would look down upon him, one gold tooth shining in the early morning sun. He blinked his wide eyes at strangers, some of whom would drop quarters, dimes, or even the occasional loonie in his cup. He'd nod and mumble at them. It sounded like "thank you" but could just as likely have been "fuck you" too.

Blood rushed to Billie's head, filling her ears with her own pulse. She closed her eyes and gripped the brick of the building with the tips of her fingers. A vision of a much younger man with a gold tooth came to mind. A man with wild eyes and a red bandana over his long, dark hair. Could it be? Wouldn't the police have let her know if they'd let the man that murdered her parents go free?

She opened her eyes and looked down at him. He scanned the sidewalk for donors, his head sweeping side to side. He noticed her, smiled, and blinked. He nodded in one quick jerk and shook his cup at her.

Her heart rammed up into her throat and she backed away, turned, and ran the rest of the way to work. She raced up the stairs, flew into the office, and dropped into her chair. Her forehead in her hands, she counted to ten then back to one, slowed her breathing and her heart.

"What's with you, sweaty Betty?"

She didn't even look up. "Leave me alone, Jeffrey."

"Well, excuuuuuse me." He dropped some papers at her elbow and put his hand on her back. "Seriously, though. If you need anything, let me know."

She leaned back, plucked two Kleenex from the box with the bright flower pattern and wiped her brow, her cheeks, and the back of her neck. "Thanks. I appreciate that." She poked the power button on her computer, chewed on one thumbnail, and bounced her prosthetic leg up and down while the computer took its sweet time booting up.

The second her desktop appeared, she double-clicked on the Firefox icon and Googled "Anthony Gerard Dickinson&1993& Murder&Fullalove." A list of sites and a few images popped up. And there he was on her screen. Younger. Heavier. Longer hair. But it was him. He was out. And living on the street, just a block from her office.

She shook her head, clenched her fists, and kicked her trashcan. It flew across the aisle separating her cubicle from Jeffrey's and clanged against the filing cabinet. It rolled to a stop at Katherine's feet.

She looked at the can, then cut her steely glare to Billie. "Bad day? Maybe take it out on your own belongings." She set her toe against the can and rolled it toward Billie. "I need the Evanston manuscript before end of day. Can you handle that?"

Billie's eyelids flickered and her red pen decapitated her boss. "Yes. I'll email it when I'm done."

Katherine nodded and carried on to the coffee pot.

"It's definitely the guy." Billie slid the open scrapbook across the table to Bruce. An article from 1993, when Gold Tooth was convicted of accessory to murder, was glued to the page, its edges curled and the paper yellowed. "He's older, sure. Looks pretty used-up. Lost the bandana. But it's the eyes. And the tooth." She tapped the picture. "That stupid gold tooth."

"He only got accessory?" Bruce ran his fingers down the newsprint and skimmed the article.

"That's my fault."

He glanced up at her. "Your fault? How so?"

"I identified him in court. And I told them that he didn't shoot my parents. The other guy did. In fact, it would appear that this guy," she tapped the picture again, "might have saved my life."

"You're kidding."

"Nope. He apparently pushed the other guy's arm down just as he was going to shoot me. The bullet that took my leg would have probably hit me in the face. Though that is just speculation by the defence. And they convinced the jury that's what happened."

"But you don't remember that part."

"No. Just the gun. I remember the gun. And the music. And the blood."

Bruce reached over and squeezed her hand. "Can you have the cops remove him?"

"Do I have that right?" She pulled her hand away and crossed her arms. "He did his time. Or I assume he did, since he's out." A bottle of chardonnay sat at her elbow. She filled her glass for the second time. "I wonder if the prosecutor still works for the Crown?"

"Maybe you need to talk to him." He poured his own glass of wine. "The guy with the tooth, I mean."

Her hands began to tremble. "I don't want to talk to him." She wanted to slit his throat. Rip his gold tooth right out of his filthy mouth and jab it into one of his wild eyes. She closed her eyes and played that scene out in her head. Her tremble eased with each flash of fake film reel and spray of his blood on the sidewalk that passed behind her eyelids.

Bruce's hands on her shoulders shook her from her macabre thoughts. He kneaded her knotted muscles, bent down and kissed her neck. "Maybe it would be good therapy," he whispered in her ear.

TUESDAY THE 21ST

"IT'S OBVIOUS SHE'S GUILTY." BILLIE SLICED A perogie in half, dragged it through a lump of sour cream, and shoved it in her mouth.

"But there's no real proof." Bruce ran his finger over the newsprint. "Even the old cases, just sudden infant death. Which, I think, is another way of saying they have no clue what killed them."

"Exactly, how can there be proof for something unprovable?"

Bruce raised an eyebrow. "Is that a word?"

She matched his arched brow. "You questioning the editor's grasp of the English language?"

He laughed. "Not anymore." He snapped the paper to straighten a crease. "Okay, so she's a total bitch. Selfish, complete lack of emotion. Didn't even cry at her trial, and look at that picture." He turned the paper around.

A photo that looked like a screen grab from a grainy video showed Janis Jones standing at a window, peering out at the media, a cigarette perched between two fingers, her elbow resting in her other hand. She looked like Norma Desmond, with that crazy-bitch, brow-arched glare. Billie nodded. "That's my point. No feeling. No empathy. Total sociopath."

"We can agree on that." He spun the newspaper back to face him. "But being a sociopath doesn't mean you're a murderer. It's not that simple. Square peg, crazy round hole."

Billie loved the way he talked. His odd metaphors, a little twisted and sideways. He was no scholar, not book smart or a word nerd. But he could paint just the right picture.

"I suppose. But I still say she's guilty as heck. If she didn't kill the first two, which they'll never prove after all this time, since the judge wouldn't grant the warrant to exhume their innocent little bodies, she definitely drowned Ryan." A shudder shook Billie's spine. How could anyone, especially a parent, lay a hand on their child? Kill them? Unfathomable.

"So what, then, is her punishment, oh judge and jury, oh wielder of the magic red pen of justice?" Bruce had finished his dinner, cleaned every speck of dough and bacon and fried onion. All that remained was a whisper of sour cream clinging to the plate. He may as well have licked it clean and put it right back in the cupboard. He watched her, his eyes alight with their shared game, her red pen in his hand, hovering above the page. "How about I shoot her?"

"With what?"

"My gun. What else?"

A tingle ran through Billie's spine. "You have a gun?"

He nodded. "I used to do competitive shooting. It's a real stress reliever."

She blinked. "I bet. What kind? Forty-five magnum?"

He raised one eyebrow. "Uh, no. Just a Glock 22 semi-auto. I take it you don't shoot?"

A vision of her father's gun case came to mind, of him emptying the magazine and putting the bullets into a separate locked box. She swallowed. "No. Never."

"I can take you to the range some time."

Her heart fluttered and sent a surge of hot ice through her veins. "Yes. I'd like that." She put the last bite of dinner in her mouth, rolled the dough and potato and cheese around, and squished it with her tongue. She picked up both their plates, her trembling fingers making the forks rattle against the glass. "But shooting her isn't the right punishment."

The beginning of the evening had her on edge. Another article. More justice gone awry. A quick flick of red ink to set the theoretical world right. Would that seal Janis Jones' fate? Would Billie wake to another report of vigilante justice and find her father's clothes in heap on her bedroom floor? But as they read more about the woman, fueled by online gossip and background checks, the less she cared. Doc was right. Strange coincidence. And damn it, Billie just couldn't stop herself from editing the news.

She scraped the wad of Nicorette gum Bruce left on the side of his plate into the garbage, set the dishes in the sink, and ran the water to rinse them. "I say she should never be allowed to reproduce again."

"I assume we're not talking about frequenting Kinko's here?"

Billie hovered over the open door of the dishwasher, the plates in her hands. She looked sideways at him. The delight on his face made her tummy flutter. "Nope, no ban on photocopying. How about someone cuts out her womb?"

"Wouldn't that kill her?" He put one end of the red pen in his mouth and held it between the peace sign made by his index and middle fingers. He sucked fantasy smoke from the pen into his lungs.

"Not if they did it right." She stood the plates up between the tines of the dishwasher tray. "But it would serve her right anyway, stealing that baby's entire life away. Taking him from his daddy."

She rinsed forks, squirted dish soap into the pot and fry pan, and filled them with water until bubbles cascaded over their rims. It took a couple minutes for the utter silence from Bruce to sink in. She turned, suds dripping from her hands. He stared at her, his face a confusion of concern and caring. And maybe just a dash of pity.

She glanced back at the sink. "What? Am I doing it wrong?"

He laughed. "I'm not sure if there's a wrong way to clean dishes." He stood and joined her at the sink, wrapped his arms around her shoulders, kissed the top of her head.

"Then what was with the look?"

"Just that, you seem to not have too many feelings about the dastardly ends you wish on these people. Like it wouldn't bother you if it were true."

Two clown faces crossed her mind. They deserved what they got. That didn't bother her. What had bothered her was that they met the end she'd written. But tonight, even that didn't bother her. What if she *was* doing it? Meting out appropriate recompense for the victims? No amount of cash would make those little boys better. And dead men can't rape.

She'd had fantasies of herself in a leather suit and cape, standing atop a tall building, overseeing her beloved Grantham. Well, the city had never been beloved before. It had been the scene of every horrific moment in her life to date. It had cuffed her upside the head every chance it got and stuck its leg in the aisle of her healing to trip her just for the heck of it. But in her superhero fantasy life, the city was held in high esteem. This is where she'd met Bruce, after all. It can't be all bad.

Maybe it was fate. Kismet. God's will. Maybe she was God's red pen, fixing what the living world couldn't get right. What He wasn't able to do without the assistance of human hands. An eye for an eye, that's what He said. Maybe she'd been wrong. Maybe God was in the revenge business. And maybe she was His eyes and ears on the ground. Or at the very least, His willing scribe.

"It's not like I'm the one doing the womb dissection. It's just for fun." She shifted in his embrace until she was facing him, rested her head on his chest. "Right? Just for fun?"

He rubbed her arms and rested his chin on her head. "Right. Just for fun." He pulled away and picked up the pen. "So, some stranger walks in and cuts out her womb."

"Well, he can't just walk in. There'd have to be a ruse. Somewhere nobody would see." Billie nodded. "Maybe a disguise."

JULY 23RD

WELL, LOOKY, LOOKY. IT'S THE GIMPY CHICK."
Bat Head tapped Billie's prosthesis with his shoe. High tops this time. Red, like freshly spilled blood. Or an ordained editor's ink.

Billie gathered her purse close to her side and held her newspaper to her chest. She looked the little bastard in the eye. "Leave me alone."

He scanned the car, his arms out, palms up. "Where's Prince Charming? Your superhero boyfriend? No one here to save you today?"

His posse must have taken the day off. Perhaps even bullies need a vacation. Only one of them hung behind him, eyeing the few riders on the car.

A mother cowered in the back and held her toddler close, unable to make eye contact. Billie didn't blame her. Why risk the safety of your baby for some stranger?

But Billie wasn't about to back down. "I don't need to be rescued."

He laughed at her. "Hear that, Todd? She can protect herself." He loomed over her, his feet on either side of hers and bent down until she could smell the weed and alcohol on his breath. "How about I prove you wrong, huh, crip?" He grabbed at her breasts over the newspaper.

She leaned back, gritted her teeth, and rammed her knee into his groin.

His breath whooshed from his lungs and he backed away, his

face scarlet. His thug buddy snickered. Bat Head regained his composure, glared at his wingman, and shut him up with one look. Clearly, this little boy was in charge of the other little boy. He jumped toward Billie and swatted the paper out of her hand. It floated to the ground in an anti-climactic swish. He poked his finger near her nose, careful to keep his legs together. "You think that's funny, bitch?"

She slapped his hand away.

He backed away, his mouth agape, eyes dazed.

She sat up straighter and leaned toward him. "You reek of booze. Aren't you a little young to drink? Is that the best use of your summer vacation? Maybe you ought to try volunteering or something. Help an old lady cross the street. I don't know ..." she shrugged. "Read a book." Her red pen drew nerdy spectacles on his face and made him buck toothed. She scratched a pocket protector where a breast pocket should be and filled it with pens. In her head, he pushed his glasses back up onto his nose and peed his pants.

His eyes clouded and he approached again. "I'm gonna fuck you up, bitch." He took hold of her cardigan and yanked her face toward his. His words slurred together and his balance faltered.

She smirked. "You couldn't keep it up long enough to fuck me, punk."

His eyes twitched. For a second he looked like a puppy that'd just had its nose smacked by a rolled up newspaper. But that second passed quickly. He released her cardigan and drew his fist back.

She closed her eyes. The impact hit her cheek and set fireworks off behind her eyelids. She slumped to the side and her hand flew to protect her face. He loomed over her, his eyes glinting with anger and smug pleasure, his hand still balled into a fist.

She patted her cheek and looked at her hand. Blood marred the tips of her fingers.

"Dude, leave her be, man." Bat Head's friend tugged on his sleeve. "I ain't going back to juvie for this." He headed for the exit at the far end of the car.

Bat Head leered at her. "I don't know. I think it'll be worth it." He pulled his fist back again.

She pitched sideways and ducked.

His knuckles cracked against the metal frame around the subway window. He bounced backward and jumped up and down, cradling his fist in his other hand. "Fuck, you stupid bitch-ass whore."

Billie tried not to laugh on the outside. She swept her good leg at his ankle and knocked his feet out from under him. He landed on his ass again, just like the last time. Billie stood up and loomed over him. "I told you I don't need to be rescued." And she'd never be a victim again.

He scrabbled backwards like a crab on an oily beach. She drew beady red eyes and little crab antennae. He hit his head against a pole; used the pole for leverage, stood, and backed away. "You think you're tough, bitch?" He curled his fingers at her, dared her to come closer, all the while edging his way to the door. "Come on, then, let's see what you got."

Bright station lights streamed past the windows. Billie grabbed the railing overhead as the subway screeched to a halt. Bat Head lost his footing and, once again, his ass found the rubber floor.

"You want to know what I got?" She took a step toward him. "I got titanium alloy." Billie brought her prosthesis back and kicked Bat Head between the legs.

He groaned and grabbed his nuts.

She sneered. "How do you like me now, bitch?" She dug into her purse and pulled out a red pen. She kneeled beside him, her knee inches from his groin, and drew circles around each eye while he moaned and called her names under his breath. She stood and admired the spectacles she'd drawn on his bully face. "Seriously, dude. Read a book."

The door opened. Bat Head crab-walked away from her and bounded to his feet. "You crazy fucking gimp." He pushed Todd out the door and they ran down the platform.

Billie dropped into her seat and pulled her purse to her chest. She shut her eyes, counted to ten and breathed with intent; willed her heart to shut up and quit screaming in her ears. She might have peed in her pants a little.

"That was amazing."

Billie opened her eyes and looked up into the frightened face of the mother who'd been cowering in the back. "Excuse me?"

"You were awesome. I'm too afraid to say anything. To stand up to them. I wish I had your strength." She reached out and touched Billie's shoulder. "Thank you."

Billie clenched her trembling hands into fists and straightened her spine. "You're welcome."

"I'm gonna kill that little bastard." Bruce dabbed at the cut on Billie's cheek with an alcohol-soaked cotton ball.

Billie loved the dichotomy between his gentle nursing of her wounds and his rough language and he-man, testosterone-fueled outbursts. "I don't think the death sentence is a fair punishment for bullying." Though she'd envisioned Bat Head hanging from the rafters by the strings of his Batman hoodie more than once on the walk to Bruce's apartment.

She couldn't face the gym. It was a hard enough day at the office. Katherine had taken her cold-hearted, don't-give-a-rats-assedness to a whole new level. She'd announced that interviews for the new editing post were delayed until better resumes came in. She stared at Billie with every word that hissed from her fork-tongued mouth.

Billie just needed some comfort. Some warmth. Damn it, she wanted Bruce's protection. And that just pissed her off.

"This isn't bullying. It's flat-out assault." He used a Q-tip to cover the cut with antibiotic ointment, then applied a Band-Aid. "There. It shouldn't leave a scar."

Not on the outside.

"And if it does," he wrapped his arms around her and helped from her perch on the bathroom counter. He kissed the bandage and then her forehead. "I'll give him a matching one. Maybe add a few more for good measure."

She hugged him, her sore cheek against his chest. The thump of his heart against the throb of the wound on her face was a healing salve. "I think I did one better. I kicked the little prick in his, well, in his little prick."

"That's my Billie. Defender of justice. Now in three-D and surround sound. You're not just an editor anymore." He squeezed her, took her hand, and led her to the living room. He arranged her on the couch with pillows behind her back.

"I'm not made of porcelain. I'm fine." She sat up. "But thank you. For taking care of me."

"You hardly need me to take care of you. But I sure enjoy doing it." He grinned. "I'll make tea."

With the heat from the teacup soothing Billie's nerves, Bruce read the newspaper to her aloud. They cherry-picked two articles where justice did not prevail and rewrote the endings.

"How would you edit the ending to your encounter this morning?" He set the paper aside and slid closer.

Billie shifted, leaned against his shoulder and rested her head against his cheek. She smirked at the picture of Bat Head's red-bespectacled face that popped into her mind. "I'd make him a different person. Change him into a good kid. I wonder how he got to be such a jerk?"

"Well, maybe it's his upbringing."

"He appears to be well off. Expensive shoes, high-end jeans. It's like the attitude and the delinquency is all an act."

"Having money doesn't make you good. And having rich parents doesn't make you well-adjusted. Sometimes it's just the opposite. Parents who don't have time for their kids. Or have all the time in the world, but prefer to spend it golfing or traveling. You don't have to be poor to be a criminal."

Billie nodded. She knew that was true. She'd been poor. Still was. And she'd never broken the law in her life. Except inside her head. But until God told her to stop — or the thought police nabbed her — that didn't count.

Bruce ran one finger along the exposed skin of Billie's arm. "My parents had money. A lot of money. But they were assholes. And look what I turned into. An asshole. You know, before the metamorphosis into the butterfly I am now." He jostled her. "Or maybe I'm just a moth. Because I am drawn to your flame." He pulled her into his lap and kissed her.

She reached her arms around his neck and returned his affection.

He stood and lifted her into his arms in one movement, swift and agile and precise, like a ballet dancer. A big, lumberjack of a ballet dancer. He was so strong, he could snap her in half if he chose to. But she trusted him more than she'd ever trusted anyone. They still barely knew each other, their relationship just a few milliseconds old in terms of a whole cosmic day. And yet she wanted to tell him everything. Be with him always.

Maybe she was nuts.

He carried her to the bedroom and laid her gently on his bed.

He began to dismantle the parts of her prosthetic leg; slid down the sheath and rolled the socks away from her skin. "Tell me if I'm too presumptuous. If you're not up for it, or if you just don't want to." He removed the leg and set it on the armchair kitty-corner from the bed.

She sat up, slid her fingers into his belt loops and tugged him closer. "As long as you don't stick your thing in my aching cheek, it's all good." She whipped his belt free and tossed it on the floor.

The bed creaked and shifted. Cool air filled the void where Bruce had been nestled next to Billie's aching body. She reached for him, her fingers trailing against his arm. "Don't get up yet."

He stood, bent over her, and kissed her forehead. "Sorry, love. I have an early meeting and need a shower. You stay as long as you need to."

"No. I have to go home to change. Just what I need, Katherine noticing that I'm wearing the same clothes." She sat up and rubbed sleep from her eyes.

Bruce opened his closet and flicked hangars with suit jackets and white shirts aside. "Maybe you should bring a change of clothes over."

Above his head, a black case rested on the shelf. The periphery blurred and the case came into laser focus. "Is that it?"

He glanced over his shoulder at her. "What?"

She swallowed. "Is that the gun?"

He followed her pointed finger. "Yeah. That's it. You want to see?"

Billie nodded.

He brought the case down and rested it on the bed beside her. His giant thumbs turned the tumblers of the combination lock.

Four. One. Nine. His birthday.

The lock opened with a click. Bruce lifted the lid. Inside, swaddled within a foam liner cut out to perfectly match its sleek body, lay the gun. Billie poked at it, prepared for its hot steel to burn her. But it was cool and icy. "Is it loaded?"

"Never. Except at the range."

"Can I hold it?"

Bruce rescued it from its nest. She held out her hands and he placed it in her palm.

"It's heavy. I always thought they'd weigh next to nothing."

"Wait until it's loaded. It weighs almost a kilo."

Billie ran her fingers along the length of it, her heart bouncing about her chest. "When can I shoot it?"

1998

"WILHELMINA FULLALOVE."

Billie mounted the short staircase, stage left. Her grandmother had taken her shoe shopping and bought her a pair of royal blue flats, all patent and sparkling under the glare of the spotlights. They matched the cap and gown to perfection, the school's primary colour. A gold sash representing her high academic achievement — highest in her graduating class — circled her shoulders. At least she hadn't lost half of her brain to a hail of bullets.

She strode across the stage. In the five years since the murders, after countless hours in rehab, she'd mastered walking with a prosthetic leg with barely any sign of a limp, thanks to her love of running. Only in the back yard at first, a few too many spills to take it out in public. But in no time, she was sprinting down the street, or jogging on the track at school. She'd even been fitted for a running blade.

The principal stood centre-stage, a scroll tied with blue ribbon in her left hand, her right hand ready for Billie to shake. "Congratulations, young lady. You should be proud of your achievements."

Billie shook the woman's hand and accepted the scroll. "Thank you, ma'am."

"Especially in your situation. Good for you to overcome such adversity."

Billie blinked. The woman couldn't leave well enough alone. Had to tack on some pity and top it off with a cliché to boot. Why couldn't they just accept that she was smart? Why did her missing leg, her dead parents, her purely and utterly crappy life get to take credit for her hard work? If they wanted to give credit, maybe they should thank all of her friends who turned their backs. The boys who wouldn't give her the time of day. It afforded her a lot of spare time to study and work. Time that other kids her age were using to drink and party, experiment with drugs, and get laid. Yep, her grades were the result of boredom and the shunning of teen society because they just didn't know how to deal with her missing leg, her all-encompassing grief.

"Billie?" The principal tugged her hand free. "Is everything all right?"

"Yes, ma'am. Just basking in the glow of the moment." Billie exited stage right to the sad and pathetic pop of pity applause and the heavy slap of her grandmother's hands clapping at a frenetic pace.

Billie walked up the aisle of the auditorium. Ronald, still in skinny jeans, still an asshole, there to support his senior buds and unlikely to graduate next year when he was supposed to, stuck his leg out in front of her and smirked.

She glared at him, veered around him, and kicked his foot on the way by.

He covered his mouth with his hand. "Gimp," he said into a fake cough.

Billie stopped, backed up, bent down, put her mouth next to his ear. "Shit head." She didn't hide it in a cough. And she didn't whisper. But she did say a silent apology to God for swearing out loud.

Students shifted in their seats, gripping their diplomas. Well, not real diplomas. Just a copy of the commencement agenda rolled into a scroll and tied with a royal blue ribbon. The real things would be mailed months later after the board of education confirmed exam results and ensured that the students had, in fact, graduated. Billie watched kids stride, dance, trip, moonwalk across the stage. She played a little game of *who's going to fail?* Most were good to go on, but a few would definitely be receiving a different kind of notice. The "you're ten credits short" kind. The girls who gave up studying to see who could get pregnant first. Reproductive Russian roulette followed by quickie abortions. Condoms were so 1987 after all.

Once all the students had received their diplomas and all the families who'd run up the aisles to snap pictures after being asked to stay seated were back in those seats, the principal addressed the convocation.

"Every year, an honour student is chosen as valedictorian. It is about more than brains and grades, about more than how many advanced placement classes they successfully complete. We also factor in outside circumstance." She paused, her palms on the podium, and swept her eyes over the crowd for dramatic effect. "This year we are very honoured to have chosen a remarkable young woman to deliver your valedictory address. She graduates with a four-point-oh grade point average. Her success in AP English, AP Creative Writing, and AP Social Studies give her a leg up at her chosen university. But there is so much more to this student than good grades."

Billie shook her head. A leg up? Seriously? She closed her eyes and clutched her note cards. Shut up, shut up, just shut the hell up. Let it be about grades. Leave it at that and just shut up.

"This student has overcome immense obstacles. Both of her parents were taken from her under tragic circumstances. That same circumstance resulted in the loss of her leg at the tender age of ten."

Billie opened her eyes. Eleven, you stupid bitch. She mentally backspaced over the principal's last two sentences. She just had to pull the cripple card. May as well just shine a big ol' spotlight on Billie's prosthesis and tell them she only got to be valedictorian because the administration felt sorry for her.

"This young woman has endured unthinkable pain, emotional and physical. I've never met a more focused individual. She buried her grief and her pain in her school work, and as a result, she is graduating a year ahead of schedule with the highest honours ever bestowed upon a Grantham High graduate." The principal beamed at the crowd, pleased as punch over her emotional introduction. "Ladies and gentlemen, please welcome Wilhelmina Fullalove. Or, as we all like to call her, Billie."

As they like to call her? That was her name, for God's sake. Long before she got cast in this high school chainsaw musical.

Billie stood. The entire audience murmured and shifted. Parents and guests clapped, some students too. A few hisses followed her to the stage. She mounted the first step, her heart in her throat and her nerves on edge.

Just don't trip, Billie. Don't give them the satisfaction.

She made it to the podium, looked out upon the crowd, and forced an outside smile.

Ronald booed. A few people giggled.

Billie straightened her note cards and cleared her throat. "Thank you, Mrs. Guilfoyle." She glanced at the notes, at the words of encouragement for her fellow graduates. The idiots and the bitches and the assholes. Even the nerds picked on her since she drew fire away from them, gave them an opportunity to be little dicks in a big dick world. They deserved no encouragement. Not a damn one of them.

She set down the cards. "As has been pointed out to you in great detail, I've had a pretty tough life so far. The first ten years weren't so bad. Although my love for God, my preference for books over boys, and of course the fact that my parents were working-class poor and couldn't afford to buy me the latest fashions, wouldn't let me wear makeup before fifth grade, or hang out after dark stalkin' the 'hood," she lifted her elbows, made peace signs with both hands and pointed down at the podium — her attempt at hip-hop cool. "Well, all those things put a big ol' bully target on my brainy forehead. Even before my parents were gunned down and murdered in a dark alley, before those same gunmen shot me and stole one of my legs, forced me into a life lived wearing titanium and rubber, yes, even before all the trials and tribulations that Mrs. Guilfoyle kindly confessed to this auditorium of mostly strangers — my life at school sucked."

She dismembered the microphone from the stand and stood beside the podium. "Enter high school. A lot of the same students I went to elementary and junior high with, but hey, a whole bunch of new faces. Maybe among them I'd find a kindred spirit. A decent soul." She bit her bottom lip. "One single friend."

The room was silent. They'd expected an uplifting soliloquy. An inspirational speech. They weren't planning on anguished tears or an angry tirade.

Fuck 'em. Fuck 'em all.

"But not one student could find a way to look past this." She lifted her robe and skirt, tapped the leg with the microphone. The dull thud echoed in the auditorium and the microphone squealed. "Pretty scary stuff, eh? Titanium instead of bone. Rubber instead of skin. How very intimidating. But I assume that's what it was. They were intimidated. Surely these students," she swept her other hand over the crowd, "your loving, well-behaved sons and daughters. Surely, they weren't so cruel and uncaring as to make the life of a girl who didn't choose her fate unliveable? Or at the very least, unenviable." She paced in front of the podium. "Well, moms and dads, here's the bad news. They *are* so cruel. They *are* so uncaring. So kudos to you for raising them well. Kudos to the school system for keeping me safe. The valedictory address, historically, offers advice to graduating students." She held the microphone in both hands. "So here's your advice."

The students stared at her, many with open mouths.

"Grow the hell up. And stop being assholes." She tossed the microphone onto the podium and stalked off stage past the principal, whose face was crimson.

FRIDAY

B ILLIE HELD HER BREATH. BRUCE PRESSED HIS frame against her back, her ass perfectly cupped by his groin, his arms over hers, holding her steady. She trembled in his embrace.

"Take a firm grip of it. No, not too tight. Gentle but firm. That's it. Now squeeze slowly."

Billie squeezed. Her arm jerked up and she snapped her neck back. The top of her head connected with Bruce's chin. A hot piece of brass flew to her right and bounced off the protective wall. The casing bounced on the cement and landed near her toes.

She spun around, the echo of the shot still ringing in her ears, and removed her protective glasses. "That was amazing. Oh, God, my heart hurts, it's beating so hard."

Bruce rubbed his chin. "Sounds about right." He guided her shooting arm away. "Always point it at a safe angle, preferably downrange. Never at my junk. And take your finger off the trigger. It should be outside the trigger guard until you are ready to shoot." He punched a button and the target swooshed toward them.

When it hit the end of the line and clicked to a stop near her, Billie scowled. "I didn't even hit the guy."

"Sunshine, you didn't even hit the paper." He took the Glock from her hand. "Your feet should be further apart, shoulder width. Get the shoulders over your hips. I prefer the Isosceles stance, your arms are straight and elbows locked." He slid her glasses back on her nose.

Bruce smacked the button and sent the target flying back to the far wall. He faced the target, held up the pistol, and fired four rounds in quick succession.

Warmth and moisture flooded Billie's panties. Her body jerked with each ping of brass casing against the concrete floor.

Bruce brought the target closer.

"Hah, you only hit him once."

Bruce cocked his head and smirked. "No, love. I hit him all four times. In the same spot."

Her jaw dropped open. She poked one finger through a hole in the paper man's heart. "Holy cow. I want to do that."

"Then get over here and practice. But first, more ammo."

"It only holds five bullets?"

"Ten. But I only loaded five." At the press of a button, the magazine dropped into his hand. He set it on the counter and pulled the chamber back, turned the gun upside down.

"I thought there were only five?"

"Just to be sure. Always be sure."

He handed her one magazine and five bullets. "Push the rear of the bullet down and slide it back." He picked up the other magazine and demonstrated.

Billie took a bullet from the box. It was cool in her fingers, smooth and icy. "This one has a hole in it." She pointed to the tip.

"Hollow point. Mushrooms on impact."

"Is that good?"

"It's not good or bad. Just depends on what you want from your ammo. The range prefers you use them because they don't damage the backstop like a full metal jacket will. In real life, hollow points decrease penetration, less likely to be a through-and-through, and won't do damage to anything but the target." He grinned. "Assuming you hit it."

"Ha. Ha. Ha." The first bullet didn't want to go in. He showed her again — push, slide. On the third try, she found the sweet spot and the bullet slid into the magazine. She did another, then a third. Soon, her thumb was black and aching. "Does this come off? Or get any easier?"

Bruce licked his finger and rubbed the black from Billie's thumb. "Yes, and yes. You're picking it up fast. The last two are the hardest." He took her magazine and turned it around. He pursed his lips. "Impressive. You loaded all ten. Now slide it in and click it into place. Just smack it with the heel of your hand."

She took back the magazine and picked up the gun. "You're making me horny."

He laughed. "Yeah, guns and sex. Good combo. Not." He pressed his lips close to her ear protection. "Although watching you handle my piece has me wanting you to handle my other piece."

She grinned, slid in the magazine and smacked its bottom, clicked the slide release and faced the target.

"Focus on your front sight." Bruce used his foot to gently kick her legs farther apart. "Bend your knees slightly." He put one hand on her belly and the other on the back of her shoulders, tipping her forward a bit. "Your target should be a bit blurry. Now, straight arms, elbows locked."

Billie nodded.

"And squeeze."

Billie moved her finger from outside the trigger guard onto the trigger. She squeezed. The recoil jerked her arms but she held stance. She squeezed again, again, a fourth time, a fifth. When the gun let out a hollow click on the eleventh pull of the trigger, she let out her breath, moved her finger from the trigger and set the gun on the counter. She slapped the button and eyed the target as it raced toward her. Ten holes in the paper. Five in the gut. Three in the shoulder. One in the groin. And one in the heart.

"And that, Billie Sunshine, is how it's done." Bruce kissed her cheek.

She picked up the other magazine. "Again."

MONDAY THE 27TH

BILLIE STEPPED FROM THE SUBWAY STATION AND leaned against the brick of an office building. If Anthony Gerard Dickinson was in the same spot, she wanted to be as prepared, as composed as possible. Show no fear, that's what her father used to tell her.

Didn't do him any damn good.

She headed up the street to where she'd found Gold Tooth the day before. She neared the concrete steps that led into the Dilly Diner. There he was, half a block up, same place, same lump of dirty fabric. He looked like a massive mound of steaming dog shit. She set her jaw and strode toward him.

She stopped directly in front of him, casting him in shadow. She crossed her arms and gave him the meanest glare she could muster.

He nodded his goofy head like he had Parkinson's or something, held up his cup and shook it. He leered at her and squinted his eyes.

She blinked a long blink and focused.

He just sat there grinning at her. No leer. No squint. Just crow's feet around his crazy eyes, deepened and weathered by the sun and the elements. Just how long had he been on the street? And why had he chosen this spot to take up residence?

He lifted the cup a few more inches and shook it again. When she didn't budge, he brought it back down and looked to the left of her for other donors. His gaze swept right and he hesitated, staring at her legs. He glanced up in a sharp jerk. He cocked his head and examined her face. His wide eyes took on a familiar wild look.

All confidence and bravado drained from Billie's bones. She turned and hurried away. Maybe she'd have to start riding the subway to the next stop and doubling back to the office. It was only a few more blocks. And the walk would do her good.

Billie hung up the phone and stared at her untouched lunch. The lobster bisque had gone cold and the thought of swallowing even one bite of turkey on rye turned her stomach to stone. She put the lid on the soup and swept it all into the garbage can under her desk. Her favourite lunch from the best deli in town, ruined. Forever linked to the realities of a conversation with the former Crown Prosecutor — now Judge — Robbins.

Model prisoner he'd said. Repentant and filled with remorse. Never missed a group session and was even counselling young offenders. This led to early parole, he'd told her. And just why was she never invited to any of these hearings? Not asked to speak to the evil he'd helped bestow upon her parents? The hell he'd made of her life?

"And put you through all that again?" Robbins said. "Billie, it wouldn't have helped. He was eligible. There was no reason not to grant parole. And you'd never come to any hearings prior, never even requested information about him."

"I didn't know about the hearings. And I didn't know I was allowed information. For God's sake, I was only eleven. Shouldn't someone have told me?"

"I'm sorry, Billie. That would be up to your legal guardian."

So it was her grandmother's fault.

"Besides. He found God. I know how important that is to you."

This smug representative of failed justice presumed to know her? Twenty-two years later? He'd never even checked up on her. Even the cop, a buddy of her father's, who led the investigation had kept in touch for a few years. He was still trying to find the guy with the gun when he dropped dead at his desk. Massive coronary. Billie had carried guilt for years that maybe his unwavering devotion to her case, his pigheaded persistence to catch the murderer had been his undoing. But his waistline and heavy breathing assured her that it was his own doing. Bad food choices. Lack of exercise. The cop lifestyle, that's what killed him.

Since his death, the case had gone cold. No new leads. No new evidence. The only evidence was bottled up inside of Dickinson's head. He knew the shooter. But he'd never identified him.

It was time he told her.

BAT HEAD

NICK FRASER PASSED A JOINT TO TODD, HIS BEST friend and partner in crime, as Nick's mother always said. It used to be just a lame cliché. Another pile of crap that his mother spewed on a daily basis. Two-peas-in-a-pod kind of crap. Like biscuits and butter. Mutt and Jeff, Frick and Frack, Thing One and Thing Two. Her bullshit knew no bounds.

But partners in crime came true. After their stint in juvie, they graduated from grab-and-run shoplifting and palming shitty Wal-Mart jewelry to pawn for chump change to drug deals in dark alleys, liquor store hold ups, and snatching purses from stupid bitches who just sling their bags over their shoulders. Easy pickings — one slice of a sharp knife through the strap and those bags were gone before the dumb broads knew what hit 'em.

Todd tapped Nick's shoulder and handed the joint back. Nick always got the last hit. He sucked smoke through the tiny nub until he was getting nothing but air, opened the alligator clip, and tossed the bit of rolling paper that remained to the alley floor. He pocketed the clip and surveyed the pedestrians who paraded past on the darkened sidewalk.

Nick discovered this location a couple nights earlier. He and Todd got all lit up, grabbed some high-end hag's purse, and took off running. Good take, that one. Coach bag. Even with the cut strap it earned them a hundred bucks at pawn. Not only was there a wallet stuffed with three hundred cash, but a gold chain and a diamond ring were tucked inside the change purse. They traded all that loot for good weed, cut it with oregano and parsley, and sold it all at the middle school. Stupid eighth graders have no clue.

They ducked into this alley, made darker than usual by three busted-out streetlights on the same block. What fucking luck. A dark street just a block from the bright lights and busy shops filled with all manner of rich twats just dying to give it away. Or at least too stupid to keep it to themselves.

He spied a lone woman wandering up the street toward them. She dug in her bag and pulled out her cell phone. She weaved side-to-side, a bit unsteady on her ridiculous stiletto heels. She grinned at the phone and tapped away at it with her thumbs, fake nails clacking against the screen.

Nick fingered the switchblade in his pocket, rolled it in his hand until he got just the right grip. He reached out and squeezed Todd's forearm. "Target, twelve o'clock."

When she got within a few yards, she tossed her phone back in her bag.

Nick shook his shoulders and bounced on his toes. He pressed the button on the knife, propelling the razor-sharp blade into the open air. When she was almost past the mouth of the alley, he pounced. He grabbed the strap of her purse and sliced through it, then turned to run.

He came to the end of the long strap in two strides. It went taut, and his momentum snapped him back like a Saturday morning cartoon dog on a short leash. He landed on his ass on the pavement.

The chick screamed and held tight to a short handle attached near the opening of the purse.

He bounded to his feet. "Grab it," he yelled at Todd.

Todd emerged from the alley and gripped the purse with both hands. He had a tug of war with the woman, and he was losing. They'd pegged her as easy pickings, but this bitch was tough. She released one hand from the purse, but kept an iron grip on the handle. She fumbled with a pendant on a long chain around her neck.

A whistle.

Nick stepped forward, grabbed her by her long, blond hair and put his other arm around her waist. He dragged her into the alley. She smelled of flowers and wine and something just a little sweet.

"Okay, okay." She let go of the handle. "Take the purse. Just take it. I'll walk away. I won't tell anyone."

He threw her onto a pile of hefty bags overflowing with kitchen garbage from the trattoria.

She kicked at his legs and tried scramble to her feet.

No one was going to get the best of him. That gimpy bitch on the subway was the last one. And she'd pay one day.

He jerked his head at his accomplice. "Hold her down."

Todd did as he was told, wrestled with her until her arms were pinned against the bags.

Nick unzipped his jeans. "Should've just let me take it the first time."

Todd stared up at him. "Dude. The fuck?"

"What do you mean, the fuck? Bitch pushed her luck. She's gonna get what she deserves."

"No way, man. You're out of control. I'm out." He let the woman go and took off into the night.

Fucking traitor.

Her arms free, the woman rolled off the bags and got her feet underneath her.

Nick put one foot on her back and stomped.

She landed face-first on the asphalt. The air groaned from her lungs.

Nick rolled her over, shoved her legs apart and yanked up her skirt.

She slapped at Nick's head. "Help me," she yelled into the empty alley. Her voice bounced off the walls of the buildings towering above the alley floor.

"Shut the fuck up," he hissed. He grabbed her hands, held both wrists with one hand, and pinned them above her head. "You yell one more time and I'll cut your tongue out. You feel me?"

She nodded, her eyes wide, tears streaming down her temples.

He ripped her underpants off, and raped her while she cried.

THURSDAY, AUGUST 6TH

S TOP HARASSING ME AND BE PATIENT. IT'LL HAPPEN when it happens." Katherine tapped her lime-green fake nails against her glass-top desk. "Or, in your case, *if* it happens. Which is unlikely."

Billie drew her hands into fists. She flailed at the made-up face across the desk, beat Katherine's surgically upturned nose into red-ink pulp and ripped her extensions out one by one. "Interviews were supposed to have been finished by now. Can't you tell me when they'll start?" She ground her teeth together.

"Nope. Can't. Not my area." She leaned forward, her elbows on the desk. "Don't worry, your resume is in the mix. Since you bypassed me and sent a copy directly upstairs."

Billie was certain that "you presumptuous bitch" died on Katherine's lips before she spoke the words aloud. Billie stood, commanded her nerves to quell and her hands not to shake, that awful tell that gave away her true nature — chicken to the core — when she tried so hard to be tough on the outside. "Fine. I'll wait." She turned and left the office, sat at her desk, and stared at the blank monitor.

No way was Katherine not the reason for the delay. She was pulling someone's strings. If only Billie could figure out whose. Someone with influence. Someone who, like Katherine, was intent on keeping Billie in the proofer's wading pool. But who would conspire with that flame-haired shrew? Who could hate Billie as much as Katherine did? Did anyone upstairs even know who Billie was?

"Still no go?" Jeffrey's hand patted Billie's shoulder.

"Correct."

"It'll happen. It's out of her control now." He winked at Billie.

She doubted anything was out of Katherine's control. One thing was certain. Billie had control of nothing.

"How can she hold me back like this? What did I ever do to her?"

Doc wrote on her notepad, the scratch of a near-dry Rollerball pen like a hot stick in Billie's ear.

"You tell me." Doc didn't look up from her scribbling.

Billie gaped at her. "Tell you what? I've not done anything to deserve this. I get my work done, put up with her bull crap, her outrageous demands and ridiculous deadlines. She just piles more on, never gives me credit, and never, ever, acknowledges my hard work."

"Maybe that's the issue."

Billie shook her head. "I don't understand."

"You're too nice, Billie. You let her walk on you. Heck, you almost encourage it. You have to be more proactive. Make her acknowledge you."

"That's what I'm trying to do." Tears threatened the corners of Billie's eyes.

"Yes. But it's too late. The pattern is set, has been in play for, what, six years? And your efforts to get out from under it now are a threat to her. She's fighting to keep the status quo. Making sure you remain at her disposal to use and abuse."

Billie furrowed her brow, opened her mouth to speak, but hesitated. She swallowed. "That's crappy advice. You know that, right?"

"My job is not to give advice. It's to help you see how you can help yourself. But if advice is what you're after, here it is. Be patient. Wait for the interview process. Forget Katherine. If you get the job, then leapfrog over the bitch and never look back."

"And if I don't?"

Doc slapped her notepad onto her lap and eyed Billie over her glasses. "Get out. Fast. Because it'll only get worse."

JANIS JONES

JANIS JONES BACKED OUT OF HER DRIVEWAY AND pulled onto the road, wipers at full tilt against the driving rain. Nothing douses the media fire better than time and bad weather.

Once the Crown Prosecutor announced that no charges would be brought, that there was insufficient evidence in the deaths of her first two children to prove any wrongdoing, the media began to lose interest. Each day, bodies and cameras would trickle off her lawn. As of yesterday morning, they were gone. Only squashed roses and footprints in the grass remained as proof they were ever there at all.

Janis missed them. Missed the attention. What was that old saying? No such thing as bad press? Well, that's a load of bull. Everywhere she went people pointed and whispered. Women gripped their children as if Janis would snatch them and drown them in the bathtub just for shits and giggles.

She wasn't a monster, for God's sake.

A frail figure limped along the gravel shoulder, one hand gripping a cane, back hunched, hood protecting him from the downpour. Why was this old man walking all the way out here? In this weather? Perhaps he was lost. Or worse, had dementia and had wandered away from home.

She glanced at the clock. Therapy didn't start for forty minutes. She did have some time to spare. Could forgo the usual three-pump, double-shot vanilla-bean latte and help the old dude out instead. Or just be late for the stupid appointment. She didn't need it. Didn't want it. But it helped to keep up the grieving mother façade. One side of her mouth turned up. She'd show her bastard husband that she was a decent person. Show the whole damn world.

She pulled up beside the drenched old fart and slowed. His face was shielded against the storm by the hood of his insufficient windbreaker. She depressed a button on the armrest of her door and the passenger window rolled down.

"Hey, mister," she yelled against the rain pounding on the roof of her Escalade. "Want a ride?" She plucked her purse from the leather passenger seat and tossed it into the empty baby seat strapped in back.

He fumbled the door open, and slid his wet, brittle figure onto the leather seat.

Janis winced. She should have thought this through. Now she'd have to get her car detailed. Get the old-man stench out. But first, the good deed. She turned the radio off, extinguishing the lyrics of Fiona Apple's *Hot Knife,* and clicked on the seat heater. "Nasty day. Where are you headed?"

He mumbled something.

"I'm sorry, where? Can you speak up? The rain, it's so loud." She glanced at his exposed hand, stared at the unexpected sight. It was too feminine, too smooth. The skin wasn't rice-paper-thin, the knuckles not gnarled from age, the veins not blue or protruding like her father's or her second husband's. She lifted her eyes to meet his gaze and was met with the brown-eyed stare of a young woman.

The woman slid her too-smooth hand into her jacket. "I'm going home." The dashboard light glinted off the edge of a knife blade. "You're going to hell." The knife sliced into Janis's belly. Her screams filled the car. Blood spattered the steering wheel. She grabbed at her stomach with both hands.

Her best suit. Ruined.

"No more children to murder." The woman sneered at her and jumped from the car. In the rear view mirror, Janis watched her run down the road, her cane in one hand, the bloody knife in the other.

Janis reached for the mirror and fumbled for the blue button. Blood smeared the glass.

"This is OnStar. How can we be of assistance, Mrs. Jones?"

"Help." It was all she could manage.

"I'm sorry, could you repeat that? Is it raining in Grantham?"

Janis mustered every ounce of waning strength she had. "Help."

"Mrs. Jones, do you need us to call nine-one-one?"

"Yes."

"OK, got it. Police are on their way."

"Stabbed."

"Did you say stabbed?" The operator's voice became muffled as if she were holding her hand over the microphone. Janis couldn't make out her words. "Mrs. Jones?" The operator's voice came back full volume. "Paramedics are on the way to your location. Just sit tight and stay on with me."

Janis stared at sheets of water on her windshield and tried to time her gasping breath to the beat of the wipers. The pain in her abdomen shot to every corner of her body. Blood drained from the wound, stained her manicured fingers, pooled onto the leather and trickled onto the floor mat.

"Why?" Her voice was only a croak.

"Just hold tight, Mrs. Jones. They're about three minutes out."

The woman's cruel words came back. *No more children to murder.* But she was innocent. The court said so.

Every blink of Janis's eyes took longer to complete. Her foot shifted off the brake pedal and the car inched forward. She put her bloody knuckles against the gearshift and pushed it up, but only got it as far as neutral. In the distance, the plaintive mewl of sirens squealed through the pounding rain.

Her eyelids fluttered and she struggled to keep them open. A wave of ice swept over her body. The car shook with the thump of rain and the quaking of her limbs. Red and blue lights bounced off the water on the windshield, distorted and twisted like a Salvador Dali painting. She raised one hand and pawed at the air, tried to touch the pretty lights.

"Ma'am?"

Janis moved her lips but no answer would come. She was drowning in ice. Through the Vaseline-haze that covered her eyes, a face popped up. The face yelled and someone stabbed her arm. Her body was jostled and jerked. The headlights of her Escalade bounced away. Rain pelted her face. A door slammed and bright lights blinded her. She closed her eyes. The beeping surrounding her became one long tone.

SATURDAY THE 8TH OF AUGUST

BILLIE SHIVERED, HER CLOTHING SOAKED. SHE SAT in a culvert in two feet of runoff, like some filthy baptism gone wrong. She looked skyward, shielding her eyes from the icy raindrops that pummeled her quaking body.

Where was she?

She scrambled to her feet, the water squelching up between the toes of her left foot. Grandfather's cane fell from her lap and plopped into the water. She snatched it before the current pulled it away. She tapped the tip of the cane against her prosthesis. Why did she have the cane if she was fully footed?

Her clothes weighed a thousand pounds. She rubbed her gloved left hand, fisted around the cane, over the mound of soaking fleece at her belly, and closed her eyes. Her father's hoodie. She searched her memory for the moment she'd donned his clothes, still stinking of chlorine since she hadn't had the heart to wash the imagined entrails of his scent from them.

Her eyelids flickered and she glanced down at her other hand. Her hammering heart picked up its pace at the site of a wooden handle and thin, curved, steel blade. Pain seeped into her consciousness. She dropped the knife into the rushing water, tucked the cane under her armpit, peeled off the wet glove, and raised her hand to her face. Blood oozed from a slice on her thumb.

Her breath came fast. Her head whipped side to side trying to find some landmark, anything recognizable to ground her. To bring her into reality. Because there was no way this wasn't a dream.

She scrabbled up the embankment to the roadside. A truck roared by, honked its air horn. Its massive tires hit a pool of rain. A wave of dirty water slammed into her and knocked her to the ground.

In the distance, sirens wailed.

Oh, God, what had she done? The knife. The cut. The clothes. Sirens. She covered her ears and shut her eyes and rocked on the shoulder of the road, gravel digging into her skin through the black cargo pants.

Another wave of puddle hit her, another honking horn. She wiped muck from her cheeks and ran one hand through her sopping hair.

Sirens neared. Through the haze of rain and the fog of memories, Billie watched flashing red lights close in. Her belly hollowed.

They were coming for her.

She scurried off the shoulder and rolled down the embankment into the culvert. She lay in the water, only her head, from the nose up, visible. An ambulance screeched past, followed in quick succession by two police cars.

Her discarded glove bobbed on the surface of the water, snagged on a branch. Billie grabbed it and inched up into a crouch. She scanned the silent road. She stuffed the glove into the pouch of the hoodie, then parted the waters with both hands, her eyes trained for the glint of steel. But the runoff was too deep, the water too muddy. And too cold. She dragged her good foot across the sludge at the bottom. When her shoe caught on anything, she fished it out and held it up. Discarded bottles, a dead rat. A few feet down current, she slammed her foot into something big enough to be a body and nearly toppled over. She plunged both hands into the murk, grabbed the object, and grunted against the weight. The remains of a blown tire surfaced. She abandoned the search for the blade after three more cars sped by.

Maybe she'd imagined it. Maybe there had never been a knife. But the cut on her thumb was all too real. As was the fact that she was wearing her father's clothes and was up to her thighs in runoff in the pouring rain somewhere far from home.

The sound of tires speeding toward her on the wet pavement was like the surf crashing against a sandy shore at night. Billie dove into the bog. A wave reared up and splashed her face. She spit and coughed dirt and silt and dead rat essence from her mouth. When only the sound of rainfall remained, Billie climbed up the other side of the gutter, shoved branches aside with the cane, and pushed her way through the brush.

Thirty yards of scratching twigs and poking limbs later, she emerged into an open field. On the other side, across the blacktop of a two-lane highway, a dying neon sign pulsated in the gloom of a late afternoon downpour and announced "GAS for LESS." She didn't give a dead rat's behind about gas. But maybe they had a phone.

A bell over the door clanged and announced her presence to the world inside the tiny station. A tiny diner shared the space, two booths and four stools at the lunch counter. All empty, thank God for small mercies.

"You're drenched!" A woman in a too-pink and too-stained polyester tunic came from around the cash desk, a roll of paper towels in one hand. She stripped of several squares of absorbent paper and handed them to Billie. "Didn't your mama teach you to come in out of the rain?"

Billie dried her face and squeezed her hair through the towel. Cinnamon and vanilla and grease filled her nose. "My car broke down. Can I borrow your phone?"

"Sure thing, honey. It's on the wall around the corner. How 'bout I get you a cup of coffee to warm up?"

Billie patted her pockets. "Thanks. But I left my purse in the car."

"On the house. Maybe a nice piece of pie too."

Billie's stomach roared in approval. "Bless you. That would be wonderful."

She found the telephone, its buttons sticky with strangers' fingerprints. Billie reached for the handset but froze. Fingerprints. She couldn't leave any fingerprints. She glanced toward the door. How would she wipe the handle down without looking suspicious? Or more suspicious.

She pulled the sleeve of her hoodie down and picked up the receiver, balanced it between her cheek and shoulder, and pressed the buttons with her finger poking the hoodie sleeve.

The phone rang two, three, four times. Damn it, please don't go to voice mail. She needed to hear his voice. Needed to know this wasn't a dream. Or better yet, discover that it was.

"Montoya."

She gripped the phone in both hands. "Bruce?" She could barely muster a whisper.

"Billie? Is that you? Where are you calling from?"

"Some diner in a gas station. I — I think I've done something terrible. Can you come?"

"Yes. Give me an address."

She looked around. A stack of menus sat on a table. She stretched the cord and snatched one with her hoodie-covered hand. "Gloria's Diner, Highway Seventeen and a Hundred and Ninety-Eighth Street."

"I'll Google it. Are you all right?"

"I don't know. I don't think so."

"Shit, Billie, you're damn near all the way to Ivy Valley. That's thirty clicks south of town. How did you get there?"

Billie swallowed. Salty tears combined with the remains of muck on her face and dripped onto her lip. "I have no idea."

Billie stood on the cool tile of her bathroom floor, one hand on Bruce's shoulder for balance.

He peeled her clothing from her limbs. The soaking wet fabric had transformed to a sort of frozen glue. Even the oversized cargos stuck to her skin and caught on the drenched stockings of her prosthesis. He cranked the faucet to hot, and steam soon billowed from the bathtub.

Bruce laid a towel over the toilet seat lid and had Billie sit. He dismantled her leg, stripped her of the filthy, stinking, sopping trappings of her misadventure, lifted her, and set her in the warm water.

Her red, icy skin was lit on fire by the first touch of hot bathwater. Billie winced, but sank into it; inhaled the lavender bath salts Bruce had scooped under the stream of soothing heat pouring from the tap. It cleansed the runoff from her body and calmed the frenetic pace of her mind.

On the drive home she'd told him how she awoke in the culvert. About the gloves and the clothes and the knife, the sirens and ambulance and police.

"That could be for anything. Car accident. Heart attack. Shooting."

His deep timbre soothed her soul, but did nothing to ease the possibility that a monster lurked within her, waiting to take over her conscious mind on a whim.

Bruce sat on the edge of the tub, dipped a sponge in the scented water and ran it over her shoulders and arms. "So," he cleared his throat. "This ever happen before?"

Billie nodded. "A couple of months ago. I found myself on the fire escape in the wee hours of the morning."

"What were you doing out there?"

"No clue. It looked like I was going to jump. I had climbed onto the railing. Woke up there." She wiped sweat from her brow with trembling fingers. "What if I hadn't come to?"

"Don't even think about it." He kissed the top of her grimy head. "You did. And you didn't jump. So it must have been something other than a suicide attempt." He reached for the shampoo bottle and squeezed a blob into his palm.

Billie inhaled the citrusy scent and closed her eyes, mesmerized by the gentle massaging of his strong fingers against her scalp. "It wasn't the first time." Or the last. But she didn't want to share the impromptu panhandling episode.

The massaging stopped. "What do you mean?"

Billie held her breath and disappeared under the water. She rubbed the suds from her head and surfaced, wiping both hands over her face. "I mean, I've done it before. Woke up somewhere unfamiliar, completely confused and unaware of my surroundings. But it hadn't happened for a long time. Not since after Grandmother died."

Bruce slid off the tub's edge and sat on the floor. He took her hand, enlaced his fingers with hers. "Holy shit. You sleepwalk?"

She laid her head on his arm. "Not exactly. Dissociative fugue. Like sleepwalking. But more rare, and much worse."

"Worse how?"

"Sometimes I go a long way. Sometimes I'm gone for hours. Sometimes I lose an entire day." She glanced at him.

"Like when you missed the movie? Was that this fugue thing?"

She shrugged. "Maybe. If it was I didn't wake up in the middle of it. So I can't know."

He rested his cheek against her head. "I see." He reached for a towel, stood, and pulled the plug. "Come on. I'll make you tea."

She took his offered hand, climbed from the tub, and balanced on her leg. "I'd rather have a drink."

"Then let's see if you have any wine." He wrapped the towel around her, wiped her face dry with one corner, and rubbed his hands up and down her back.

An odd memory crept in, of her mother after bath time when Billie was little, maybe four or five. The big towel, sitting on her mother's lap. The good times before she reeked of booze and before Billie knew that the other smell was cigarette smoke. Billie would lay her head against her mother's shoulder and her mother would rock her and hum a lullaby.

Billie leaned into Bruce's body and rested her head on his shoulder. He engulfed her with his arms. "It's all right, Billie Sunshine," he whispered into her wet hair. "I've got you."

Billie held the teacup in both hands, the heat easing the remaining chill from her bones. In retrospect, she was happy to be out of wine. Chamomile was working its magic, warming her from the inside out, letting her shed most of the panic. But not all of it. Nothing was that magical.

Bruce breezed about her tiny kitchen, setting about to fry and boil some of her meagre refrigerator offerings into something edible. He manoeuvred the cupboards and countertops with such ease. He reached to pull a knife from the dusty block that Billie's grandmother had given her when she moved out on her own.

Billie froze. Her gaze focused in on an empty slot in the wood. A missing knife. Her gut turned to stone and she fumbled the teacup. It crashed to the floor and sent shards of kiln-fired pottery scattering about.

Bruce swung around, a chef's knife in his hand.

The room spun and Billie's vision blurred. She wavered on the stool and tipped to the side.

Bruce raced around the breakfast counter and grabbed her before she hit the ground. He carried her to the sofa, laid her down, and tapped at her cheeks. "Billie, are you all right? Did you faint?"

She brushed his hands away and sat up. "I'm fine." She looked past him to the knife block, now with two empty slots. She stood and hopped to the kitchen. "Where is it?"

"Where is what?" Bruce was behind her.

She pointed to the knife block. "The knife." She pulled each knife from its allotted space and dropped each to the counter. "The long skinny one. It has a curved blade." She yanked the dishwasher open, but it stood empty. She scanned the sink, shoved plates and mugs aside.

"A boning knife?" Bruce put the other knives back into the block.

"I think so." Billie pulled drawer after drawer open and rummaged through them. Only steak knives and dull dinner knives to be found.

She gripped the counter's edge. "It was my knife." She turned to Bruce, searched his face for answers.

"You mean the one today? The one you dropped in the culvert?"

She nodded with vigour, her dizzy spell creeping back in.

"Come on, sit." He guided her back to the sofa. "You've cut your foot on the cup."

She sat in a haze while he tended to her injury, cleaned the broken glass, and wiped splotches of her blood from the floor. When everything was returned to normal, he sat beside her. "It makes sense, doesn't it?"

She blinked. "What makes sense?"

"That it was your own knife. If it wasn't, where would you have gotten it?" He brushed hair from her forehead.

She swallowed. Yes, that made sense. If anything that happened this crazy day could possibly make sense. She touched his cheek. "Thank you."

His face scrunched up. "For what?"

"Are you kidding me? For reassuring me. Cleaning up after me." She leaned forward and kissed him. "For rescuing me. Again."

"My beautiful Billie, I didn't rescue you. I just drove out to get you." He settled in beside her and picked up the phone. "I'm ordering Chinese. You okay with that?"

"If that means you stay beside me and we don't use any knives, then I'm thrilled with that."

"How about I come to church with you tomorrow?"

She pulled back and eyed his face, searching for signs of sarcasm. "You hate church."

"Yeah. But maybe it would do you good. I can be there for moral support, so to speak."

She snuggled into his side and pulled his arm over her head and around her shoulders. "I don't want to go." The instant she stepped inside the door, she'd probably burst into flames.

SUNDAY THE 9TH

BILLIE SAT UP IN BED AND GASPED. SHE WIPED sweat from her brow and out of her eyes, but couldn't wipe the dream from her mind. Spewing blood and a flailing knife, the open mouth of a screaming woman, all of it drenched in a lake of sewage and ooze.

Bruce moaned and snorted sleep through his nose.

Billie dried her hand on the comforter and reached for him. She hesitated, didn't want to wake him, but needed to know he was real. She touched her hand to his chest and let the rise and fall of his breathing ground her back to reality. She breathed in time with his heartbeat, tried to satisfy herself that the images in her head were just that. Images.

Maybe satisfied was a stretch. She scanned the floor for a mound of her father's clothes. The coast was clear. Besides, Bruce had washed them, boxed them up and put them in a closet in his apartment.

She glanced at the bedside clock. Four forty-five. Bruce would be out for a couple more hours, but she knew the thrum in her own veins all too well. She may as well get out of bed and do something useful. Sleep would not be coming back.

She slid from beneath the covers and hopped to the chair where her cane rested its horse's head against the upholstered armrest. One touch of her warm flesh to the cool brass and a new wave of pseudo-memories rushed at her. The dirty smell of rain on pavement and the shush of rubber tires racing past.

Billie dropped to the chair, her head swimming and spinning, her stomach hard and ready to jump out of her throat. She put her head between her knees and struggled to breathe.

"Billie, what's wrong?" Bruce's bare feet thumped onto the carpet and scurried to her side. He lay on the floor at her foot, his head under hers. "You all right?"

She giggled at the sight of this grown man, burly in all the right places, lying on her floor just to get a good vantage point. "I just had a dizzy spell."

He bounded to his feet and rubbed her shoulders. She sat up slowly and leaned against the backrest, one hand on her forehead, her other still gripping the head of the cane.

"Why don't you come back to bed." He eyeballed the clock. "Shit, love, it's not even five."

She shook her head. "No, I'm too awake. You go back. I'll get some work done. I promised that manuscript to Annabelle before the fifteenth." She patted his arm.

He leaned in for a kiss. "Okay. I could use a couple more hours. When I get up, I'll make pancakes and bacon."

Her mouth filled with saliva. "Sounds perfect." Billie eyed the cane. "Will you hand me my leg?" She rested the cane against the wall. Releasing it let go of the sensation of being thigh-deep in freezing water that smelled like asparagus farts. She fitted her apartment prosthesis over her stump and kissed Bruce on his morning-breath lips. At the threshold, she admired the view of him climbing back beneath her comforter and stuffing her pillow under his curly hair. Peg Leg meandered across the room and weaved his way between her legs, rubbed his inky fur against her bare flesh, and the fake flesh too. Billie pulled the door shut with a quiet click.

On her way past the breakfast counter, she poked the power button on her open laptop. Peg Leg crawled onto the couch, stepped over the end table, and made the short hop to his morning perch on the window ledge. His tail flicked about, side-to-side, up, down. He mewed at the line of orange and lilac on the horizon and demanded the sun hurry up and rise already.

Sunday was coffee day. But she was going to edit, so that demanded tea. What a conundrum. Which ritual would she uphold? She hedged her bets, put a pot of her favourite dark roast on to brew, filled the kettle with water, lit a burner, and put it on to heat. Once they were ready, she'd make her choice. Or maybe just have a cup of both. The extra caffeine might clear her brain.

She turned the television on with the volume down. A years-old habit she learned from her grandmother. The voices kept her company and provided white noise as if she were in the office. It helped focus her thoughts on the task at hand. Silence drove her bonkers.

Billie checked her email while water burbled through the coffee filter and into the pot. By the time the teakettle whistled, she'd cleared her inbox and opened Annabelle's manuscript to the last page of completed edits.

Coffee smelled of Sunday, rich and heady, with just a hint of cinnamon. The thought of tea bored her silly. Coffee it was, with too much half-and-half and a generous spoonful of brown sugar. Her other Sunday ritual had taken a backseat to more exciting pastimes of late. But sweet, creamy coffee won out every time.

She set the mug and adjusted the angle of the handle, interlaced her fingers and popped her knuckles, twisted her neck until a crack crunched in her ears. She re-read the last few paragraphs to get her bearings, then carried on. It wasn't a bad little story. The construction was good, the plot decent. Grammar and spelling were passable. Some punctuation issues, but heck, nobody was perfect. Least of all authors. They focused on the story and left the grunt work to the professionals. Maybe that was best.

The newscast in the background kept spouting words that

interrupted her focus.

Murder. Stabbed. Ivy Valley.

Billie froze, her fingers hovering above the keyboard. She trained her ears on the low volume of the television but couldn't bring herself to turn around.

"Janis Jones, recently found not guilty of charges that she murdered her son by drowning him in a bathtub, was pronounced dead en route to Grantham General. Police are canvassing the area, but without an eyewitness account, have little to go on."

Billie shifted in her chair and turned to the television.

"Mrs. Jones' husband, Harold, showed little emotion when the police delivered the news," the female anchor read from the teleprompter. "He was questioned in connection with her death and released due to a solid alibi. He was in his office in downtown Grantham on Saturday afternoon at the time of the attack."

"Mrs. Jones," the male anchor to the woman's left tapped the desk with his fingertips, "is predeceased by all three of her children." He turned to the woman.

"With any luck, this incident will spur the construction of the new hospital," she said. "Perhaps if there were a rural location, she could have been saved."

Billie pointed the remote at the set and pressed the mute button. She stared at the silent screen, at a commercial for a cooking show, a close up of chef's knife slicing a rack of lamb into chops, followed by a scene with young children eating hamburgers. "I'm loving it," scrolled across the screen.

Her fingers numb, her eyes unblinking, Billie turned to her computer. Ivy Valley. Wasn't that where Bruce had said she was? She Googled it, Googled the diner. There it was, on the outskirts of that tiny town in the rural 'burbs outside Grantham.

She left her computer and flopped onto the couch; grabbed a pillow to her belly and rocked. The image of a woman's face, her mouth twisted, her eyes contorted in pain, popped into Billie's head. She felt the wooden handle of a knife in her hand. Her body reeled at the sensation of plunging it into the soft folds of the woman's flesh, and the flow of her hot, crimson blood.

Nausea rolled up Billie's body, but before she spewed coffee into the air, it quelled. She was overcome by a new sensation.

Power.

"You make any progress?" Bruce padded out of the bedroom, his hair askew, pillow lines etched into his face.

Billie tossed the pillow aside and jumped to her feet. She threw her arms around him and inhaled the musky odour she so loved, reveled in the warmth of his ruddy skin, sticky with sleep sweat. She laid her head on his chest and listened to his heartbeat in her ear, closed her eyes as his arms closed around her body. "Yes." Her blood coursed through her veins and delivered its energy to every extremity. Even the missing one. "Yes, I think I did."

MONDAY THE 10TH

I WANT TO GO BACK ON MEDS." BILLIE TOOK A LONG gulp of her caramel macchiato.

Doc Kroft nodded, her lips puckered. "I see. That's quite the one-eighty." She tapped her pen against her cheek. "What happened, Billie? Why the emergency appointment?"

Billie set the coffee on the table and lay back on the chaise. She dropped her hands to her belly, her gaze focused on the tin ceiling maze. "I had another fugue episode."

Doc's pen scratched on the lilac pad. "When?"

Billie explained the events of Saturday.

"I see. How long were you in the fugue state?"

One thing Billie appreciated about the doc. When it came to talk of disorders and other serious shit, she was all business. "Well, I remember Friday night. But not waking up Saturday morning."

"So sometime after, what, midnight? Until late in the afternoon. At least seven hours, maybe up to fourteen or fifteen."

Billie nodded. "Sounds about right."

"So that's the farthest you've travelled and your longest state yet. And, to be frank, the weirdest." Paper rustled and the pen scratched.

Billie couldn't bring herself to sit up and face the doc.

"Have you checked the news? Found out if anything happened out that way?"

"Happened?" Billie wasn't sure if she was ready to share the potential realities.

"Billie, you had a knife. You cut yourself. I doubt anything happened, but have there been reports of any ...." Doc's linen pants shushed against her leather chair. "Have you checked to see if anyone has been stabbed?"

Billie sat up and swung her feet to the floor. "Yes. I did. And yes, someone was stabbed. And she died. In the exact area where I woke up, or whatever you call it. Well, a couple of miles away." Damn her motor mouth of guilt. And damn her ping-ponging psyche. Overcome by the likelihood that she'll rot in hell for bringing her justice fantasies to life one minute. Ready to punch strangers in the face for cutting in line at the coffee shop the next.

Doc nodded. "I see." She set her notepad aside and tented her fingers. Her cheeks pinked. She stared at Billie for what seemed like an hour. "I'm going to suggest ..." she clamped her lips together. "No, I'm going to insist that you avoid the newspaper. No more editing the endings. No more red pen of appropriate justice."

Billie stared at her psychologist, a woman trained to find answers, to get to the bottom of the truth of Billie's own special brand of psychosis. "Really? You think I should just avoid the whole thing?"

Doc sighed. "For now. Is there any chance you could stay with this boyfriend of yours? Have someone with you at night in case you wander? Does he know about this?"

Billie nodded. A little white lie. He didn't know about the dead woman in Ivy Valley.

"As you know, we have confidentiality between us." She bit her lip. "But do you trust this subway man to keep his mouth shut?"

"I do."

"Good." Doc reached behind her and picked up a prescription pad. "Get this filled and start taking them today. That's step one. Step two is support. As in regular counselling. Maybe we can nip this thing now and prevent any further ... incidents."

"Have you seen the paper?" Bruce slid the Grantham Herald across the island between his beer bottle and her wine glass and tapped the open page.

Billie shoved it back to him. "Nope. Can't. Doctor's orders. Just like staying with you, I'm to avoid the news. And I'm not to edit." Her fingers itched to pull a pen out of her purse. But what ending would she give this crime? What fate did she deserve?

"Billie, a woman died just miles from where I picked you up. Stabbed." He put his hand over hers. "Just tell me, do you think it was you?"

She yanked her hand away. "I don't know." Her voice screeched from her throat. She dropped her chin and shut her eyes. "I'm sorry. I really don't know. But — maybe."

She couldn't bear to look at him. Didn't want him to see the truth. That she was drowning in a cesspool of disgust and fear and sin and hell. But at the surface of that pool was the divine light of power and strength and righteous indignation. That woman deserved her fate. And if Billie was the hand of God, wasn't that her own fate? Her destiny? Her super-power? And didn't she owe it to God to carry out his bidding?

"Look, I know you were in that foog state of mind thing."

"F-you-g."

He cocked his head. "Billie. Whatever." He circled the island and slid behind her stool, draped his arms over her shoulders, and rested his evening whiskers on her cheek. "It's a real disorder. It wouldn't be your fault." He kissed her cheek and perched on the seat next to her. He smoothed her hair and ran a thumb across her forehead like half a baptism. "I mean, damn, it's scary as hell, the possibility. But shit. Pretty sexy. In a sick, twisted, warped, Batchick kind of way."

She held her breath for a few heartbeats. "Do you think so?"

"Hell yeah, I think so." He tugged her off her stool and pulled her toward him. "Except that I can't see you harming a soul."

"No souls. But what about the living? The soulless and the callous and the murderers." She smacked the newspaper. "The rapists."

"No one. It's just not in you." He grabbed her waist with both hands and shimmied her hips back and forth. "But if it *was* you, well, hell. I knew it the first minute I met you, Billie. You are badass."

"If not a little crazy." Her cheeks flushed with heat.

"Crazy good." He kissed her.

She gripped his shirt in both hands. "What if it is me? What if I get caught? I mean, it's justice, right? But it's illegal too. That whole eye-for-an-eye thing I grew up with. They killed someone, I took their life. They raped someone, I took their ability to rape away." She swallowed. "Theoretically." She rested her head on his chest. "If I've taken lives, should I not die as punishment? And what about whoever puts me to death? Is it their turn next? I mean, where does it end?"

"And that little realization is just one of many reasons I skip church and God and just live my life my way. Because no matter what you do, you just can't win." He hugged her hard. "I think you'd be less murderer, more vigilante superhero."

She pulled away. "I'm no superhero."

"Aren't you? Fighting for truth, justice. The Canadian way?"

She laughed. "The Canadian way? So after I fix their wagons I should apologize and offer them a double-double?"

He roared. "Yeah, that's about right." He scratched at the stubble on his chin.

Her body flushed with warmth at the memory of his whiskers against her cheeks when he kissed her. Against her breasts and her belly. Against her inner thighs.

He took a gulp of beer. "You need a name. For the press. You know, just in case. If you have a name, you'll gain a following. No one will want to convict you."

"You're having a little too much fun with the possibility that I slice people up in my off hours."

He shrugged. "Maybe. Maybe I'd be okay with it. Maybe I'd even join in your crusade."

"I doubt that. But I'll play along. What is my superhero name?"

"Billie the Badass? Or Billie with the sweet ass." He flashed his eyebrows up and down grabbed her behind with both hands.

She grinned and slapped his arm.

He pulled her body to his and stared into her eyes. "And I can be your sidekick. Robin to your Batchick." He kissed her forehead. "Your Kato." He licked her cheek. "Your Bucky Barnes." He nibbled her lips. "Your, your ... Your Jimmy Olsen." He buried his nose behind her ear and kissed her neck.

Adrenaline flooded her body and pooled between her legs. "More like my Dum Dum Dugan."

He snickered into the tender skin at her collarbone, swept her into his arms, and headed for the bedroom. His long arm reached around her body and he caressed her breast with one hand.

She closed her eyes and leaned against his shoulder. "Maybe my Jughead Jones."

FRIDAY, AUGUST 14TH

B ILLIE HIT THE SEND BUTTON AND CLOSED HER laptop. First freelance job complete. Money in her bank account. Or at least her PayPal account. She guzzled what remained of her tepid tea and checked the stove clock.

Plenty of time to shower and put on her best business suit. The one she'd never worn. Never had a reason to. But today was different. Today blossomed with possibilities. Today she was going upstairs to be interviewed. Her chance to vault out of the proofing pool and lounge by the side, champagne glass in hand, with the other editing elite.

After that? The perfect topper to the day. Her regular Friday dinner with Bruce. Not that they were on a schedule anymore. He slept over at her house, and she at his. They went to the gym together any day of the week they felt like it, met for a quick lunch when he had meetings in her end of town. Her normal scheduled existence had become life by the seat of her pants. It scared her at first, but she'd grown into the randomness of it. But Friday dinner, that was a staple. No matter what. And that tiny slice of schedule brought her a huge helping of peace and comfort.

Two hours later, she sat at her desk, licked her fingers, and glued a stray hair to her head. She'd worn her hair in a high ponytail, but not confined to a bun. Bruce's recommendation. He said it made her look sleek and professional, but not uptight. She dabbed rose gloss across her lips and used one fingernail to separate a clump of mascaraed lashes. She'd never felt less uptight in her life.

She blinked against her new contact lenses. It was like there were shards of glass in each eye instead of malleable plastic that didn't hide her beauty behind thick rims. Bruce meant well, but Billie couldn't reconcile beauty with brains. Contact lenses with accomplishment. But he had more experience climbing ladders than she did, corporate or otherwise.

"Are those pants?"

Katherine had snuck up on her, stealthy despite her clunky Guess heels and her jingling jewelry.

Billie cleared her throat. "Yes. A suit."

Katherine's doom brow shot up. "Huh. Looks nice." She twirled one pointed finger in the general direction of Billie's face. "I like the lenses." Katherine walked away.

Billie sat in stunned silence. No zinger? No threats to her safety? Was that an actual … compliment? Her hand trembled. It was a bad omen. The calm before the shit storm. Katherine had pulled some nasty trick and doomed Billie's chances at the job. Undermined her, cut her off at the pass.

Breathe, Billie. She closed her eyes and gripped the edge of the desk with her fingertips. There was a chance that Katherine was being sincere. That she simply liked Billie's suit.

When 7-Eleven closes on Christmas Day.

She opened her eyes and shot red ink poison darts through Katherine's open office door.

A calendar reminder popped up on Billie's screen. Fifteen minutes until the interview. She gathered her editing samples and tucked them in her briefcase alongside references from authors and the editor of Dreckula's business card.

She clicked the case shut, tossed a piece of gum in her mouth, and chewed it one hundred times before spitting it into the garbage. She stood, smoothed the front of her suit jacket, and shook her leg. The rayon of her pants dislodged from the sheath. She knew there was a reason she didn't wear pants.

"You'll be great." Jeffrey came out from behind his cubicle wall and looked her up and down. "Twirl."

Billie giggled and did as he asked.

"Whew, honey, your ass looks hot in those slacks. You ought to ditch the librarian garb and update your closet."

"Well, if I get this job, that'll be first order of business." She'd wanted to expand her choices, add some figure-flattering tight-fitting clothes. Bruce seemed to think she had the body for it.

"It's a date!" Jeffrey clapped his hands.

"A date?"

"You don't think you're going shopping without me, do you? Girl, I can hook you up."

Billie nodded. "All right. A date. I'm ready to be hooked."

"I didn't stumble once, didn't say um or er or any of the obvious nervous tells, and she kept zinging questions my way and I fielded them all, deflected the onslaught with my gold bands of justice, *ptiu, ptiu, ptiu.*" Billie held her arms up and mimed Wonder Woman's patented wrist action.

Bruce laughed. "I'm not surprised. I knew you'd kick ass. When do you hear back?" He shoved a big bite of rare steak, dripping blood and juices, into his mouth. He gestured to the waiter, tapped his empty beer bottle and Billie's mostly empty glass of Petit Verdot with his fork.

"They interview through Tuesday, thin the herd, and bring the shining stars back for one more interview. With the editor-in-chief."

"Right to the top dog. This must be quite the position."

"Well, if I do get it, I'll be catapulted about three rungs ahead of where I am. A few years later, who knows? Maybe I'm the editor-in-chief." She wiggled her eyebrows.

The waiter set a full bottle of beer in front of Bruce and another half-carafe of wine next to Billie's glass.

"Jeffrey is so sure I'll get it, he's already planning a shopping trip so I'll have the right wardrobe for the position."

Bruce screwed up his face. "Jeffrey? Isn't that the weasel?"

Billie nodded and swallowed a mouthful of prawn risotto. "He's not so bad. Ever since I stopped him from getting beat up, he's kind of become my best friend."

"I thought I was your best friend."

"Okay, he's my gay best friend."

Bruce raised his bottle. "To Billie. Future editor-in-chief. Superhero to Grantham's victims of crime." He reached across the table with his other hand and brushed a thumb across her cheek. "Woman of my dreams."

Her face flushed with warmth and she averted her eyes. "Aw, gee. Thanks." She clinked her wine glass to his bottle. "Cheers." She downed the remaining wine and filled her glass. "Can we have pie?"

Tuesday Morning

BILLIE STARED AT THE POLICE ARTIST'S RENDERING on the front page. A sketch of two suspects in a string of robberies and assaults on women, including one rape.

She scanned the article, her finger traversing the newsprint. Police were concerned that the dynamic duo would escalate and end up murdering someone in the commission of one of their crimes. Women were warned to avoid dark streets or alleys, never walk alone, keep their purses close to their bodies.

It's always up to the women to change their habits. To avoid becoming a victim. How about the cops catch the perpetrators and the courts actually prosecute them for their crimes and keep the streets safe for law-abiding citizens? That would be a nice change.

She eyeballed the familiar tribal neck tattoo and the bandana. That was new. She opened the page to find grainy screen grabs from a shitty security camera. No matter the quality of the pictures, they were easily recognizable. Bat Head and his disciple. What was his name? Tom or Tim or … Todd. That was it. But Todd had walked away from Bat Head the day he'd assaulted Billie on the subway. Maybe bullying a woman with one leg wasn't enough for Todd to risk arrest, but clearly Bat Head was in charge and Todd had fallen right back into step.

She read the article three times. They had no fingerprints, only eyewitness testimony and a few security videos. Anyone who knew Bat Head's swagger and his habit of yanking his pants up every other step might recognize him. Or might write it off as just another anonymous teenager, like so many others roaming the streets after dark without proper parental supervision.

But Billie knew. It was him.

She dialled Bruce's number. "You aren't going to believe who made the morning paper."

"So, what's his fate?" Bruce sat at her breakfast counter hunched over the newspaper. "The little bastard has really taken a bad turn. Rape?" He shook his head. "Shit." He reached across the counter and snatched a red pen from her pencil cup.

Billie put her hand over the pen and pushed it away from the paper. "No editing, remember? If I do, and something happens, it might prove it's me."

"And if we don't, and something happens, what does that prove?"

Billie shrugged. "That I'm not a murderer?"

Bruce put the end of the pen between his lips and sucked on it. "Vigilante superhero, remember?" He touched the red tip to the page. "Come on. You know you want to."

Oh, yes, she did. "He needs real jail time. He's a good-looking kid. He'd find out soon enough what rape is."

Bruce nodded. "I like it. An eye for an eye. Theoretically speaking." He winked, and began to edit.

"Or maybe he should meet the same fate as those clowns. Except for the dying thing." Though that wouldn't be so bad either.

THURSDAY, THE 20TH

BILLIE VIEWED THE SIDEWALK AS IF THROUGH A glass tunnel. The periphery blurred, shadows jumped, and light refracted, her focus laser sharp on her target. Gold Tooth sat hunched in the same spot he'd occupied for more than a week. Perhaps longer, but had he been there before, she'd never noticed. His presence only became clear when she was overwhelmed by her own guilt, by the possibility she was no different, no better than him.

If she had murdered, it hadn't been with intent. And if Gold Tooth really had saved her life, if he hadn't pulled the trigger that killed her parents and took her leg — how could she judge him? The courts had already done that. And he still had to answer to God.

She stopped two steps beyond his rumpled form, took a deep breath, turned back, and plopped down on the pavement beside him, her eyes firmly on his face.

He smiled at her and shook his cup. He cocked his head and squinted. "Saw you the other day." His voice was old and gravelly. "You never help a poor man out." He shimmied the cup again.

"Help you?" Her voice spat from her mouth. She took a breath. "Why should I help you?" She couldn't hold his gaze. She looked away and stared at an ad on a bus stop bench across the street. She focussed on the hefty bosom of a scrawny model selling vodka and struggled to keep her breath steady, to keep her butt planted on the cement. To not jump up and flee.

She could feel his googly eyes boring into her.

"I know you?"

She cut her eyes his way then refocused on the boobs across the street. "I think you do."

"You work in a shelter?"

"No."

He shifted his weight and extended his legs. One real leg. One peg leg. He tapped her prosthesis with his. "Me too."

Her heart sank. Did he have that back in 1993? She scoured her memory and tried to focus her eleven-year-old's eyes away from the blade, away from the bandana and the tooth, away from the barrel of the gun. But she just couldn't see anything else.

She swallowed. Sympathy would be the last thing this monster posing as a regular man deserved. He must remain a monster. If he wasn't, her whole life was a lie.

"How'd it happen?" She mustered a hoarse whisper. Her red pen drew a pig's nose over his, though his wasn't much better. He had the bulbous, open-pored, glowing proboscis of a lifetime drunk. She added ink fangs protruding from his mouth. Gold ones.

"Lower extremity arterial calcification."

She gawked at him. "Excuse me?"

"Don't make me say it twice, lady."

"No, of course not." She tugged at the hem of her jacket. "When?"

"Five years back. Doc hacked it off in prison. Can't afford no fancy foot like you got."

She nodded, returned her eyeballs to tits and vodka. "Why prison?"

"I done something real bad." His voice cracked.

Billie gave him a sideways glance. "What was that?"

"I was messin' where I shouldn'ta been messin.' Cop and his lady died. Little girl got sho-." His body went rigid. He inched his head around until his eyes met hers. "Oh, no. No way."

She raised one hand and gave him a tiny wave.

Tears sprung from his eyes and left clean tracks on his dusty cheeks. "Is it you? Is it really you?" He rested the back of his head on the brick wall behind him and squeezed his eyes shut. "Wilma? Willie?"

"It's Wilhelmina. I go by Billie."

He nodded, his eyes still shut, a crooked grin on his face. "Billie. I remember now." He opened his eyes and turned to her. "He was gonna kill you." He looked away and wiped his face with one hand.

A man in a suit that probably cost a month of Billie's salary dropped a toonie in Gold Tooth's cup. He smiled and nodded at the man who didn't even slow down. "Fuck you. Fuck you very much."

Billie snorted. "You are saying that. I couldn't tell before if it was thank or, well, that other word."

"Fuck. Go ahead, little girl, say it. It don't bite."

She rubbed her palms together. "The Crown Prosecutor, Mr. Robbins, said you'd found God. Had you lost him before?"

"Oh, yeah. Lost him big. I'd been doing everything wrong. Thinking that God was watching all that? Well, I couldn't deal with it. So I just let him go."

"You found him in prison?"

He chuckled. "Nah. I found him in my heart. I was just lying on the exercise yard floor with a shiv in my gut when it happened."

"But you say that word out loud. He doesn't like that."

"Well, my God likes it. Out loud is honest. And I like it too. Says everything all in four little letters. Now don't get me wrong. I appreciate the cash. But most folks ignore me or dig a quarter out of their pocket. Five buck coffee in the other hand. So that's my sanity keeper. Mumbled thanks that flips 'em off at the same time." He grinned wide. Next to his gold tooth, the rest were rotted, some down to stumps.

"How long have you been out of prison?"

"Ah, they didn't tell you, did they?"

She shook her head.

"Paroled a while back. Been three winters." He swallowed and wiped fresh tears from his face. "I always wanted to tell you how sorry I was. But you never came to any of the hearings."

"I wasn't invited."

"Well, I still am. Sorry, I mean. More than ever. If I hadn't been doing that deal in that alley, you'd have parents. And a leg."

She wiped her own cheeks dry. "Too late for that." She dug a five-dollar bill from her purse and tucked it into the cup. "Well, Mr. Dickinson. I've got to get to work." She stood.

He fished the bill out and handed it back to her. "Call me Tony. And I don't need your money. Don't deserve your kindness. I've taken enough from you."

She took the money and tucked it in her pocket. "Most everyone deserves kindness." She turned and walked away.

FRIDAY THE 21ST

BILLIE ROLLED THE SCROLL WHEEL ON HER MOUSE and read line after line of garbage on the screen. How did these people get past the slush pile? She had no appetite for proofing, each spelling misstep, each rule of grammar murdered on the page like a bite of liver dripping with ketchup and onions when she was nine. Cover that shit up with all the metaphors and adjectives you want, she still couldn't choke it down.

"Fucking crap," she mumbled. She smiled. Gold Tooth was right. Saying it out loud didn't bite. She bit a section of apple in two.

The ring of her phone, shrill and intense, startled her. Her hand jerked and tightened against the mouse's body. In one movement she'd highlighted and deleted most of one shitty paragraph. The literary world should thank her.

She eyed the call display, not in the mood for Katherine, or for cold calls from office supply companies that dial every number until they find the one dolt in the building willing to commit to buying toner at criminal markups. Her brows arched. It was Debra, executive assistant to the editor-in-chief.

Billie lunged for the receiver, dropped it on her desk with a clatter, snatched it up, and put it to her ear. She swore a blue streak in her head, but her mouth said, "Good morning, Debra, Billie here. What can I do for you?"

"Hello, Billie. We're letting everyone know the result of the interviews. We've shrunk the candidates down to a short-list."

Billie swallowed and closed her eyes. Next was the easy let

down.

"Can you come for a follow-up interview on Tuesday at ten?"

Billie squeezed her closed lids more closed and hit the rewind button. Follow-up interview. Tuesday. "Yes. Yes, I can do that." She opened her eyes and glanced around the office. Jeffrey had rolled his chair into the aisle.

She gave him a thumbs up.

He flashed both of his thumbs up and grinned like a lunatic.

"Tenth floor, in Ms. Armbruster's office."

"I'll be there." Billie knew all too well where the editor-in-chief's office was. "Thank you so much, Debra." She eased the receiver back on its cradle and stared at it for a few seconds.

"You're in, right? I told you!" Jeffrey put his hands on her shoulders and gave her a playful shake. "Tonight. Shopping. You and me. Girl, I'm going to deck you out."

Billie laughed. "I'm in. But not tonight, tomorrow. Tonight is date night."

Jeffrey pouted. "Aren't you living with him or something? Isn't every night date night?"

"Not living. We just stay over once in a while." Like, every night for almost two weeks. But it didn't matter. Date night was sacred.

Billie flung the glass doors of the office building open and freed herself from its crumbling cocoon. She skipped down the marble steps and strode toward the subway, her eyes making contact with every face, offering each passerby who dared to share her zest for life a sharp nod and a heartfelt "good afternoon." Not that there were many of them.

The business end of downtown cleared out early on Fridays, and she'd chosen to work late, clean up some of the backlog of proofreading, and meet up with Bruce directly from work. The sun slipped behind the tall buildings on its descent into nighttime. The towers cast the sidewalk into eerie shadow. Billie shivered at the evening chill.

A breeze caught her hair and tossed it about. A wave of tresses flew in front of her face. She pushed it aside and tucked it behind her ear. A month ago, she'd have captured it, tethered it to the base of her skull with an elastic band, and wrapped it tightly in a bun. Heck, she'd have never allowed it loose to begin with.

She fluffed it with both hands and let it fly free, let the wind have its way with her hair and twist it into knots.

A man jostled her from behind and rushed on past, his suit jacket open and flapping in the wind. A bike courier, his basket empty of deliveries, nearly ran her down, his eyes averted. Did no one want to share her good vibrations?

Her path crossed in front of an alley. She made eye contact with a young man in the shadows, leaning against the brick building.

He pushed away from the building and stepped from the anonymity of the alley. He held his arms out, both hands pointing at his crotch. "Hey momma, you want a piece of this? 'Cause I'm gonna get me some of that." He gestured at her chest with one hand and assaulted her with his eyes.

The bandana, the neck tattoos, the swagger. She'd recognized him immediately. But he didn't seem to have a clue who she was.

He blocked her path, looked up the sidewalk past her then over his shoulder. "Come on, baby." He grabbed her around her waist and pulled her into his body, his other hand in his pocket. "Don't scream and don't try to run or I'll shoot you, bitch." The stench of whisky rolled from his mouth, his hoodie stunk of sweet, acrid smoke. His pocket bulged with what could be a gun.

Or probably just his pointed finger, the little faker.

He pulled her into the alley and she let him do it. He dragged her behind a Dumpster and she didn't resist. Adrenaline pumped through her body, her hands trembling. Not in fear. In anticipation. This was no fugue incident. This was real life. And she was ready for it.

She elbowed him in the ribs and ripped herself free of his grip. "Get your hands off me." She dug her hand into her open purse. Her fingers found her can of pepper spray.

The boy pointed at her and laughed. "Shit, maybe you're too dumb to fuck."

She glanced down. Her prosthetic foot rested in the gutter that ran down the middle of the lane. Mucky water dripped into her snakeskin flat. Filth wicked up her pant leg. She raised her eyes to meet his. "What's the matter, Bat Head? You not man enough?"

He cocked his head. "Bat Head?"

"Yeah. Bat Head. You don't have what it takes, do you? Can't get it up for the gimpy chick?" She shook the swill from her foot and took a step toward him.

He took two steps backward. "No fucking way." He rubbed his eyes.

Billie advanced. "I hear you've graduated from bullying innocent bystanders on the subway to actual crime. Theft. Drugs." She raised one hand and pushed on his chest with her fingertips. "Rape."

He tripped on a crate that had fallen from a pile of wood stacked against the brick building. He landed on his ass and scrambled to his feet. "It can't be you."

"Can't be who?"

"You. Gimpy chick. Shit, look at you. You're hot." He smirked. "But if it is you, then this is my lucky day." He shoved his hand in his pocket. "You owe me, bitch."

"I owe you?" She laughed. "What do I owe you, you thug? Comeuppance? Another kick in the pants? Retribution perhaps?"

He pulled a knife from his pocket and launched the blade. "Then maybe I owe you." He lunged at her.

She jumped sideways. His knife sliced the air, his body bolted forward. She caught the seat of his pants with the toe of her wet foot and shoved him to the ground, face first. He rolled onto his back and jumped to his feet. "You crazy bitch. I'm done playing with you."

He raced toward her and grabbed her hair. He pulled her head back, shoved his face into hers, and pinned her arms. "You're mine now." He pushed her to the ground. She landed on her knees and dropped her purse. At the sound of his zipper coming down, she spun around and shot pepper spray at his face.

He swore and swiped his face, his cheeks red from pepper, one eye watery.

She'd been too far away.

He covered one eye with one hand and held the knife out with the other. "Shit, I'm gonna cut you, whore."

She focused on the glinting blade and froze. Wet garbage, filthy asphalt, tall buildings closed in on her. She shut her eyes and shook her head. No. This was not 1993. She was not a helpless little girl.

She bounced to her feet, stood in fighting stance, her good leg in front, prosthesis behind, her fists raised and ready, the pepper spray still in her firm grasp.

He dropped his arms to his sides. "Seriously? You think you can take me?" He shook his head and pounced.

She weaved left, planted her good leg and brought her prosthetic foot to his groin.

He stopped mid-attack, like a DVD on pause. He fell to his knees and grabbed his crotch. His knife skittered across the pavement and came to rest in the gutter a few yards away.

Billie bent over him. "Yeah, I think I can." She shot pepper directly into his face.

He screamed, his hands flew to his face.

Her head ping-ponged, her gaze cutting from his face to the knife that rested a few feet behind her and back. Her fingers itched to snatch it up. To slice him into ribbons, to feel his hot blood against her skin. To make him truly pay for his vile crimes. There had to be more victims than the reporters knew about. He was ripe to reoffend. Hell, he was probably a serial killer in the making.

He swept one leg up and kicked her in the stomach. The air left her and she stumbled backwards, landing hard on the alley floor.

Bat Head scurried toward her and pinned her to the ground.

She stared up into his swollen eyes, blazing with hatred and oozing tears. She spat at him.

"Oh, that's it, you fucking bitch. Now you're going to know what being a whore feels like." He backhanded her across the face.

Her head snapped to one side. Her mouth filled with liquid metal and rage.

"Get off me, you fucking little bastard." She jerked her body and tried to buck him off.

He laid one forearm across her chest. "I'm done talking, skank." He ripped her blouse open with his other hand.

She grabbed at the sleeves of his hoodie, squirmed beneath him and struggled to breathe, unable to scream.

He fumbled with his pants, undid the button of hers and tried to yank them down. "Fuck, why you bitches gotta wear skin-tight jeans?"

Billie got one knee up, planted her heel and pushed. She scooted back a foot.

He scrabbled along the payment with her and took her by both shoulders. He lifted her upper body until their noses were so close she could hear his inhale whistle through snot. "Stop moving," he said, his voice a low growl, "or I'll bash your pretty head in." He pushed her.

Her shoulders and head hit the pavement. Her right arm flopped to the side. Something cut into her elbow.

Bat Head shoved one hand in her bra and squeezed her breast, his other hand grabbed at her pants and tried to rip them from her body. His waistband was around his thighs, his erection tenting his loose boxers.

She'd figured he'd have Batman briefs.

She scanned the ground, her eyes wild, her heart about to explode. That'd show him. She'd die during the commission of his crime. That was first-degree murder.

No, God damn it, that was not the way she and Bruce had written it. The little prick had to go to jail with not one more victim. But maybe it was too late for that.

Out of the corner of her eye, she spied the knife. She cut her eyes to him. He was all wrapped up in the difficult task of stripping tight jeans from a woman who wouldn't quit kicking and bucking. He had them down far enough that she could see most of her white cotton underpants. And he could see them too, his thug eyes on her private underthings. His grimy, disgusting hands on her flesh, touching things he had no right to.

She shook her head.

No. Fucking. Way.

She scooted the blade closer with her elbow until it was close enough to grab.

Bat Head curled his fingertips around the elastic of her panties and smirked. He looked into her eyes and yanked on them.

She thrust the blade into his belly and held her breath. It slid in easier than a steak knife through tenderloin.

His face twisted and contorted. His boxer bulge deflated on impact. He squeaked something unintelligible.

Billie pushed him off of her and rolled away. She crawled a few feet, filth and rocks and broken glass digging into her palms, until she bounded to her feet. She ran to the alley entrance, the knife still gripped in her hand. At the sidewalk, she screamed for help.

The street was empty except for a lone woman exiting Billie's office building. The woman ran to Billie, stiletto heels clacking against the cement. "Oh my God, Wilhelmina?"

Billie looked up into the confused face of Katherine. "Call the police."

Katherine dug in her purse and pulled out her iPhone. "I need cops and an ambulance at Seven-fifteen Fourth Avenue. The alley entrance on the east side." She squatted in front of Billie and examined her. "Assault," she said into the phone. She pulled what was left of Billie's blouse over her partially exposed breast. "Make that rape."

Katherine tossed her phone into her bag, took off her silk blazer, probably Holt Renfrew, and draped it around Billie's shoulders.

Billie's body began to tremble. "I think I killed him."

A patrol car careened into the mouth of the alley, sirens wailing and lights flashing.

Billie winced.

The doctor put one final stitch in the knife wound on her elbow.

She sat on the hospital bed in a scant gown that opened in the back. Her skin crawled with gooseflesh from the air conditioning and the remnants of Bat Head's hands on her body.

She'd already undergone the debasing experience of a sexual

assault exam, even though she told them he didn't get the opportunity. For evidence, they said. The crime geeks made her strip, took her clothes, swabbed her and scraped her and clipped her nails. She felt like victim and criminal at the same time, like she was being assaulted all over again.

"Billie, what happened? Are you all right?" Bruce stormed into the tiny room and filled it with his presence and his voice and his cologne.

Billie put on her best outside smile. "Sorry, I can't make date night tonight."

He touched her cheek near the stitch on her swollen upper lip.

"Billie," the doctor laid a hand over her knee.

She flinched.

"We'll get you some morphine for the pain. Try to rest."

"No, I just want to go home."

The doctor sighed. "All right. I'll get you some pain killers to go." He turned to Bruce. "Take care of her."

Bruce glared at him. "She does a fine job of that on her own." He waited for the doctor to leave the room before turning to her. "What the hell? Who did this to you?"

"Bat Head."

His ruddy complexion boiled over with rage and turned the colour of a red velvet cupcake. "How? Did he follow you?"

"He didn't know it was me at first. When he figured it out, all hell broke loose."

"Billie," Bruce looked at the ceiling and inhaled until his chest puffed out, "you didn't bait him? Didn't try to make our edits come true?"

She squinted and shook her head. Was he blaming her for being attacked? She was the victim, for God's sake. "It was coincidence. You know, those things you and Doc Kroft keep saying all of this is? I say baloney. It's fated. I just know it."

He put his arms around her. She rested her undamaged cheek on his chest and closed her eyes.

"Billie, did he—?" he whispered, his voice more raspy than usual.

She shook her head. "He tried." She pulled away, tears dripping into the stitch on her lip, the salt stinging through the numbing cream that was fast wearing off. "I stabbed him."

Bruce's brow furrowed. "Is he dead?"

"I don't know. They won't tell me. But I had to. He was going to …." She looked away. "And the hate in his eyes? I honestly figured he would kill me after. We said he'd become a serial killer, right? I'd be victim number one. His trigger." She gathered the hospital sheet into both fists. "What if he dies? I didn't mean to kill him. I just wanted to save myself."

"Did you have a chance to get away? Could you have run?"

The threat of tears stung her eyes and snot dripped from her nose. "Maybe."

He nodded. "But you chose to play superhero? Billie, it's not real. You're not Batman for God's sake."

"Of course I'm not Batman. I'm not an idiot, Bruce. I'm not crazy." She crossed her arms over her chest and grimaced at the pain in her ribs.

"Hey, how you doing?" Katherine stood in the doorway, her designer-clad shoulder leaning against the jamb.

Billie mustered a weak smile. "I'm okay." She gestured at Bruce. "This is my boyfriend, Bruce. This," she looked at him and raised one eyebrow, "is my boss, Katherine."

Bruce stepped around the bed and held his hand out. Katherine smiled and shook it. "Nice to meet you. Billie, you never told me about Bruce."

Billie blinked. Had they become girlfriends now that Katherine had shown a modicum of human kindness? Was Billie obligated to reveal her private affairs to the harridan in the corner office? "Sorry." It was all she could manage.

"Well, I just wanted to check in on you. If you need to take some time off, just let me know."

"I'll be in on Monday." And at that interview Tuesday morning. Maybe that was Katherine's plan, to sideswipe Billie's chances with faux kindness. "I'm sorry about your jacket. They took it for evidence. I'll replace it." And her life's savings would be out the window.

Katherine waved her hand in the air. "Don't worry about it. I got it at a thrift shop for ten bucks."

Billie gawked at her. "But, wasn't it Holt Renfrew?"

"Hell yes, it was. Three or four seasons old. You have to dig, but sometimes there are good brands and designers with the original tags still on." She huffed. "You think I can afford to look this good on the pittance they pay me to manage the proofing pool?" Katherine rolled her eyes. "Puh-lease." She nodded at Bruce. "Well, it was nice to meet you. And seriously, Billie, call if you need some time off." She waved and slipped into the hallway.

Billie listened to the click of thrift store designer heels echo down the hallway and stared at the empty doorframe. She was left stunned in the wake of Katherine's Chanel cloud.

"Isn't she the shrew?" Bruce sat on the edge of the bed and took Billie's hand in his. "She seemed pretty nice to me."

"I don't know who that was, but it's not the Katherine I know." Thrift stores? Actual concern? No name-calling or backhanded compliments? What was happening to the world?

"Maybe she's got a good heart under that mask of makeup and hairspray and fake nails."

Billie snorted. "No way. You be careful around her. She discards men like used dental floss. She's a succubus."

"A what?"

She smiled at him. "Never mind."

"Billie Fullalove?"

She turned to find a police officer standing in the doorway, his uniform pressed and tucked in, his hat under one arm. A wave of comfort and safety blanketed her. It was an old and familiar feeling that she hadn't experienced in years. The same feeling she got every time her father donned his uniform, every time she helped him starch his collar and iron crisp pleats into the sleeves and the pant legs. "Yes, that's me."

"I'm Constable Donnelly. I have to take your statement."

She nodded, ready to tell her story, eager to hear of Bat Head's fate. "Will he be all right?"

"He's in recovery. Apparently, you nicked an artery or an organ or something. Serious, but he'll live."

A heady mix rippled through her. Relief with the distinct aftertaste of disappointment.

The officer walked her through the attack and made notes.

As she told her tale, the heat rose in her cheeks and she sat straighter on the gurney. When she told of the stabbing, she mimed the action and thrust her empty hand into a mental red-ink reproduction of Bat Head's lean torso.

"And the knife you stabbed him with. That was his?"

"Yes. He dropped it when I pepper-sprayed him." She bent her arm and held it up for inspection. "I think that's what cut my elbow."

"Well, some cops say you should never fight back. That it's better to give in to save your life." He approached the bed and put one hand on her shoulder. "I come from the 'fight like hell' camp." He held his hand out. "Keep up the good work, Billie."

She shook his hand. "I'll try."

"I'll have this typed up. You'll need to come by the station and sign it over the weekend. But for now, go home and relax." He tipped his hat and left.

"Billie?" Bruce kneeled on the floor and pulled the legs of hospital pyjama pants over her feet.

"What?"

He helped her stand, pulled the pants up and tied the drawstring around her waist. "Next time you play superhero? Call for backup first."

WEDNESDAY

EVERY MORNING PLAYED OUT THE SAME. GOLD Tooth, Tony Dickinson, sat in his usual spot. Billie nodded at him on the way by. He would smile and put his hand over his cup, sometimes offer her a quiet good morning.

Each day her desire to see him dead waned. Her fantasies of his dismembered body parts strewn in the alley, or him hanging by the neck from one of the gargoyles on her apartment building, faded. He looked less like a giant mound of shit, and more like a huge, slightly melted, Oh! Henry. Her red pen quit drawing horns on his head and a trident in his hands and replaced them with a fedora and a submarine sandwich. She even bought him food. But she knew he wouldn't accept if from her, so she gave her offerings to Bruce to deliver.

Every day, Billie summoned the strength to ask Tony the one question she needed an answer to. Finally, after a week of avoiding it, she steeled herself for the truth, and eased her body, still aching from her run-in with Bat Head, to the hard cement next to Tony.

"You're not going to try to give me money again, are you, Billie?"

She shook her head and handed him a cup of hot black coffee and a bag with two apple fritters. "Just breakfast."

He peered in the bag. "Oh, bless you." He took a huge bite of sweet pastry. "What happened to your face?"

She touched the stitch on her lip. The story had been numero uno on the office hot gossip list. By the time she went for a follow-up interview yesterday, even the barista in the lobby coffee shop knew what had happened. There was no question it was Katherine who spread the story around. Billie hadn't figured out her motives. But if the sympathy gave her a leg up with the editor-in-chief, well, dang, who was she to complain? "I got attacked last Friday."

"Attacked? You okay? He get arrested?"

"I'm fine. He's still in the hospital, but cuffed to the bed."

"Hospital? What you do to him?"

"I stabbed him with his own knife."

Tony laughed and nudged his shoulder against hers. "Good for you. You have to testify?"

"Eventually. But you know how slow the system works. And he has to recover first. But whenever they get around to trying him, I'll be there." She scratched a non-existent itch on the back of her hand. "Tony, I have to ask you something."

He nodded and stuffed another mouthful of fried dough in his mouth.

Billie took a deep breath and blew it out slowly between pursed lips. "What's his name?"

Tony froze. He swallowed hard and took a swig of coffee. "Who?"

"Come on, don't mess with me. You know who."

He looked at his lap. "I can't."

"Why not? It's been twenty-two years. He got to go about his life like nothing ever happened. Live free and out in the open. It's more than my parents got. Heck, it's more than I got." She shifted and turned to face him. "Please, I need to know."

Tony's head shook in that Parkinson's-like wobble he had. "He hasn't been free."

"What do you mean? You keep tabs on him?"

"My parole officer keeps in touch. She fills me in. That no-good scum is out now, but he was in jail most of the last fifteen years."

"For what?" She could barely eke out a whisper.

"Rape. Of a fourteen-year-old girl."

Billie shut her eyes and balled her fists. If only Tony had told the truth back in ninety-three, this guy would've been arrested and convicted. He'd have never had the chance to rape anyone. That's two young girls whose lives he'd ruined. Billie bet there were many more.

Her eyes flickered open. "I need his name."

"He'll kill me." His face contorted and pleaded with her.

She squinted. "I don't care," she deadpanned.

"I deserve that." Tony turned his gaze to his lap. "And it don't matter anymore."

Billie sighed. "What do you mean?"

"I got some cancer."

"What kind?"

"It's in my liver. Don't have a lot of time left."

"I'm sorry."

He huffed. "No you're not."

She touched his arm. "Yes. I am."

He burst into tears. "I'm so sorry, Billie. I think the cancer is my proper sentence. It's what I deserve for what happened to your family. For what happened to you. I've hated myself. Hated him. It didn't have to happen." He slumped forward and his shoulders convulsed.

Billie put her arm around him and hugged his body into hers.

He sobbed, his tears soaking through her light cardigan and into her skin.

They sat that way for several minutes, oblivious to the stares of passersby. He was probably accustomed to stranger's stares. She certainly was.

His sobbing subsided and he pulled away, swiped at his face

with his sleeve and sniffed. "Douglas."

"Pardon?"

"Art Douglas. That's his name. Arthur Richard Douglas." He ripped off a chunk of the fritter and tossed it at a trio of pigeons.

Her heart skipped one beat, two, four. Arthur Richard Douglas.

"He's all over the system. Shouldn't be too hard to find." He turned to her. "Tell them to get him soon. I'll testify. But hurry. I'll be lucky if I make it until autumn."

Billie took Tony's hand and squeezed. "Thank you."

She got to her feet with tears in her eyes, pulled a twenty from her pocket, and stuffed it in his cup. She turned and walked away before he had a chance to protest.

Arthur Richard Douglas. Murderer. Rapist. All-around waste of human skin. A real life Joe Chill.

Time to die.

ART DOUGLAS

ART DOUGLAS DREW SMOKE DEEP INTO HIS LUNGS and watched the tip of his cigarette burn red in the dark. He lounged on a stack of crates, sated and content in his favourite haunt, the abandoned end of the docks, where the stench of rot and filth and sewage kept the pussies away. Even the cops had given up all hope on this area, just ignored it and assumed no one would want to spend more than one second there.

Cops were morons.

Blue smoke trailed into the sky. A perfect night. Not a cloud, every star visible from his vantage point in the shadows, far from the hot lights of downtown Grantham. When ash neared filter, he reached out and butted his smoke on the peach fuzz of a young hooker's ass.

She didn't notice. Dead girls don't flinch.

Nobody could call him a moron. He'd learned from his mistakes. No more little girls from good neighbourhoods. People cared too much about them. Searched for them when they went missing. Demanded justice when he popped their sweet little cherries.

Since they opened those jailhouse doors and set him free for the last time, he'd sworn to be smarter. He knew he'd never stop. How could he? It was as much a part of him as his arms and legs, as his hot breath and his cold heart. But from that day forward, just whores and skanks, junkies and hobos. He'd only cast his line into toxic waters and reel in whatever mutant took the bait. They didn't need to be pretty. Didn't need to be skinny. They didn't even need to smell good. He couldn't smell anything anymore anyway. Nope, they just needed to be part of the landscape. Part of the invisible background that regular folks never see, never remember. Women, or when he was lucky, girls, who nobody noticed had gone missing. Who nobody gave a rat's ass about if they never came back.

The other lesson he'd learned? No witnesses. He knew he could only get it up for rape. What he'd discovered about himself is that he got a powerful orgasm if he came as he choked the life from them. Shot into them when their eyes could no longer see. Yeah, that was a pleasant surprise. But like all cravings, all addictions, he had to feed it. And like all crimes, he had to cover it up. Shooting his load into a rubber lacked a certain satisfaction that filling a whore's pussy held. But no condom equalled jail time. Bastard cops had his DNA on file. There ought to be a law against that. No damn privacy left in the world.

Except in his little slice of dock heaven. Private. Peaceful. No one around to hear them scream. He patted her naked bottom and flipped her over for one more go. One look into those open, dead eyes, and he was ready and able. And when he was done, he'd slice her into chum and toss her to the fish. They would feast tonight. She was a hefty one.

SATURDAY, AUGUST 29ᵀᴴ

BILLIE SIPPED ON HER MORNING COFFEE. SUN streamed in the window and laid a hot slice of light across Peg Leg's blackness. How that cat didn't fry up into kitty nuggets was beyond her.

She sat at her laptop, typed "Arthur Richard Douglas" into the search field. Her pinkie hesitated over the Enter key. Was she ready to dive headlong into this man's world?

"Screw it."

She flicked the key and the Google gods responded in a nanosecond with a long list of links. A goldmine of potential leads. Tony was right, Art Douglas was all over the system.

She pulled up an article dated seven years ago. An op/ed piece about convicted felons and re-offending. It discussed the case of Art Douglas, convicted of rape and aggravated assault. As if taking the virginity of a young, innocent girl wasn't enough, he piled on by burning her with the tip of a lit cigarette. He served the full ten-year sentence. Not even a month after his release and still on parole, he robbed a convenience store and snatched a young girl from out front. Before he could do her any physical harm, a citizen called the cops when they heard muffled screams in an alley.

Joe Chill still loved his dark alleys.

He did another three years for robbery and attempted rape. The author of the article felt he should have done harder time, second conviction and all. And since he was still bent on rape, his inability to complete the nasty deed notwithstanding, it showed a pattern. Citizens needed to be protected from scum like him. Well, that's not what the article said. But that's how Billie edited it.

She nodded through the article. Damn straight, they all needed to be protected. And if protection wasn't going to come, then someone needed to take the threat off the streets. Put justice right. Something the courts seemed incapable of doing. Or at least doing well.

Another newspaper clipping had him walking out of prison five years ago. It appeared he'd begun living a normal life. Gone straight, or so his parole officer claimed. Though she found some internet chatter that maybe he was responsible for the rape and murder of two prostitutes whose bodies were discovered floating in the Grantham River. Speculation was, he must have worn a condom, and the water had washed away any other evidence. Except the cigarette burns on their bodies, his signature move. But that clue went nowhere without an actual cigarette with spit or a fingerprint still intact.

Forums filled with angry citizens demanded Douglas and his ilk be strung up, imprisoned for life, put to death, or castrated, chemically or physically. Sprinkled in and among the insanity and blood lust was the occasional cry for forgiveness. For understanding. For reform.

Billie crinkled her nose. Fuck forgiveness.

She returned to the Google homepage and typed his name in again. She took a few deep breaths, hovered her cursor over the link to images, and clicked.

Her screen filled with pictures, some of old men, some little boys. As with all searches, the page was peppered with bare breasts and the occasional penis. But most of what came up were mug shots. Close-ups of an angry man, with a crooked nose and bushy eyebrows. Those brows matched the mouse beige of his hair. In some pictures he was younger, his hair long, bangs nearly covering his eyes. In others he had aged, his nose more crooked, scars on his cheeks and forehead. His hair was cropped short and his face was never fully clean-shaven, though he didn't have a beard or moustache. Time and prison life had not been kind.

She clicked on one of the pictures of a younger man. Stared intently at the face that had been behind the muzzle of that gun. He wasn't an ugly man. Not back then. He was only in his mid-twenties. Life had only beaten him down on the inside and hardened his soul. The outside would have fooled anyone into thinking he was just your average Joe. She would have passed him on the street, sat beside him on the subway, ordered a coffee from him, and never known he was the man who had gunned down her family. Not realized that he cared so little for other human beings that he was willing to snuff out the life of an eleven-year-old girl with just the pull of one trigger.

The squeal of the shower tap turning off cut through her thoughts. She sped her mouse around the counter, favourited some of the sites with Douglas's history, shut down her internet and email, and opened her new client's manuscript.

Bruce came out of the bedroom with one towel around his waist and rubbing his hair dry with another.

Billie poured him a coffee and handed him the steaming mug. They were taking turns staying at each other's apartments. Just like Doc insisted. It was lovely to snuggle into his warm frame each night, wonderful to have company and not be so lonely.

But damn. She needed some time to herself.

"So, I was thinking. I haven't had any episodes. You know, no fugue, no murderous rampages."

Bruce took a gulp of coffee. "Nope. Just one unofficial judicial intervention that won't happen again without your sidekick." He grinned.

"I think I'd like to go to church tomorrow."

"Okay. We can stay here again tonight if you like, then it's just a quick walk. Better than the subway ride from my place."

She put her mug on the counter, took his hand, and pulled him toward her. "I was thinking I'd like to go alone." She traced a cross through his chest hair, then encircled it inside a heart. "Do you mind? You don't even go to church."

"I don't mind. I can watch the game. Keep Peg Leg company."

Might have to hit him over the head with it. She drew out a long sigh.

"Oh, I get it." He put one finger under her chin and lifted her face. "You need a break. Had enough of old Bruce already?" He planted a dry peck on her nose.

"Not at all. But I wouldn't mind some time to myself. Catch up on laundry, maybe seek out some new clients."

Stalk Art Douglas.

She looked up at him, her eyes as saucer-like as she could muster without vomiting. "Is that okay? You're not upset?"

"As long as you're not breaking up with me, it's totally cool."

She took his mug from his hand and placed it beside hers. "Definitely not breaking up." She slipped her T-shirt off her Saturday-braless body and slid off the stool. She snatched the towel from his waist, hopped to the bedroom, and lunged for the bed.

Bruce landed beside her.

SUNDAY

THE GARAGE DOOR SQUEALED ITS DISPLEASURE AT being forced open after so many months sitting idle. Dust billowed up from the concrete floor and the smell of old oil and paint thinner sent a spasm of memories through Billie.

She ran one finger along the side of the eighty-five Impala, its black body marred by a thick, ashy layer. She rested a bag of rags and cleaners on the floor, pulled on the latch of the driver's side door, and inhaled the scents that reminded her of her grandfather — Armor All and pine air freshener. The dust on the inside was just a mist across the dashboard and the steering wheel. She folded the old bedsheet that covered the seat and slipped it from the car, then set to work making the interior sparkle. An hour later, she slid into the driver's seat and gripped the wheel.

She didn't have many occasions to drive, the subway being so easy and convenient and cheap. If the new owners of Grandmother's house hadn't let her keep the car in the garage, she would have had to sell it. But they did. So she didn't.

How many times had Grandpa let her sit on his lap and take the wheel while he barrelled down the highway at twice the speed limit? Her father would have killed him had he known. Too much bacon and salt did the job for him instead. Grandpa keeled over on bowling night, his teammates' attempts at CPR fruitless. His heart gave out two years before he had to witness the death of his son.

She held her breath and turned the key. The engine turned over with a rumble. She gunned the gas pedal and the motor sputtered out the cobwebs, filling the lines with oil. It was the sound of power and freedom. Of the open road and endless possibilities.

Her heart pitter-patted. She'd have to go driving more often. Maybe take Bruce on a road trip.

She eased the car into gear and manoeuvred into the driveway, climbed out, and closed the garage door. She clicked the padlock shut, climbed behind the wheel and found the nearest touchless car wash.

Billie read the slip of paper again: checked the street sign and the address over the door of the rundown garage. This was definitely the place. The last known employment for Arthur Douglas. But that was a year ago. He could be anywhere by now.

She crouched down in the seat and sipped her coffee, her eyes glued to the building. It took almost an hour, but finally someone appeared inside the open overhead garage door. He rolled out from under the body of a rusty sedan, got up from the creeper, pulled a rag from the pocket of his coveralls, and wiped his hands.

It was the face from Google images. Hardened, scarred, angry. Wider than before, like freedom came with a better menu. Or maybe a less-healthy one. His hair remained short-cropped, like a military cut, but with more forehead, his hairline receded, his hair thinner. His brows were bushier than ever, that weird opposite thing that happens as men age. More hair in the ears, nose, and brow. Less and less on the head.

Adrenaline filled her belly, like hot wax dripping into her stomach.

He picked up a pack of cigarettes that rested on the trunk of the car, lit a match with his fingernail, sucked smoke into his lungs, then exhaled. His body shook with uncontrolled coughs.

Maybe she didn't need to do a damn thing. He was killing himself, slowly but surely. She smirked. No way. He didn't deserve a natural death. He didn't deserve to walk this earth one day longer. Her hatred for him had been all-consuming for twenty-two years. It began the moment her father's knees hit the alley floor. With every passing year and everything she'd learned about Douglas in the past week — the rapes, the allegations of serial murder — her hatred turned malignant.

Every moment of every day was scarred by the vision of him, by her memories, as fuzzy as they were and as focused on the gun. She was traumatized anew by her imagination conjuring the sight of young girls, raped and ruined and never able to be the same.

The man had no right to live.

He guzzled from a greasy travel mug, slammed it down on a scarlet tool chest, and butted out his cigarette. He disappeared from her view. Seconds later the articulated door rolled down with a shudder and a bang. He reappeared at the side door, followed by another grease-stained man who slammed the door shut and locked it behind him. He waved at Douglas. Douglas offered a lame salute and climbed behind the wheel of a rundown Chevy Malibu. The engine groaned and the car shook. Just like accountants who don't balance their own chequebooks, he was a mechanic that didn't care for his own vehicle.

She started her car, took a right, and followed from a distance.

Half an hour later, they neared the abandoned docks. She scanned the street, her stomach in knots and her body quaking. The farther she drove, the fewer cars occupied the streets. Traffic had been camouflage for her stalking endeavour. But as the gut-wrenching stench of dead fish overtook the Impala, she was alone with Art Douglas in the worst end of town. Alone with a murderer and a rapist. No sidekick. No other living soul knew where in the hell she was.

Douglas kept glancing in his rear view mirror.

She lost her nerve, put on her signal and turned left at the last street before the docks. At the next corner, she turned left again, then a third time, and parked behind an abandoned building. She crawled through a broken window on the main floor, partly covered with plywood, and picked her way through the dingy building until she found a window at the back. In the distance, he stood next to his car smoking another cigarette, safely behind a chain link fence just inside the dock entrance, padlocked against the outside world. He paced the locked gate and scanned the roads.

She'd spooked him. Gotten too close. But she had him now. And she wasn't about to let him go.

FRIDAY, SEPTEMBER 11ᵀᴴ

BRUCE RAISED HIS GREEN BOTTLE OF TSING-TAO. "To Billie, superhero of my heart, able to edit piles of literary shit into bestsellers with a few strokes of her magic red pen." He clinked his bottle against hers. "Congratulations. Not that there was ever any doubt that you'd make editor."

"I had a lot of doubt." She sipped her beer. "You should have seen the look on Katherine's face."

"You mean the nice Katherine I met in the hospital?"

"Yeah, she was back to bitch on heels by Tuesday. Pulled me in her office and demanded I tell no one about the thrift store thing. Now she's all pissed that she has to waste her time finding my replacement. And more pissed that they want me upstairs a week from Monday. Got all in my face about how backed-up the pool would be. I told her to take it up with the editor-in-chief."

"That's my girl. Kickin' ass and takin' names."

"I have to email my freelance clients tonight and bow out. No way I have time for that now. And I won't need the money." Billie made a crucifix with her chopsticks, dragged them across a dumpling and hacked it in half. She picked up one piece and dipped it into soy sauce spiced with chillies and cut with rice wine vinegar. Her favourite part of Chinese food — fried balls of meat covered in greasy dough, dripping in hot salt.

She tapped her sticks against her bowl and chewed, her eyes on the General Tso's chicken, her mind on the stinking dock that Art Douglas made his home. And probably his body dump. She'd begged off going to Bruce's twice this week to continue her surveillance. So far, all she got was a repeat of the first time. Chain link fence. Padlock. Murderer disappearing in the darkness.

She needed to get inside. Maybe it was time to call on her Robin. Especially since he was beginning to think she was avoiding him.

She put her chopsticks down and took a deep breath. "So, I have to tell you something."

Bruce froze, his own sticks in his mouth, Cantonese noodles dangling from his lips. He gave her a slight nod, slurped the food up, and wiped his face with a napkin. "Am I going to hate this something? Because I know that you're pulling away. I've been afraid to bring it up."

She reached across the tiny table and put her hand over his. "I'm not pulling away from you. I've just been kind of … Well. Obsessed with something."

"Who is he?"

"Arthur Richard Douglas."

Bruce tossed his napkin on his plate and pushed it away. "I figured." He lifted his chin and looked at the ceiling, his hands on his thighs, both knees bouncing up and down. He rubbed his face with both palms. "Look, I'll get the bill and drop you at your apartment. But if this Arthur guy ever does anything to hurt you, call me. I'll take the bastard down."

"No, you don't understand. I'm not dating him. I'm stalking him."

Bruce's eyebrows shot up. "And this is better for me how?"

"Stop being silly." She shook her head. "I'm not interested in him like I am in you. I don't want to sleep with him or anything." A shiver passed over her body. She glanced around the restaurant and leaned in. "I'm going to kill him," she whispered.

Bruce shut his eyes and gave his head a shake. "Sorry, what?"

"He's the man who murdered my parents. I've been following him, studying him. I'm going to kill him." She plucked a piece of deep-fried chicken laden with red sauce from the dish and popped it in her mouth. "Not sure I can pull it off by myself," she said through the General Tso's. She swallowed and took a sip of tea out of a tiny cup. "It's not like cracking nuts in an alley. I need my sidekick." She flicked a gnarly piece of putrid squid from the noodles and pulled the plate closer. "You in?"

"So ... You're not breaking up with me?" Bruce snagged the squid from the table and bit it in half.

"Why would I do that? I love you."

His cheeks pinked. "I love you too. But killing?" He shot a sideways look at a nearby table and hunched forward. "That's kind of crazy."

"Crazy good, right? Besides, we talk about doing it all the time. And I might have already murdered as many as four people." Almost five if she'd aimed that knife just three inches higher in Bat Head's gut.

"That's different. The editing, that's all fantasy. And if you were in that fugue state, you couldn't be held responsible. If you did anything. Which I still can't believe, despite evidence to the contrary." He plucked the napkin from his plate and pushed noodles around. "How do you know this is the guy?"

"Tony told me."

"So why not go to the cops and tell them? They'll arrest him, try him."

"Because Tony is dying and wouldn't be around for the trial. And without him, there's no evidence. What if they don't convict? What if I go through it all again and nothing happens and they just let him go free?" She pitched her chopsticks on the table. "He doesn't deserve to be free. To walk this earth on his two good feet. To breathe." She picked up a fork and stabbed a dumpling. "He has to die."

The waiter shuffled up beside Bruce, filled their teacups and gestured at the food. "You finished?"

Billie nodded. "Wrap it to go, please."

The waiter pulled a bill and two fortune cookies from his apron and gathered the plates.

When he walked away, Billie turned to Bruce. "I'm doing it. I need your help. But if you don't want to, I understand. But I'm doing it. No matter what."

Bruce, his eyes unblinking, his jaw set, ripped the cellophane off a cookie and snapped it in two. He popped one-half of the cookie in his mouth and pulled two fortunes from the other.

"Ooh," Billie said. "That's good luck. Like double cupcake liners, or a folded potato chip."

"You are so weird."

"Thank you. Thank you very much."

He read both the fortunes to himself and huffed. He handed the slips of paper to Billie.

"You are a true and loyal friend." She smiled and looked up at him. "Well that's the truth." She dropped the tiny paper to the table and looked at the other one. "One must dare to be himself, however frightening or strange that self may prove to be." She raised her eyebrows. "Oh, my. That's different." She cocked her head and analyzed his face. "What part of yourself are you holding back, young Padawan?"

He smirked. "I've told you about my past. But sometimes, and I think you've seen it, that side of me wants out. The rough guy. The pushy guy." He sipped his tea. "The guy that wants to pound the shit out of anyone who looks at you sideways or makes you feel like you aren't perfect as you are." He tossed her the other cookie. "You go."

She brought her fist down on the cookie and smashed it to bits. The cellophane ripped open, spraying the table with crumb spatter.

A woman at the next table jumped and her baby started to cry.

Billie fished the fortune from the cookie's belly and stared at the words. "Well, that seals it then. Time for some retribution."

He took the paper from her fingers. "You are people's hero, you will always be." He smiled. "Well, that's true." He sat back and put his palms on his thighs. "Billie, I know you want this guy dead. I get it. But real murder isn't like editing the news." He reached across the table and took her hand. "You aren't that person. You're too good. There's no way you did any of the things you think you did. It's just not in you. Maybe you need to see Doc Kroft before your next scheduled appointment?"

Her eyelids fluttered. Should she tell him she'd skipped the last two appointments? Tell him she couldn't bring herself to take the meds? Every time she picked up that bottle, her skin crawled and her mouth filled with cotton. She thought he understood. Thought he was an ally in her fight for justice. Maybe he wasn't who she thought he was after all.

"Billie, promise me you won't do anything crazy. Promise you won't go after this man. You could be the one who winds up dead." He rubbed his thumb across the back of her hand. "Promise?"

Her head nodded without her consent. She wouldn't promise. Couldn't promise. Not out loud.

SATURDAY

B ILLIE PULLED ONTO THE DIRT LOT BEHIND THE abandoned building and parked in the shadows, out of sight of the entrance to the dock. She snatched the small carry-on bag from the backseat and pulled the latch to open the door. A thick fog of putridity rolled in from the river and reached into her nostrils. She ignored it. But she couldn't ignore the surge of adrenaline quickening her heart and making her limbs come alive.

Billie squeezed between the broken glass and rotting plywood covering the window. She stood at the first-floor window facing the entry to the docks and let the consistent routine of Arthur Douglas play in her mind.

Arrive around six. Unchain the fence, drive through, padlock it back up again.

Except for that one night he didn't show up until after eight. It was almost dark.

Billie fished a pair of binoculars from the suitcase and trained them on the dockyard. She scanned the length of the chain-link fence. No holes. No breaks. She scanned left then swept right. And there it was. A section that wasn't blocked by crates or barrels or rusted-out shipping containers. Her stomach gurgled. She pressed on a spasm until a bubble of gas exploded from her mouth. She giggled.

"See you next Saturday, Art Douglas."

MONDAY THE 21ST

BILLIE STOOD AT THE WINDOW OF HER TWENTY-fourth floor office and stared out at the city below.

Ants.

All those miniscule people really did look like ants scurrying around in their little downtown tunnels. She scanned the office towers around her, peered into windows to see if anyone else watched the insect melee in the streets. Last week, she'd have been one of those little ants. Technically, she still was. She just had a better vantage point.

She sat in her ergonomic leather chair and ran her fingertips over the glass top of her desk, its surface area at least three times that of the tiny workspace in her proofing pool cubby. The editor-in-chief had already dropped by to welcome her and hand her a stack of manuscripts. There were more in her email inbox.

The office smelled of good coffee and clean carpet. It lacked the fetidness of peon-sweat and lost hope. There was no lingering odour of Katherine's perfume that was less subtle and more like a caveman whack to the head. No yappy little dog, nor any of its shit to pick up.

Billie flipped through the first pages of each manuscript. Errors the proofing pool missed jumped from the pages like bad grammar jacks-in-the-box. Billie tamed each with a swipe of her red pen and made a mental note to tell Katherine to do a better job managing her staff.

After sifting through seven candidates, she settled on an action novel of intermediate length for her first official project as associate editor. She couldn't resist the title.

Kill. Or Die Trying.

She sipped at her creamy sweet coffee and snapped off half a chocolate chip cookie from the cookie bouquet the third floor sent her. She'd bet it was Jeffrey's idea, his signature on the good luck card the biggest and most flouncy, surrounded by little purple hearts. Katherine barely signed it at all. Couldn't even bring herself to break out the cursive. Just her first name, printed in small block letters. In red ink.

Billie handed Tony a submarine sandwich, thick with meat and cheese and calories and fat. His body jerked, and his legs quivered with restless spasms. His cheeks were sunken, like those skeletal Somali children who dominated the news shows her father always had on in the early nineties.

"I'm not too hungry." He placed the sandwich on the sidewalk beside him. His breath wheezed and rattled in his chest.

"You need a doctor." She held the back of her hand to his forehead like her grandmother used to do. "No fever. But you look like hell." More so than usual.

"I'm fine. Just a little off."

Billie filled in his cheeks with her mental red pen and tucked a crimson rose into the lapel of his imaginary suit jacket. "Just be sure to eat. Keep your strength up." She didn't have a good reason for stopping by. The anticipation of the coming events had made her jumpy and excited. Scared to death but elated at the possibility of ridding the world of evil incarnate. She'd toyed with the idea of sharing the murder plot with Tony. But what if he tried to talk her out of it? How could he ever understand her driving desire to see his former partner's blood spilled? To see the life drain from his eyes?

"Can I bring you anything? I'll grab you a coffee before I go back to work. And some water."

He patted her hand. "You're too kind to me, Billie. I don't need nothing like that." His eyes teared up. "But there is one thing."

"Yes. Name it."

He looked away, then turned his head until their eyes met.

A wave of concern and compassion overtook her. She reached out and held his hand. "What is it, Tony?"

"I don't deserve it. I'd understand if you said no. But I was hopin' — prayin' — that before I die, maybe you'd forgive me for the terrible things I done?"

Billie's eyes filled with tears. "That's a tall order."

"I know. And I got no right to ask. Only if you want to. If you truly feel it. Only if it's real."

She nodded and stared across the street, the dry skin of his dirty hand rough against hers. The events of that night in nineteen ninety-three rushed through her mind. She closed her eyes and looked for Tony, looked past the gun and the fear and focused on the younger version of the man seated beside her. The muzzle of that gun trained on her face, the sudden movement of an arm knocking it down, the flash of light glinting off a gold tooth in Tony's open mouth, yelling words she didn't hear. He had saved her life. And for the past few months, she believed it was a life worth saving.

She squeezed his hand and released him, got to her feet and looked at his crumpled form. "I do forgive you, Tony. You gave me a second chance at life. And I appreciate that."

He closed his eyes, rested his head against the brick and nodded, silent tears streaming down his cheeks, a twisted grin on his lips.

Billie turned and walked away. Half the weight of two decades of anguish, hatred, and guilt lifted from her like a helium balloon.

It was time to release the other half.

SATURDAY, SEPTEMBER 26TH

ILLIE PRESSED A BUTTON ON THE SIDE OF HER watch. The glow from its face lit hers. It was getting late. Maybe Art Douglas wasn't coming back.

She stared out the window of the abandoned building and tapped her toes against the concrete floor. Damn it, he had to come back. Tonight was the night, she was so ready. The same satisfaction that came over her when she saved Jeffrey flooded her body. And when she took Bat Head out of commission and probably saved countless women from being raped, maybe even killed. Righteousness and action had filled her with power.

She pulled on the snug leather gloves she'd picked up just for the occasion. She opened a new box of bullets, loaded a magazine, and smacked the magazine into Bruce's gun.

How could she have ever known that this was what she was built for? To be a vigilante. A defender of justice. Just like her name means. Maybe her father knew that. Named her Wilhelmina on purpose. But he probably never foresaw this for his little Billie Angel. No, he probably thought she'd be a cop like him. Or maybe a lawyer. But a hired gun? Shit, she wasn't even hired. She'd do it for free as long as it was justice.

A slice of headlights across the window flashed in Billie's eyes. She pulled back and peered out. She grabbed the binoculars that dangled from a leather strap around her neck. There was someone in the car with him. Someone short. Or drunk.

Three weeks of stalking and planning. Twenty-two years of

anguish, pain, and hate all wrapped up in survivor's guilt and tied up with a fugue ribbon. It all led to this moment. "Okay, Billie Sunshine, are you ready?" She bounced on her feet and shook her arms, rolled her neck until it cracked.

She nodded. "So fucking ready."

She crawled out the window, ran across the abandoned lot, her body crouched low. Douglas had done what he always did — drove in through the gate, closed and chained it, and secured it with the giant padlock.

Like that could keep her out. Maybe he'd never heard of bolt cutters.

She pulled out the section of chain link fence that she'd cut open the prior Sunday and laid it gently on the ground. She was as quiet as possible in case her prey had hearing like the dog he was.

The stench that took her breath the first few times she'd approached the docks no longer bothered her. Now it smelled of sweet vengeance.

She traversed a labyrinth of teetering rusty shipping containers — some Seussian landscape from an R-rated horror movie. Wooden crates were strewn about, alongside oil drums that stunk like toxic waste. So many places to hide bodies. Or pieces of bodies. And no one around to look for them.

The rotting flesh of the containers gave off a metallic stench that swirled with dead fish and dead hookers in an eddy of putrefaction. A waft of jasmine caught in Billie's nostrils. She searched the darkness for its source. Among the trash and filth, creeping through pavement and rooted in rot, sparse vines dotted with white flowers were scattered about the dockyard. The scent made her feel a bit drunk with its sweet, sensual power. She plucked a blossom and inhaled the elixir. It mixed with the adrenaline flooding her veins until purpose and confidence coursed through her.

Breaking glass shattered the silence. Billie dropped to the

ground and duck-walked behind a stack of crates and barrels. She peered out between two drums.

Douglas's silhouette was backlit by the dim light cast from a bare bulb above the door to the Quonset hut. He pulled a bottle out of his car and lobbed it at a pile of trash; brought another one out and uncapped it, tipped it to his lips, and gulped down the remaining contents. That bottle died alongside the others, splintered glass spraying the tarmac.

Douglas pulled his car mate from the passenger seat and dragged her toward the Quonset. Her stiletto heels scraped against the pavement.

Whoever it was, she was passed out cold. Or dead.

Billie slinked through the night until she was hidden behind corrugated cardboard.

Douglas dragged the body to a stack of crates and tossed her on top. She landed hard and sent the sharp crack of breaking wood through the night. He arched his back and stretched his neck. A flash of flame lit his face, then the red tip of a fresh cigarette glowed in the shadows. He pulled on the cancer stick, his full attention on the corpse atop the crates. Between puffs, he leaned in. There was an audible intake of air when he sniffed her hair. He ran his fingers down her back, over her behind, and down one leg.

"Definitely dead," Billie whispered. She eyed the body on the crates. Short skirt, crop top, high heels. Another hooker. Easy prey and nobody looking for her. Bastard had learned his lessons all right. Go for the invisible victims and chances are, the cops won't give two shits about them. Won't even look for them. Just assume they moved on to more profitable territory.

Cops needed a wakeup call.

Douglas sucked the last of his cigarette and tossed the glowing butt into the air. It bounced on the blacktop and rolled. He unbuckled his belt and whipped it from his belt loops with a snap.

He smacked the dead woman's ass with the belt, then threw it aside. The buckle clanked against the tarmac. Douglas cut the woman's skirt off with a knife. He tossed the blade aside. Its metal edge sparked against the blacktop and came to rest a few yards away. He dropped his pants and bared his ass to the audience he didn't know was watching.

Billie looked away.

The squeak of crates blessedly masked his groans and grunts. Billie took a deep breath and squeezed her hands into fists.

It was now or never.

She tiptoed through the darkness and around the edge of the dim spotlight created by the bare bulb. Art and his date went about their business in the shadows, which allowed Billie to get within spitting distance.

Billie fingered the gun in her pocket. Her eyes caught the glint of Art's discarded blade. She scooped it from the ground and rolled the handle in her gloved hand. Oh, irony, you have a wicked sense of humour.

Billie sidled up to Douglas. When she was within arm's reach, she held his knife to the side of his face.

He froze mid-thrust, his gulp audible. He glanced sideways until he caught Billie's eye. "Well, what have we here? You want a threesome? It must be my lucky fucking day."

His voice turned Billie's stomach. "Dream on, pig. I'm going to watch you die on the pavement in a pool of your own blood." She drew the blade across his cheek and marveled at the crimson oozing from the cut. In the dim light, it looked black, like evil escaping his veins.

Art Douglas winced. Then he laughed at her. "Seriously? Some scrawny bitch thinks she can do me in? How 'bout you just do me instead."

He pushed off the dead girl, knocked Billie sideways, and stood in the dark with his pants around his ankles.

Billie recovered and stood in front of him, her eyes glued to his face. "I want a fair fight. Pull up your trousers."

He huffed and bent to pull up his pants, his eyes never blinking, never leaving hers.

"Besides," she said. "I can't bear to look at your pitiful excuse for a dick. No wonder you fuck dead people."

His face contorted. Billie readied for him to rush her.

Douglas threw his head back and roared. "I like a little trash talk before I slice a bitch to pieces."

"You like that?" She jerked her head at him. "You have huge feet. So I guess that whole 'big feet, big dick' thing is just an urban myth."

He snickered. "That's funny, bitch. But your trash talk could use some work. It's a little stiff." He eyed the ground.

"Looking for this?" She sliced the air with his blade. "Yeah, I cut you with your own knife. Thought it would make our little encounter more personal."

He put his hands on his hips. "Who the fuck *are* you?"

"Wilhelmina Angelina Fullalove. In nineteen ninety-three you murdered my parents in an alley."

He snorted. "Which parents? Which alley? Ninety-three was a long year, sweetheart. You'll have to be more specific."

Billie went cold at his callous words. "Police officer and his wife, out for a stroll after a nice birthday dinner for their eleven-year-old daughter. That would be me." She tapped her chest with her fingertips. "After you murdered them for no reason, you shot my leg off."

"So, Tony finally ratted me out, eh? He saved your life that night, you know that, right?"

Billie nodded. "I'm aware."

"Now I'm gonna have to go kill his sorry ass."

"No point. He's almost dead already. Cancer."

"Well, ain't that nice. I love it when God does my dirty work."

The hair on Billie's neck bristled. God would never give someone cancer. Not on purpose.

Douglas pulled a cigarette pack from his breast pocket and tapped one out. "You mind?" He lit the smoke.

"Not at all. Consider it your final wish before you die."

"No. My final wish is to fuck your stupid brains out. But I think I'll do you while you're still breathing, then carve you up piece by piece while you watch. I'll toss your juicy bits to the slime that swim in the river. They love them some whore parts. Gobble it up like it's their last meal. I bet they even eat the bones."

She tossed the knife into her left hand and pulled Bruce's gun from her pocket. She aimed it at Douglas's dick.

An almost imperceptible twitch in his eyelids gave him away. Fear was creeping in.

Billie squinted and lowered her chin. Her lips quivered and her jaw clenched. She couldn't take her eyes from his face. Refused to fall victim to him again.

"You got a silencer on that thing?" He swallowed hard. "You shoot, gonna be cops swarming all over this place."

"No there won't." Billie closed her fist on the knife and kneaded the handle like a stress ball. She memorized his every movement, every jerk of muscle in his arms, shuffle of feet and shift of his eyes. "There's nothing for miles. Police don't give a crap about this place. Isn't that why you're out here?" She jerked her head at the body on the crates. "For the privacy?"

He snorted. "You been following me. I knew it. Could feel it." He eyed her from bottom to top. "You got skills. Maybe I could use that." He sucked on his cigarette, reached behind and butted it on the hooker's cold thigh. "We should team up, you and me."

Bile rose in Billie's throat and her balance wavered. No, she would not fuck this up.

She launched the knife at Douglas. It penetrated his right shoulder and crunched into bone. The handle protruded from his flesh at a right angle, erect, aroused.

He reared sideways and grabbed his arm. His jaw clenched and he straightened. He glared at her, and yanked the blade free. In one swift movement, the knife sailed through the air.

Billie dove over a pile of garbage. The blade pinged off an oil drum and skittered along the pavement, coming to rest against an apple core. Through her heartbeat banging in her ears, she heard footsteps and grunts of pain.

She rolled onto her back and raised the pistol, focused on the front sight and aimed for the centre of his looming blurry figure. He lunged for her. She shot once, twice. Three times.

His body jerked with the impact of each bullet. He looked her in the eyes, his face a mask of shock and pain, before he crumpled and fell on top of her.

His hot breath, sweet with whiskey and laden with tar and nicotine, expelled from his lungs and onto her face. Her stomach clenched and roiled.

A roar built up inside Billie and exploded from her mouth. She thrust her arms out and pushed him off, propelling his limp form and the gun a good metre. She scrambled to her feet, wiped his grimy touch from her. She shook out her arms and stood over him.

He gasped and drew in a gurgling breath. Bubbles of blood trickled down his chin. He grinned and lifted one hand, made a lame attempt to grab her leg before his arm flopped to the asphalt. "Well shit." He coughed up blood. "You got me."

Bastard was hard to kill.

A scream bellowed from deep inside her. She kicked him in the groin, the side, the arms. His knife lay on the ground. She stormed at it, snatched it up, and turned to him. She dropped to her knees and stabbed him in the stomach and the throat, pummeled his head and his neck with her other hand.

She switched the knife to her left and stabbed him until her body ached. Without the energy for another thrust, her arms went limp. The knife hit the pavement and sent a spark into the air. Her head rolled back. She let out a long wail, wrapped her arms around herself and crumpled to the asphalt. Her body undulated with relief and rage, guilt and grief.

Sirens keened in the distance. Billie's heartbeat accelerated as they neared. She backed into the shadows and scurried behind a stack of oil drums. He was right. Cops would be all over the place.

She held her breath until the screaming cars sped away, probably blocks from the dock, and dissipated in the darkness. She let the air out of her lungs and snorted a small laugh from her nose. Like the cops gave a damn about this place. About Art Douglas.

Billie wiped the tears from her cheeks, leaving smears of greasy blood in their wake. She lifted her hands into the moonlight and stared at the evidence all over them. All over her.

"Come on, Billie. Time to move."

She got to her feet and approached the dead woman on the crates. Billie studied her face, the dark brows in contrast to the hair dyed platinum, cropped short, and spiked with gel. The woman smelled of sex and smoke and hopelessness. And this would be her final resting place.

Billie pocketed the knife and retrieved the gun. By the light of the moon, she scrounged for bullet casings, counting each as she snatched them up. How many times had she pulled the trigger? She closed her eyes and rewound the night.

Bang. Bang. Bang. Her shoulders tensed with the memory of each shot. Three shots. She opened her palm. Three casings.

She grabbed Arthur Richard Douglas by his evil clown feet and dragged him to the edge of the dock.

Billie sat on an upturned wooden crate and slid the knife in and out of Douglas's body. His flesh put up little resistance.

Dead men don't fight.

She ran her fingers over the bars of her gold crucifix and stared across the wide expanse of river at the lights of downtown Grantham. The strains of an old Adam Ant song rang in her ears.

Goody two-shoes, my ass.

Bullets. She had to get back those bullets or the cops might be able to tie his murder back to Bruce. She stripped off Douglas's bloody shirt and found one bullet hole among the stab wounds. The blade of Douglas's own knife slid inside his dead flesh. She shoved her gloved fingers in the hole and dug around until she felt the bullet. She held it up to the moonlight. It looked like a brass banana, peeled and exposed, with a Claymation mushroom for bloody flesh. She dug out the other two and dropped them into her pocket, along with the gun.

She rummaged around the area for rocks and anything heavy that would sink Douglas in the brown ooze.

Half an hour later, she'd filled his clothing with rocks and bound him in rope to secure the weights. She raised his knife into the air and stabbed the blade into his chest.

She slid Douglas off the edge of the dock. His life, abundant with evil and notoriety, ended without fanfare. With zero splash. He slipped into the water without so much as a slosh.

"It's over." She looked up into the face of the moon and raised both arms. "I did it, God," she yelled at the sky. "Justice delivered. An eye for an eye. My father's life for his. If I could kill him again, for my mother, I would."

Her mouth filled with saliva and her guts revolted. She dropped to her knees and leaned over the roiling water. Vomit hurled from her mouth. She gagged and puked, tears running down her cheeks and mixing with her dinner and the dirty grave water of the man whose murderous actions had ruled her life.

She kneeled at the altar of Arthur Richard Douglas's death and prayed to God for forgiveness. For understanding. And she prayed that Douglas would burn in hell where he belonged, for all eternity.

THE FOLLOWING MONDAY

BILLIE WAS SO HIGH ON LIFE, SHE NEARLY SKIPPED toward Tony's regular spot. News of the demise of Art Douglas was tingling on her lips. It was all she could do not to brag about it to every sidewalk robot who passed by. But there was only one person who needed to know. Then Tony could relax and live out the rest of his short life without worrying that his former partner in crime would seek him out and shove a knife in his gut.

She neared the stoop of the Dilly Deli, her step light, her mood lighter. It was an elation she hadn't felt since … well, since never. It was better than meeting Bruce, better than saving Jeffrey, even better than getting Bat Head behind bars. Hell, it was better than sex. And that was pretty damn amazing.

But the closer she got to Tony, the darker her vision became. His spot was empty. No rumpled heap of homeless man. No cup jingling with coins. No fuck you, fuck you very much.

She stood where he sat and scoured the sidewalk, eyed across the street past the boobs-and-booze ad and along the edges of the buildings. He was nowhere, the only sign of him a dried up chunk of apple fritter being picked apart by pigeons.

An ache hollowed her gut. She shook it off. Perhaps he'd had enough of the same crowd and moved on. Found some more fertile sidewalks to troll. But damn, he hadn't even said goodbye. No, something was wrong.

She picked up her pace and hurried to the office. Three phone calls and six transfers later, Tony's parole officer's phone rang and rang.

"Jamison."

"Good morning, Mr. Jamison."

"Ms. Jamison."

Billie held the receiver from her ear and stared at it for the blink of an eye. The deep bass on the other end did not sound female. "Sorry. Ms. Jamison. My name is Billie Fullalove."

"No shit? As in Wilhelmina, the little girl in the alley way back in ninety-three?"

"So Tony talked to you about me?"

"Lady, what happened back then ate that man alive. I'm guessing that's where his cancer came from. Stress and remorse. If that's possible."

Billie nodded to herself. Maybe it was possible. "He wasn't in his usual place today. I just wondered if you knew where he might be."

"Last we talked, he told me about your visits. He seemed happy for the first time in years." Paper shuffled on the other end of the line. "Let me make a few calls. What's your number?"

Billie reeled off the digits of her work and cell phone numbers and ended the call. She leaned back and ran a hand through her hair. She fluffed her tresses and clicked open her latest manuscript.

Every few minutes, she glanced at the clock, clicked the lock on her phone to be sure she hadn't missed any calls. An hour later, she paced in front of the window, her arms crossed, her mind anywhere but on the work. "Damn it, how long do a few phone calls take?"

Her chair creaked and bounced when she flopped into it. She slouched in the seat and dragged her mouse around, clicking between the manuscript and an empty Google page. She jumped at the ring of her phone and snatched the received up without checking caller I.D. "Ms. Jamison?"

"Uh, helloooo. It's twelve-ten. You were supposed to meet me in the lobby. Lunch, remember?"

"Oh, Jeffrey. I'm so sorry." She became aware of the rumble in her stomach. "I'll be right there. Can we walk up to Dilly? I don't want a pre-wrapped soggy sandwich from the coffee chick." And she could spy on Tony's spot and see if he'd shown up.

"Sounds good to me. I could use a big fat pickle."

"Jeffrey, no penis jokes about food, please? Now I can't have a pickle."

"You get pickled at least four times a week. Lucky bitch."

He was crude, but she couldn't help but giggle. "I'm coming."

"Oooh."

"You know what I mean. Give me five."

Billie yanked the bottom drawer of her desk open and pulled out a cosmetics bag. She tugged a brush through her hair and checked her face, tossed the bag back, and slammed the drawer shut. She ran to the hall and jabbed the down button for the elevator four times in quick succession, like that would make it arrive any faster.

In the lobby, she burst free from the elevator and ran-walked across the marble floor, polished to a mirror sheen, to meet Jeffrey at the door. She entwined her arm with his and they exited into a bright and sunny Indian summer day. It was Billie's favourite time of year. Past the heat of August, the leaves just beginning to turn, but not yet threatening to plunge from the trees to their death on the ground below. And before the God-awful snow hit. Running was easy. Navigating icy walks with one leg that had a delayed reaction to slipping was treacherous at best.

They walked with their heads together, catching up on office gossip.

"And he dumped the bitch, just because her Fendi was a knock-off and her Holt Renfrew suit was a Value Village hand-me-down. Serves the bitch right."

"Come on, Jeffrey, that's not fair. Katherine is definitely the bitch of the century, but that guy sounds like a horrible snob. She deserves better."

"Whatever you say, Saint Billie."

They wended their way through the gauntlet of lunchtime pedestrians. Near Tony's regular spot, Billie slowed and eyed the empty sidewalk.

Jeffrey tugged her along, in a rush for a fat slab of meat and salty pickles.

They placed their sandwich orders and slid along the cafeteria-style line with their retro brown plastic trays that had seen better days. Billie opted for a bottle of sweet iced tea, a brownie for dessert, and, damn it all to hell, a big fat dill pickle to cut the cholesterol-and carbohydrate-laden Reuben on rye.

She slid into one side of a booth for two, Jeffrey facing her. She picked up her pickle and hesitated. "Look away, Jeffrey."

"Why?"

"If you watch me shove this pickle in my mouth, I'll probably spew pickle juice in your face."

Jeffrey fanned himself with one hand. "Don't tease me."

Billie giggled. She'd let the hatred of that titter go and had come to enjoy it. A spontaneous expression of joy and hilarity, embarrassment and anxiousness, all rolled into one bubble of girly laughter. A sound she used to make with regularity before nineteen ninety-three ruined her life.

Her phone vibrated against the cool stainless of the tabletop. She poked the screen and the number of Tony's parole officer stared back at her. She pressed the icon and fumbled to get the phone to her ear, her fingers quaking with anticipation. "Hello? Ms. Jamison?"

"Hi, Billie. I've got some news."

Billie closed her eyes. Ms. Jamison told her of Tony's fate. How he'd spent weekends in a nearby shelter because there wasn't enough foot traffic downtown to bother begging.

"He spiked a fever Saturday afternoon. They called an ambulance and got him to the hospital, but it was too late. He died late Saturday night."

Billie rubbed her eyelids with her fingertips. Saturday night. "What time?"

"I'm not sure. Is that important?"

"No, just curious." Perhaps Tony was finally able to rest once Art Douglas's evil presence was erased from this earth. "What about his funeral?"

There was a long pause on the other end. "Billie, there won't be a funeral. He has no family, no one to mourn him. And, frankly, no one to pay the bill. He'll be cremated and buried in an anonymous grave outside the city. They do write his name in the cemetery ledger, though."

"No." Billie shook her head. "How do I claim the body? I want to give him a proper burial."

"I'll find that out and let you know." Ms. Jamison breathed into the phone a few breaths. "Billie, I just have to say, you're the oddest victim I've ever run into."

"The woman's body has been sent home to Calgary. Funeral services will be announced." Bruce slid the newspaper to Billie and handed her a red pen. "When are they going to catch this bastard? Shit, this one wasn't even a hooker. Just a screwed up kid with less-than-perfect parents and a yen for adventure."

Billie swiped a tear from her cheek. If she'd acted quicker, not spent so much time planning, maybe that girl would still be alive. She just couldn't leave her out there to rot like the fish. One mumbled emergency call from a lone payphone on a dark street corner brought the cops to the hellhole on the dock. Billie was long gone before their flashing lights bathed the dock in red and blue.

"Hey, you're taking this pretty hard." Bruce slid off his stool and stood behind Billie, massaged the tension from her shoulders. Or at least, he tried to. "I know it was the same guy that killed your parents, but this isn't your fault. You know that, right?"

She rewound the article in her head. Art Douglas's fingerprints and DNA all over the dead girl's body. His blood all over the dock. Evidence of other murders the cops were matching up with missing persons. All-points bulletin, warrant for his arrest, and BOLOs across the country.

What a waste of effort. But he'd surface one day. Billie didn't tie good knots.

"Hey, Sunshine." Bruce kissed her cheek. "Not your fault." He spun her stool and held her shoulders. His eyes implored hers. "Right?"

She didn't say a word. Just stared at him and let tears pool in her eyes.

He sighed. "You know, I'm feeling a lot less like Robin, and more like Lucius Fox."

She reached up and touched his cheek, ran her thumb along the wisp of a scar under his eye, and smiled.

He closed his eyes and kissed her palm.

She wiped her cheeks dry and dragged the newspaper closer. Her eyes wandered to the pencil cup filled with red pens. "Maybe we can't fix everything. But we sure can fix some things."

Or at least, she could.

She flipped the pages and scanned the crime section, snatched a red pen from the cup and jabbed it into the newspaper. "This one. Let's edit this one."

TUESDAY, SEPTEMBER 29TH

BILLIE SAT IN THE HOLE ON THE SIDEWALK LEFT IN Tony's wake. She rested a paper cup filled with daffodils on the pavement in front of her crossed legs and pulled a bag from her purse. She tore pieces of fried dough from an apple fritter and tossed them at a crowd of pigeons a few feet away.

The birds raced each other for the offering, pecked at the chunks of sweet pastry, and bobbed their cooing heads. Pedestrians shuffled by, disturbing the birds' feast and sending the feathered rodents scattering across the sidewalk just long enough to turn right around and continue pecking at crumbs once the coast was clear.

Billie lifted the small bouquet from the cup and brought the canary blooms to her nose. She'd wanted the flowers to mean something. To be more than just an empty gesture. Google to the rescue again. She spent more time worshipping the Google gods than her own God of late. Daffodils meant beginning anew and leaving the past behind. They were the perfect choice, not only for Tony, but for her, too.

Passersby absent-mindedly dropped coins into the empty cup. They didn't look at Billie, didn't notice her clean, pressed clothes, her tidy hair, her fresh-washed scent. Sitting on the periphery of their lives, she became part of the landscape in an instant. Their anonymous donations were their penance, their Hail Marys, forgiveness for their perceived sins.

She tossed the last bits of fritter to the birds, spread the flowers over Tony's empty spot, and pocketed three dollars and eighty-two cents in coins — pennies? Seriously? They don't even mint those anymore — to be given to the first homeless person she met.

FIRST SATURDAY IN OCTOBER

A BREEZE RIPPLED THROUGH THE LIMBS OF THE giant elm, sending a few bright yellow leaves to their final resting place atop Tony Dickinson's shining oak casket. Billie stood under the tree's shade, her head bowed in prayer and respect.

"Amen." The street minister, a regular at the shelter where Tony spent his weekends, raised his head and looked to the skies. "Tony went through his rough times. He did some bad things in his day. But he paid the price that the courts demanded. He did his time, not one day less. And we ask God to consider that to be good enough. To welcome him with open arms."

Each of the mourners, a small crowd of Tony's homeless brethren, two shelter volunteers, and Ms. Jamison, his parole officer, took turns tossing a handful of dirt onto the lid of his coffin. Tears glistened on Ms. Jamison's cheeks when she passed by. She placed one hand on Billie's shoulder and nodded. "Tony would have loved this. Thank you."

Billie waited for the others to shuffle away before she kneeled in front of the grave. She dug her fingers into the dirt pile and squished the soil into her palm. She closed her eyes and opened her fist one finger at time. Clods of dirt knocked on the lid of Tony's casket.

Billie prayed for his soul to be saved. For God to accept him into heaven. She had forgiven him his sins against her. Against her family. Would God forgive the rest?

She stood and stared at Tony's final resting place for a few minutes, then sprinkled the coffin with five daffodils. One for her mother. One for her father. One for her grandmother, who never recovered from the loss of her son. One for Billie. And one for Tony.

None for Art Douglas. He could burn in hell.

She leaned into Bruce's body. He'd been within inches of her the entire service, his hand on the small of her back or at her waist, a gentle reminder of his presence. His support. His love. She looked up at him. "I'm ready."

He nodded. "Are you hungry? Maybe a submarine in Tony's honour."

Her stomach grumbled in protest.

"Can we have pie?"

Thank you for taking the time to read **Goody One Shoe**. If you enjoyed it, please consider telling your friends or posting a short review. Word of mouth is an author's best friend and much appreciated. Thank you.

Julie Frayn

ACKNOWLEDGEMENTS

I ACKNOWLEDGE MY CHILDREN. I HAVE TO, THE courts said so. Kidding! My kids are everything. Without Baby Girl and Baby Boy, I would be one miserable dude.

This version of Goody has a new cover. My dear systir, Carolyn Frayn, created the original. I loved that our individual brands of art can grace the same product. She was working on a reboot of the Goody cover when her cancer jumped up and grabbed her again. She died in December 2015.

The new cover is thanks to Dane Low of www.Ebooklaunch.com. A custom character of Billie Fullalove in all her vigilante, superhero-wannabe glory.

Thanks to my brother, John Frayn. He is a cop, now retired, and my go-to guy for all things cop-related. And this time gun-related. Between him, Steve Johns and Scott Morgan (the civilian gun guys), I hope to have gotten the details right. I hate guns. Luckily, these guys know their shit.

To Tracy Todd, an old friendship renewed (seriously, met the girl in grade school), for her eagle eye for literary oopsies.

Thanks to author JD Mader, and author and editor, Laurie Boris. JD's 2minutesgo! flash fiction exercise on his blog got this Goody party started, and Laurie (after a flip comment I made about being called goody two shoes in school but now I'm just goody one shoe) told me *Goody One Shoe* was my next book title. Be damned if she wasn't right. Thanks also to Laurie, author and editor, David Antrobus, and my own wonderful editor, Scott Morgan, for giving me tips and insight into what it's like to be an editor, including all of their idiosyncrasies, rituals, and pet peeves about us fellow authors.

And speaking of my editor - countless thanks to Scott for two full edits plus a final read through. He makes me a better writer (even though he disagrees), and I love him for it. That, and because he's just so cool.

ABOUT THE AUTHOR

BY DAY I COUNT BEANS. THE REST OF THE TIME, I revel in the written word. When I'm not working or writing, I spend as much time as possible with my babies. Well, they're grown adults now, but they still think I'm cool. Right kids? Right? Hello?

I am working on my fifth and sixth novels. One will tell the fictionalized story of my parents' love affair. The other is a more gruesome tale of murder and suspense.

I also pen short stories and pour my heart out on my blog, www.juliefrayn.com, as mental floss between novels.

I love, love, LOVE hearing from readers. If you'd like to contact me, you can find me here:

- Website/Blog: www.juliefrayn.com
- Twitter: www.twitter.com/juliefrayn
- Facebook: www.facebook.com/juliebirdfrayn
- Amazon: www.amazon.com/Julie-Frayn/e/B00BH47C3G

OTHER WORK BY JULIE FRAYN

MAZIE BABY

Winner of the 2015 Indie Reader Discovery Award for Literary Fiction

Named to three Best of 2014 lists by Suspense Magazine, IndieReader.com and Readfree.ly

"Just finished reading this story and I'm still holding my breath. I could have been Mazie and this very well could have been my story. The characters were so real and the action so authentic my head is still reeling from its emotional impact. Excellent, and thank you to the author for pulling back the curtain on spousal abuse." ~ Veralisa Fresh

"The dialogue is raw, the character development happens at a life-like pace, and the story line — though depicting a desperate mother — never wavers on the edge of fantasy. Though fiction, MAZIE BABY could arguably be a firsthand autobiography for someone." ~ Jessica Czarnogursky for IndieReader.

IT ISN'T CHEATING IF HE'S DEAD

Winner of the BigAl's Books and Pals 2014 Readers' Choice Award for women's fiction

"Jemima, struggling to understand how she lost her fiancé and trying to make sense of her life after his death, is so utterly human that she blooms off the page." ~ Laurie Boris

"Jemima Stone, Jem for short, is one those characters I found myself caring about almost immediately. She isn't without faults (who among us is?), but she also has a way of taking a negative and turning it positive, which is a quality we could all emulate." ~ BigAl's Books & Pals

ROMEO IS HOMELESS

Winner of double gold medals in the Authorsdb.com 2013 cover contest

(Formerly titled *Suicide City*)

"Suicide City is gritty, unrelenting, tragic, desperate, sad, heart-warming, heart-breaking, and gut-wrenching." ~ Sean P. Farley

"Hands down, the best ending line of any book I've read in the thirty-one years I've been a reader. Please, do not miss this exceptional novel!" ~ Amber Jerome Norrgard

A TRILOGY OF UNRELATED SHORTS

A collection of three short-short stories

"These stories are difficult to read, powerfully written, emotionally draining and awesome. Frayn's writing is flawless. There is nothing with which I can find fault. Frayn gives us a glimpse into a world that might seem bleak but is not without heroes." ~ Rabid Readers Reviews

TWO WINS AND AN HONOURABLE MENTION

Another collection of three short-short stories

"A roller-coaster ride of pity, punk, repulsion, and redemption."

"Unique and quirky."

"Sick, twisted, scary but with a bit of macabre humor too."

CONTACT THE AUTHOR

Website/Blog: www.juliefrayn.com
Twitter: www.twitter.com/juliefrayn
Facebook: www.facebook.com/juliebirdfrayn
Amazon: http://www.amazon.com/Julie-Frayn/e/B00BH47C3G
Email: juliefrayn@juliebird.ca

www.ingramcontent.com/pod-product-compliance
Lightning Source LLC
Chambersburg PA
CBHW020336180626
46812CB00001B/228